SuperGuy 2: Electric Boogaloo

by

KURT CLOPTON

Copyright © 2019 by Kurt Clopton

All rights reserved.

Published in the United States by
Not a Pipe Publishing, Independence, Oregon.
www.NotAPipePublishing.com

Hardcover Edition

ISBN: 978-1-948120-42-5

Cover art by Jeremy Whittington
www.jeremycreates.com

This is a work of fiction. Names, characters, places, and incidents either are products of the writer's imagination or are used fictitiously. Any resemblance to actual persons, living or dead, events, or locales is entirely coincidental.

Author's Note: I mention iPads several times in the text and want readers to know that this is not product placement. I have not received any iPads or related products for mentioning them in the book. However, I'm not against that. I also mention a Jeep, a Tesla, a PRS McCarty 594 guitar in Orange Tiger finish, and a Harley Davidson, although some of those only in this note.

For all the people out there
who don't read books

1

ALEX knew something was wrong. Very, very wrong. He didn't think he was dreaming. He was pretty sure about that because of the pain. He thought you couldn't feel pain in dreams. That was what the whole pinching yourself thing was about, right? So, logically, if you felt like you were being pinched all over your entire body by a hundred blue mutant lobsters, then you had to be awake. Not happily so, but awake, no matter the color of the mutant lobsters. So at least that was settled. Not surprisingly, this conclusion didn't make Alex feel any better, although it didn't make him feel any worse. How could it? A hundred blue mutant lobsters? Couldn't get much worse.

Well, he could have bowel issues. Alex detested bowel issues. He maintained an insanely bland diet with little variation for that very reason, as well as having alcohol wipes on his person at all times to fend off any germs that might be passed around. In addition to this fear of germs, Alex was also just a very clean person, usually showering at least two times a day at minimum—not counting workout days—and he wouldn't go within fifty yards of a public restroom. He'd just hold it, thank you very much. But right now, he did seem to be having issues, and not just of the bowel variety. Weird smelling stuff was leaking out of everywhere. Oily liquid in a surprising range of colors oozed out of every natural hole in his body, as well as several unnatural ones that Alex was only now noticing. Still, despite all the pain and leakage, he remained pretty upbeat, at least in one small corner of his twisted mind. Regardless of what was so wrong at this moment, he somehow knew it was just part of a process; a forging in fire of something new, something better, something extraordinary. Sort of like becoming a butterfly, if the time inside the chrysalis involved extreme mutant lobster related pain and being drenched in very iffy smelling fluids.

All the fluids brought back a memory of falling, which seemed strange to Alex. Of course, most of the past few hours qualified as strange at this point. He tried to concentrate on that feeling of falling, attempting to get a grasp on that particular memory, but it wasn't easy. His mind wasn't exactly a steel trap at the moment. Sounds and images and sound images and image sounds were crashing into each other and exploding into hundreds of other sounds and images and stranger things that were neither of those. Really. It was making that much sense to him. Amidst all the chaos swirling in his head, Alex finally zeroed in on the memory of the giant hero quality metal vat filled with noxious, bubbling liquid. He felt himself falling toward it. He knew what it contained. He himself had helped Gray Matter create the mixture of toxic sludge and rotten super serums. Looking up,

SUPERGUY 2: ELECTRIC BOGALOO

Alex saw SuperGuy above, watching him as he plunged toward his hideously monstrous fate. Gray Matter and SuperGuy. Those two figures had been bouncing around in his mind since his fall, slipping in and out of his pain-ravaged thoughts, never leaving him alone, never giving him a moment to make sense of anything.

Yet, in all this mind-melting disarray within his head, Alex saw what was really responsible for his pain. Yes, Gray Matter and SuperGuy were to blame, and they would pay, but there was more. It wasn't just those two individuals. It was also the structures behind them that propped them up, that gave them power. The monolithic forces that created them and continued to support them in their pathetic thirst for power. It was a never-ending cycle of greed. This sickness stretched out over the world like a web and managed to catch him— one small, insignificant man—in the middle. It was The System. This huge faceless thing that encompassed both good and evil and all the space in between, and didn't care which side won as long as it was in control. And The System certainly didn't mind crushing tiny, innocent pawns like him. But Alex wasn't so tiny anymore and that would be its downfall. He would take it apart piece by piece until there was nothing left, and he would start with the most obvious pieces. He would start with the ones who caused him all this pain: SuperGuy and Gray Matter. Alex would have his vengeance! He would destroy both the hero and the villain, and then wreak havoc on the foundations that propped them up. He would tear the world apart until there was nothing recognizable left, and then he would remake that world and rip it apart again, and again, and again—

Alex felt an abrupt jolt. He had crashed through something. Again. It kept happening. It was constant at first, right after he had broken out of the vat, but once he was outside the factory, it had become less of an issue. The problem was that he couldn't see very well, with his eyes being one of the many places from which fluids were leaking. This time, like all the previous times, Alex didn't stop when running into whatever he ran into, he just went right through it. However, after breaking through whatever it was this time, he slowed his pace and finally stopped. Even without being able to see, he could tell he wasn't outside anymore. He wiped at his eyes in an effort to clear his vision. After a minute, he could make out the blurry world around him. The first things he recognized were boxes. Cardboard boxes. Dozens of them, varying in size, stacked somewhat precariously against a wall. Next to the boxes leaned a mattress and two bicycles. There was also an old weight bench and a couch. It was a storage unit. He had walked through the back wall of a storage unit. Alex would have guessed it smelled musty, if he could smell anything other than the liquids leaking out of his own body. Suddenly he was very tired, feeling as if he had been wearing a hulking suit of armor and trudging along for days. He desperately wanted to rest.

Turning back toward the hole he had made in the wall, it slowly dawned on Alex how huge that opening actually was. He looked at his massive hands and slowly flexed them. Eventually, he pushed the twisted metal back in place to close the breach in the wall and then set the mattress against it to shut out the last of the incoming light. Light that was beginning to brighten with a new day. Slumping down on the couch, Alex exhaled. It felt good to sit. His hand hit something on the couch next to him and he saw it was another cardboard box. He wondered how he could still see anything since he had just blocked the outdoor light, but then he realized it was emanating from him. Not everywhere, but here and there cracks in his skin were emitting a light blue glow. Yet another thing that wasn't entirely normal, but for the moment, rather useful (Alex was trying to remain positive). Something in the box caught his eye, so he reached inside and pulled out a copy of an old movie. He fell asleep with the old VHS tape on his lap, words from the cover floating through his torn up wasteland of a mind, a very large piece of which was focused on vengeance. *If you can't beat the system...break it!*

2

BEING *a superhero is definitely a prestigious occupation. Heroes can be seen on television, on news and entertainment sites on the internet, and constantly dominating social media, sometimes trending several times a day. But you don't often hear about the people behind the heroes, the everyday folks who support our costumed defenders of law and order. Recently, our very own Milwaukee Times Herald News Observer Entertainment Editor, Les Williams, sat down with the guy behind SuperGuy, Roger Allen.*

\#

LW: What's it like to work with SuperGuy?

RA: It's great. Of course, in my previous job I spent 90 percent of my time resetting people's passwords, so it's not hard to beat that. But now I get my hands on some amazing tech on a daily basis. The supercomputers, the gadgets…the various machines we get to use, they're all really cool. Well, mostly. It was cooler in the beginning when we used more vehicles.

SUPERGUY 2: ELECTRIC BOGALOO

LW: But that's not needed now that SuperGuy can fly?

RA: Sadly, no. I had a lot of fun with the flying machines when we first started. And not just those. We had a couple of super fast motorcycles, a submarine, and even experimented with a high-powered hoverboard for a week or two. But then Oliver got the flight booster and well, that was that. It was just easier to fly everywhere. Even underwater. Total waste of the mini-sub. Although we still take it out on the lake on the occasional hot day. That's pretty sweet.

LW: Are you happy with your current position, or would you consider a move? Maybe take a support position with a state or federal level hero where there's more money and more tech? There have been rumors of The Titanium Turtle needing a new tech guy…

RA: I've heard that, and The Titanium Turtle uses a lot of toys. I mean, all capitals A LOT. He's kind of the holy grail of gadget heroes. The Turtle Tank alone is enough to make a tech guy cry. And, with the name The Titanium Turtle, you know he's not going to go out and get a serum booster for flight, that's for sure, so all those toys aren't going to disappear. But no, I'm not looking to move anywhere. I really like working with Oliver, and now that GLAND (Great Lakes Area New Defenders) is operational, I'm also handling all of their tech stuff. That's tech support for five other heroes, a whole regional superhero team, not to mention their new HQ. That thing is amazing. It's a freaking floating base over the Great Lakes. How cool is that? Anyone can have a plain old HQ, or maybe spice it up a bit by making it a cave hidden underneath your mansion or a giant room hidden behind the bookshelves, but to make it hover wherever we want over the Great Lakes? That's just…Hell, it *hovers*.

KURT CLOPTON

Enough said. You gotta love those extra super group funds. So yeah, I've got plenty to keep me happy.

LW: Well, let's take it a step further. Now that you've gotten a taste of the superhero life, what about becoming a sidekick? Any interest in that? I know the Mayor and his people are looking at the options right now and I would think you'd have the inside track.

RA: I'd consider it. Who wouldn't? But it is just a sidekick position, it's not a hero. By the very definition, you're not hero worthy. The powers usually aren't as good, or the gadgets either for that matter. And SuperGuy is only a city level hero, and a small city at that, so how good could the sidekick spot be?

LW: True. And besides the flight booster, SuperGuy is the lowest level hero possible, isn't that right?

RA: Yes, or as we like to call it, the basic, no perks.

LW: So, going by the power level definitions of a hero and sidekick you've set forth, won't it be hard to get a sidekick for this position who isn't almost more powerful than the hero they are supposed to work with?

RA: Yeah, probably. Especially if it's an already established sidekick looking for a job. You could create a new one, just a basic without flight and they'd be lesser powered to that degree, but that's about it. Still, there are plenty of situations where the hero and sidekick are comparable in abilities but it's experience that defines the relationship, like a veteran hero getting a newly created sidekick. They can have similar power levels, but it's really about mentoring. And then there's always the control factor.

LW: Control factor? Like with their powers?

RA: No, they can control their powers just fine, they just can't control themselves. They get too angry and lose their temper, which leads to bad tactical decisions during a fight. Or they run off and do something stupid on their own. Impulse control problems. They take everything personally, even though the villain is trying to kill everyone, not just the sidekick. Sometimes it's hard to even know what a sidekick is thinking. Do you remember the Sonic Worm and his sidekick? The Inchworm stole the Sonic Jet and disappeared for five months. By the time he showed up again, he was a wreck and they had to send him off for "supplemental training." I hear he does equipment testing for the Department of Superhero Funding now, at least when they can get him out of bed. And nobody's seen the Sonic Jet since. I'm sure you could ask any parent of a teenager, it's a frigging mystery sometimes. And then some of these sidekicks are going on their third or fourth jobs because they can't find a way to make it work, so that can't help. But there's always another hero who sees the raw talent and thinks they are the one who can turn the sidekick around, and boom, the sidekick's got another job. I mean, how many chances do they deserve?

LW: Well, to avoid the sidekicks with issues and one who's basically the same level as SuperGuy, could the city apply for someone with say, three-quarters of that basic level? Just settle for a lesser powered sidekick without the baggage?

RA: Unfortunately, that's not possible. That basic, no perks level Oliver got is the hero minimum. Every hero gets that, whether it's a muscle guy or a brainiac, and you can't go below it. That lower limit probably has a lot to do with the near invulnerability every hero gets just to make sure they don't die the first week on the job. It is a big investment, after all. So they are made to survive a lot of physical harm, not to mention not needing sleep or food or air for long periods of time, if ever. I guess all that must add up to the minimum level. Obviously you can go quite a bit above, but the DSF brains haven't ever figured out how to dial it back. Here's a fun fact: Do you know how the super serum was invented in the first place?

LW: No.

RA: It was meant to be a cure for the common cold. Some pack of scientists just trying to get rid of the sniffles created superheroes. Heck, next to Viagra or Rogaine, it's gotta be on the Mount Rushmore of "Whoops, look what we made" success stories. So while the formula they eventually came up with could indeed make people immune to the common cold, it also made them immune to essentially anything else. Any virus, any kind of poison, radiation, you name it. The test subjects didn't need to eat or sleep. They could fall off buildings and walk away. Basically, they were just hard to kill, whether it was with a little virus or a big truck. That is the bottom line invulnerability that comes standard with every serum. But once the code was cracked, so to speak, they could create the add-on boosters for additional powers and abilities, and therefore make real, big-time superheroes. That's when the government stepped in, of course. Can't have some drug company deciding who gets to fly around and shoot beams out of their eyes. They're only ethical enough to decide how much to overprice their life-saving medications. So the government seized it all and eventually made it into a nice, shiny, bureaucratic mess. But hey, we got guys in tights.

LW: What about the extra bit of fame you've experienced since being on the reality show *New Hero?*

RA: Oh, that. Well, I blinked and it disappeared.

SUPERGUY 2: ELECTRIC BOGALOO

LW: True, the episodes focusing on SuperGuy didn't manage to extend to a whole season. That must have been disappointing.

RA: Heck, it was only four episodes, and then just parts of the last two. Those spent more time introducing that rookie hero from San Diego. The producers couldn't get us off the show fast enough. They were all excited to jump in with a brand new hero who had just defeated a supervillain and was learning to fly, but all they got was footage of court hearings, press conferences, and Oliver jumping a little bit farther than the time before until he could just take off and fly. They had missed all the excitement. No battles with the supervillain and his army of robots, no watching the superhero figure out the evil, world-enslaving plan, even missed the big surprise of discovering who the supervillain was. They really blew it. And once the producers figured out none of us were drama queens or wanted to be famous for a third-rate reality show, they bugged out.

LW: I suppose it's best to take the high road and keep your dignity.

RA: Oh, no, don't get me wrong. I totally would have tossed my dignity out the window if it were a first-rate reality show. Probably even second-rate. Most definitely.

To read the extended interview, go to the Milwaukee Times Herald News Observer's website. To hear more of Les Williams, make sure to check out his podcast, Les With More, where Les gets together with a local celebrity each week to cook processed noodle foods and talk about books they've heard of that they want to read someday.

3

OLIVER could hear the bullets whistling past him as he flew down and leveled off just a few feet above the water of Lake Huron. There were four speedboats ahead, each with a heavy machine gun mounted on the front that Oliver thought were unfairly focused on him. He really needed to talk to the group about always being the one cast in the diversionary role. Obviously in this case it had to be one of the three members of GLAND who could fly, which left out Metal and Buffalo, and while The Creeper didn't technically fly—he teleported—you couldn't see him while he was teleporting so he really didn't make a good diversion. That left Oliver, Stormfront, and Ohio Man. And, in what was becoming a disturbing pattern to Oliver, it came down to power. The other two were more powerful and therefore more effective on the attack, so that's how it was decided. Still, in this case it was just a bunch of guys in speedboats, not any supervillains. It's not like the team had to use the best tactics every time they

SUPERGUY 2: ELECTRIC BOGALOO

went into a fight. That seemed to be a little OCD. Plus, this particular strategy got Oliver shot at a lot. And occasionally blown up. Speaking of which, Oliver spotted two shoulder launched rockets being fired from the boats ahead.

"Wonder who the target is?" Oliver muttered. "I sure wouldn't mind fighting some criminals who didn't fall for the diversion every time." He barrel rolled to one side to dodge the rockets. "Seriously, look to your left or right once in awhile," he yelled vaguely in the direction of the boats.

On cue, Stormfront and Ohio Man, carrying Metal and Buffalo, flew in from either side of the formation of speedboats and slowed to match their velocity. Once in position, Stormfront dropped Metal onto one of the boats while Ohio Man dropped Buffalo onto another. Unsurprisingly, chaos erupted on those two boats. Stormfront and Ohio Man peeled away, chased by a hail of bullets from the other two boats. That didn't last long as The Creeper teleported on board one of the them. A thick gray fog enveloped the boat, throwing the men aboard into a shadowy nightmare. In an instant, that boat became the darkest, most filthy alley in the worst part of the worst city they had ever imagined, and a grotesque man in a tattered, grungy bathrobe flitted around them like a skipping film, jumping from place to place while he cackled with sickening delight. Four of the men on the boat peed their pants, while the other three failed to maintain their composure even up to that standard. Seconds later, they were all abandoning ship, leaping over the side and into the water, leaving the speedboat to careen away from the group, still enveloped in its thick fog.

Oliver had closed the distance on the speedboats and flew directly over the top of the one with Buffalo battling a few henchmen in the back. The bad guy manning the mounted machine gun on the front was still firing at Stormfront and Ohio Man, so Oliver grabbed him with one hand and the gun with the other and removed them both from the boat, managing to knock a second man overboard with the machine gun in the process. As he banked back around to the fight, Oliver dropped both the man and the machine gun into the lake.

"You guys should really be wearing life vests," he said as he dropped the bad guy. "It's just a good policy. And sunscreen. I can't stress that enough."

Ohio Man advanced on the last unengaged boat and unleashed a succession of water blasts, picking off five of the occupants and either knocking them overboard or just plain knocking them out. Stormfront approached from the opposite direction and threw a small tornado onto the front of the craft, which proceeded to dispatch the other three men with chain lightning. Buffalo was finishing off those left in his boat, so Oliver streaked toward the last boat with Metal in it. She had mostly cleared hers, but Oliver was able to pick one last guy off the back to help her out. He was still conflicted whenever working with her. On one hand, he felt somewhat obligated to help her whenever he could because he was still embarrassed by the fact that he didn't know for the longest time that Metal was a woman, but on the other hand, if he helped too much, then it could seem as if he was doing it because Metal was a woman. Oliver didn't know how to get past it, he just felt guilty for not knowing. In his defense, Stormfront hadn't known either and she had spent much more time with her. But it really wasn't at all obvious by looking at Metal. She was just a giant, hulking mass of rusty, dented metal. No real gender indicators and a voice that

SUPERGUY 2: ELECTRIC BOGALOO

sounded like a small car accident. They really couldn't be blamed. Still, they both felt bad about it, even though Metal didn't seem to be bothered by it at all.

After the last of the fighting was over, the team tied the boats together and fished the rest of the bad guys out of the water, piling them in with their cohorts to wait for the Coast Guard. The Creeper kept them company while the rest of the team headed back to their new headquarters to debrief and celebrate. Ohio Man was big on the debriefing, Metal and Buffalo on the celebrating, and none of them wanted to stay behind with The Creeper.

The new GLAND headquarters was an amazing structure that brought the phrase "space age design" immediately to mind, probably because that's where it was supposed to be: out in space, orbiting the Earth. Originally produced to be part of the Superhero Earth Protection System (SEPSys), late stage design changes cut this particular module from the overall plan. The Department of Superhero Funding (DSF) decided to make it available to supergroups as a terrestrial base, with priority going to any team that either didn't have an HQ at all or one that was obsolete. Due to an extreme amount of luck, GLAND happened to be the only newly formed superhero group without an HQ and no current groups qualified with a base needing replacement. That included Metal and Buffalo's former supergroup, GLAD (Great Lakes Area Defenders), whose members tried to make their base qualify as obsolete by "accidentally" blowing part of it up. Of course, once the news of the space module was out, lots of heroes tried to throw together last minute teams to get it, but the paperwork for a supergroup was stupefyingly complicated (Ohio Man called it average) and couldn't yet be completed online for some baffling reason. A hero could buy missiles specifically designed to detect and lock on to the radiation signature of a particular supervillain from an app on their phone but they couldn't fill out a couple of forms so a bunch of them could have weekly meetings and get labeled with a not-well-thought-out acronym. GLAND, on the other hand, happened to have all their paperwork in already, thanks to Ohio Man, and still had their new supergroup federal grants to pay for it, so they got their state-of-the-art headquarters.

It was cool enough that the base looked like a spaceship, with its futuristic smooth rounded edges and sleek white surface in a stretched out ovoid shape, but it had the added bonus of floating. Sure, it would have floated in orbit, but it wasn't originally going to be able to do that on Earth. DSF scientists had been working on new structure suspension technology for another project and needed a test subject for their research when the module conveniently became redundant, so they used it as their guinea pig. That left GLAND with an upgraded headquarters that could hover anywhere from five to twenty-five thousand feet above the ground. It could also fly to different locations. This was not done at breakneck speeds, more like hot air balloon floating velocity, but it got there. The one downside of the base's hovering system being a prototype is that there were occasional hiccups, like it drifting a bit in heavy winds or suddenly dropping a few thousand feet without warning. Stormfront could correct the drifting easily enough but the abrupt altitude adjustments (a.k.a. Triple As) were still an

SUPERGUY 2: ELECTRIC BOGALOO

ongoing issue. At the moment, the base floated near the southern edge of Lake Huron, coincidentally within sight of the old, non-hovering GLAD base. Part of which was still smoldering.

Oliver, Stormfront, and Ohio Man, the latter two carrying Metal and Buffalo once again, flew up over the top of the base and descended onto the flight deck, which was a recessed section in the top. Roger liked to joke that it was the hole in the elongated oval donut that was their headquarters. Obviously the heroes could land there, but it was also large enough to accommodate flying craft like helicopters or planes that could land and take off more or less vertically. While the flight deck was excellently designed for its intended use, the GLAND members liked to use it for recreation, mostly in the form of cookouts. Additionally, there was an ongoing discussion about how to get a decent sized swimming pool up there despite the problem with Triple As. This openly ignored the fact that the base was almost always floating above one of several very large lakes.

Roger was waiting on the flight deck when the group landed, and he carefully greeted them from a distance at first, having learned that he definitely did not want to be within high five range of Metal and Buffalo. They didn't break any bones, but they seemed to know just how close they could get. After the others went ahead inside, Roger fell in beside Oliver.

"Another successful GLAND mission," he said. "You guys are really racking up the wins."

"Well, it hasn't exactly been against stellar competition," said Oliver. "Low-end criminals and smugglers aren't exactly supervillains."

"Give yourself some credit, that was probably the best bunch of smugglers we've encountered yet. I mean, how nice were those speedboats? High quality equipment and they kept a pretty tight formation until The Creeper dropped in. The rocket launchers were a nice touch, too."

"If you say so."

"I do," said Roger, as they entered the base. "By the way, you only have a limited amount of time to celebrate this win. Emma called to say we have a meeting with the Mayor at six. Sounds like they've come to some kind of decision on the sidekick thing."

"You get any clue if you've got a shot at it?" asked Oliver.

"No clue. Emma said they didn't tell her what they decided."

"Okay, I guess we'll find out at six."

Metal suddenly rushed up to them and grabbed Oliver's arm, pulling him toward the main control room. "Hurry, it's an emergency," she said.

"What's going on?" asked Oliver. He didn't recall ever seeing Metal this worked up about something. "What's happened?" He wondered if The Creeper had somehow gotten into trouble with the smugglers he was left behind to guard.

"We need you to moon GLAD," said Metal, still dragging Oliver by the arm. "Come on, hurry up. Over here by the window."

"Wait, what? Moon?"

Buffalo was waiting by the window. He was waving them over as he kept looking between them and the old GLAD base down below. "Hurry," he said. "I think a couple of them are there."

SUPERGUY 2: ELECTRIC BOGALOO

Oliver finally shook off Metal's hand as they reached the window. "Seriously, you want me to moon your old base?"

"Exactly," said Buffalo. "We can't do it."

"Yeah, he's a fur ball and I'm a big hunk of tin," explained Metal. "No butts to be seen. Not really effective. We need you."

"Yeah," said Buffalo. "We can't ask Stormfront to do it because that's not cool, at least for me, and Ohio Man is too uptight, so that leaves you." Buffalo looked pleadingly at Oliver.

"What about The Creeper?" asked Oliver. "Surely he'd be happy to do it."

"Oh, yeah," replied Buffalo. "He was more than willing. Way, way more. That was the problem."

"Yeah," chimed in Metal. "Why do you think we had him stay behind with the boats? No way I'm giving that guy a reason to drop his pants."

"Does he even wear pants under that bathrobe?" asked Buffalo.

"So it's just me?" asked Oliver.

"No, not just you," said Roger as he strolled up to the window. "I'm here to do my heroic deed for the week."

"That's my man," said Buffalo with a smile.

"How do you know they're even looking up here?" asked Oliver. "Seems kind of useless if they aren't."

"It's really just the principle of the thing," said Metal. "Plus we had Roger hack their system to aim a camera up here and play it on all their screens. On a loop. For a couple of hours."

Oliver thought about it a little more and then shrugged. "For the team," he said, turning around and dropping his pants. Roger followed suit. Metal and Buffalo cheered, jumping up and down beside them and gesturing rudely at their old base. Stormfront walked into the room at that moment to witness all the mooning and rude gesturing, and see how the heroes in question reacted to a Triple A happening a second later.

4

"**So**, have you two worked out how to decide who gets the sidekick spot if it's offered?" asked Oliver. He walked alongside Roger and Emma as they climbed the stairs of the city government building, on their way to meet with the Mayor to learn his decision on the sidekick proposal. Emma and Roger were dressed a little more formally than usual for the meeting, and Oliver was in uniform as he always was these days. Even though he had been the city's hero for the better part of a year now, people still stopped and stared when he walked through the building. Whether that was due to his celebrity status as a hero or just the tightness of his costume was up for debate. Oliver had gotten somewhat more comfortable with the suit, which was all white in the body and was complemented with a black barcode on his chest and black gloves, boots, and mask. His mask only covered his eyes and wrapped around the back of his head with a thin band so his blond, superhero hair could wave in the breeze. Roger had previously augmented the mask by combining it with lenses from used goggles he got from the DSF Superhero Surplus Warehouse that provided Oliver with some useful options, such as a night vision mode, a telescopic mode, and a camera, but he had further refined it so the mask wasn't so bulky and the lenses even slid out of the way completely. This made Oliver feel more comfortable when speaking with people in normal situations. He hoped to add a cape to his uniform someday, not just because it was cool as DSF polls showed, but to help hide the extreme tightness of the suit.

"Well, obviously becoming a sidekick would be a huge deal for either of us. Something that completely changes the course of our lives," said Roger. He had pulled off his round-rimmed glasses and was wiping them with his shirt. "So we're going to rock, paper, scissors the hell out of it."

"That seems logical," said Oliver. "Best of five, I'm assuming."

"Five," scoffed Roger, putting his glasses back on. "This is best of nine if it's anything. I did say it was a once in a lifetime opportunity, remember. Huge deal."

"I was pretty much assuming we would apply for the position and they would pick one of us," said Emma. "Not as cool as rock, paper, scissors, but more, you know…realistic?"

"So you're interested in it?" asked Oliver.

"I'm interested in their decision," she replied. Emma had the blond hair and blue eyes of Scandinavian heritage and she pushed a bit of that wavy blond hair behind one ear as she thought. "I still don't know that I'm definitely interested in taking the job. You recall I've seen what all you've had to deal with being the hero. I'm not convinced a sidekick position would be worth the trouble."

SUPERGUY 2: ELECTRIC BOGALOO

"I'm sure it's not," said Roger. "But I'd do it. I'm counting on the whole serum brainwash effect to make me believe it's worth it. Plus I'll be able to eat Thai food more often without the alarming aftereffects."

"So basically this life altering opportunity comes down to Thai food for you?" asked Emma.

"No, not only Thai food. I have my problems with spicy Mexican too," replied Roger. "I'm just saying that I've gone over all the aspects of the job, like the good stuff of powers and great hair—I'm going to have the biggest afro you've ever seen, by the way—and the bad stuff of getting knocked around by supervillains and ogled by the old ladies of the Milwaukee Flower and Garden Society because of my incredibly tight costume, and not having bathroom issues after consuming certain foods is kinda tipping the scale right now."

"Well, here's a tip," said Emma. "You might not want to lead with that in the interview."

"Oh, don't worry. I'll be all about truth and justice and defending the peace in that."

"Well, regardless of how this all shakes out, I want you both to know I'd be happy to have either of you as a sidekick," said Oliver as they approached the Mayor's outer office. There were a couple of desks for assistants and some chairs along the wall for people to sit in while waiting. "And whoever loses out I will ridicule relentlessly for being a failure and an embarrassment to your parents, and really, all of humanity."

"That's touching," said Emma.

A woman at one of the desks smiled at them as she picked up her phone and pressed a button, presumably to announce their arrival. A second later, the Mayor's executive assistant, Lily, opened the door and beckoned them inside. Oliver and Emma started toward the office, but Roger stayed put. He was texting furiously on his phone.

"Come on, Rog," said Oliver. "Now's not the time."

"Yeah, save it for while driving," said Emma.

"As an officer of the law, I cannot condone that comment, but...nicely inappropriate," said Oliver. "I like it."

Emma shrugged a thanks. "I blame you two for the bad influence."

Roger paused in his texting and squeezed his eyes shut while holding up a hand. "Shh, shh, shh," he shushed. "I'm in the zone here. Gimme a sec."

Oliver looked questioningly at Emma. She rolled her eyes. "It's Joyce. They've been texting all afternoon. Apparently trying to build up the courage to not ask the girl out again this week." Raymond Joyce, CEO of Joyce Industries, was also known as Gray Matter, the supervillain whose plan of world domination Oliver had thwarted several months before in his first big victory on the job. Joyce had managed to escape any real penalties due to a really impressive team of lawyers and had somehow begun a relationship with Roger and Emma based on dating advice. It was a weird reality in which they now lived.

"Wait, I thought you were a part of this little evil love connection," said Oliver.

"Oh, I was, last century at least. But it's been months. I gave up. Just couldn't stand it anymore," said Emma. "The nice thing is that after beginning to feel empathy for the lovelorn diabolical supervillain in the first few weeks, the next five months really beats that out of you. Then you remember he's a bad guy and cheering for him to get a girlfriend probably isn't the nicest thing for the girl. Kind of a sisterhood thing there. Anyway, Roger won't quit. I think he's got a problem."

Oliver and Emma waited a little longer as Roger finished his text and slipped his phone into his pocket.

"Finally push him over the edge?" asked Emma.

"Maybe," replied Roger. "I just channeled some serious mid-nineties coming of age romantic comedy seize the day and/or girl stuff there. Or maybe it was mid-eighties. Either way, real second level motivational crap."

"So now you're just throwing melodramatic movie quotes at him?" asked Emma.

"Pretty much."

"And that qualifies as second level?" asked Oliver.

"Yep."

"Remind me not to ask you for advice with Janice," said Oliver. "Come on, let's go." He turned and led the other two through the door into the Mayor's office.

"Welcome, welcome, welcome!" said the Mayor, as soon as they entered. He was always extra enthusiastic when things were going well, and he'd been riding a wave of good publicity and approval ratings lately, largely due to Oliver's exploits. That wave had begun several months earlier with the foiling of Gray Matter and his plot to take over the world using a mind control drug delivered via breakfast cereal. And while the supervillain avoided punishment, that was blamed on the justice system's failings and not the Mayor or Oliver. The good press had continued after that big victory with some much publicized foiling of multiple smaller crimes in the city, highlighted by a couple that really showcased Oliver's new flying ability. His high visibility as he zipped around Milwaukee and its suburbs grabbing up small time crooks was a big hit with the public according to polls. And just recently there had been a succession of victories with the GLAND group, one or two of which made national news, which didn't hurt at all.

"Please come in and have a seat!" said the Mayor, vigorously shaking Oliver's hand as he led him to a couch in the office seating area. This was a collection of two couches and four chairs arranged around a big coffee table on the opposite side of the room from the Mayor's desk. "Roger, Emma, great to see you both too. Excited to hear what we've decided, I bet, huh?" Emma took a seat next to Oliver on the couch while Roger grabbed a chair next to Lily. The Deputy Mayor stood by one of the windows, busy texting on his phone, but managed a nod in their direction as they took their seats, and the Police Chief sat a safe distance away in one of the chairs across from the Mayor's desk. He gave Oliver the slightest of nods. The two of them had begun an arrangement when Oliver first started as the city's hero where the Chief showed dislike for Oliver in public while secretly providing information and support in private in order to protect the city. It had played a vital part in defeating Gray Matter because the supervillain had had informants within the police department. Now, while the arrangement was probably no longer needed, the Chief still persisted in bashing Oliver in public. Often in private, too. He just seemed to really enjoy it.

"I think all of us are excited to hear what you've decided," said Oliver.

"I bet you are, I bet you are," said the Mayor. "Well, we've put a lot of time and thought into it. Really, Lily here did most of the heavy lifting, with researching all the possibilities and seeing how they would fit with our budget and all that. The Deputy Mayor and Police Chief were kept in the loop too, so we could have their input."

SUPERGUY 2: ELECTRIC BOGALOO

"I was against it," said the Chief, looking over for a second before going back to staring at the nearby shelves. He did it all with a nice bit of distaste.

"Yes, yes, of course," agreed the Mayor. "Quite a surprise there for all of us, Chief. Thank you." He gave the Chief a bit of a disappointed look, not because of the Chief's position on the matter, but because the man was getting in the way of the Mayor's big reveal. The Mayor didn't like it when others messed with his spotlight. He paused a second, trying to get back on track. Taking a couple of steps over to one of the empty chairs, he set both hands on the back in what he thought must look like a pretty "in control of the room" sort of way. Unfortunately, it was a pretty high-backed chair and he wasn't all that tall, so it had the effect of making him look even smaller than he was. Nonetheless, he forged on.

"I was actually amazed at the amount of possibilities once we started getting into it. I thought we'd just be writing up a position description for a sidekick and sending it in, but Lily found so many other options." Oliver didn't need enhanced hearing to detect Roger's groan at this point. The Mayor continued, "You see, applying for a brand new sidekick is easily the most expensive option. But did you know there are sidekicks already out there looking for jobs? Sidekicks that are already sidekicks. They've already been created. We don't have to foot the bill to make them. They've got their powers and abilities and gadgets and stuff, and we just hire them. We can even bring them in for interviews and tryouts for a couple of weeks. See who works well with you. And then it's just a matter of the salary, which is really nothing next to the position creation and super serum costs."

KURT CLOPTON

"Okay...but aren't these sidekicks you're talking about ones who have already failed at other places? Otherwise they'd have jobs, right?" asked Oliver.

"I wouldn't say failed," said the Mayor. "Yes, some of them were let go from sidekick positions, but others were available after their mentor hero positions were eliminated."

"You mean they got their hero killed," said Roger.

"Well...I don't know if there was ever anything proven," said the Mayor. "There's a lot of gray area there. At least no charges were filed."

"Oh brother," said Emma in a barely concealed whisper.

"Look, don't worry about that, because we're not going that route either," said the Mayor, trying to regain control of things. A big smile spread across his face. "There's a way where we get a sidekick, but the DSF pays us."

"Oh god," groaned Roger, in a way that made his previous groan sound utterly optimistic. "Not STraP. Please tell me you're not talking about STraP."

"YES!" exclaimed the Mayor. "STraP!"

"STraP? What's that?" asked Oliver, really fearing the answer. He knew if Roger was unenthusiastic about something hero related, it had to be bad.

"It's the Sidekick Training Program," answered Lily politely from her chair. She smiled serenely as she stared at the Mayor's deliriously happy face. She was never happier when the Mayor was happy. It was oodles of happy.

"Yes," said Roger. "Instead of permanently hiring just one of those out of work, incompetent sidekicks, we get to bring them all in individually and train them for several weeks at a time. An infinite supply of the unfit and inadequate."

SUPERGUY 2: ELECTRIC BOGALOO

"Exactly," said the Mayor, pointing at Roger. "And we get paid by the Department of Superhero Funding for doing it."

"And they aren't all unemployed former sidekicks," said Lily. "Some will be newly created sidekicks getting training before going to their permanent positions."

"That's just what the DSF says in their STraP propaganda," said Roger. "It's really just an unending line of degenerates. The whole thing will have the feel of a horribly run halfway house, but without the optimism."

"This sounds like a mess," said Emma. "And considering it seems like someone will have to try to organize this mess, I'm going to go out on that good old limb and guess that I will be getting the pleasure of doing that particular job?"

"Well, you will be the coordinator," answered Lily. "You'll be working with the STraP program to schedule the sidekicks, get them settled in, complete evaluations, all that sort of thing."

"Yeah, all that sort of thing," repeated Emma. "And I'm sure these additional duties come with a little bump in pay?" Emma said this in a dispirited way that clearly meant she didn't believe it to be the case.

"Yes, in fact it does," replied Lily, much to Emma's surprise. "STraP pays us to be in the program and part of the money goes to cover the administrative costs of supporting the sidekicks. So there's a pay bump. It looks like this." Lily handed a piece of paper to Emma.

"Oh. Well, I didn't expect that," said Emma, taking the paper and giving it a look. "Oh. Wow. Okay, I'm good with this."

"Nice bump?" asked Oliver.

"Well, just don't blame me if I'm nicer to the sidekicks than the hero."

"You're nicer to everyone than me," said Oliver. Emma shrugged.

"That doesn't seem very fair," said Roger. "After all, won't Oliver and I be doing most of the training?"

"Yes, that's true," said Lily, " but the program provides for that too." She handed Oliver and Roger sheets of paper detailing their pay increases due to the STraP participation.

"Whoa," said Oliver. "Is this right?"

"Oh, yeah," said the Mayor, nodding like a maniac. "There's a lot of money in this program. Apparently there aren't a lot of participants so they've been increasing the benefits. Gotta use your budgeted money or you'll just lose it."

"Well, this will still be a mess, but you've bought my compliance," said Roger. "And a really nice motorcycle."

"Glad to hear it," said the Mayor. "Lily's got all the details for you, including all the information on the potential sidekick trainees. But I do want to say that while I'm wholeheartedly behind this program for financial reasons, we need to keep in mind that this can't become a problem situation for us either. We do it, we put a nice public relations spin on it, and you guys don't screw it up."

"In other words, don't let the never-ending parade of incompetent, overpowered dipsticks we'll have coming through blow up anything of significance," said Roger.

"Ooh, or get me killed," said Oliver.

"Precisely," said the Mayor. And so the meeting was adjourned.

SUPERGUY 2: ELECTRIC BOGALOO

Alex was pretty sure he was bigger. When he woke up after falling asleep on the old couch in the storage space, he found the couch crushed beneath him and both of his feet sticking out of the far wall into the adjoining room. Yes, he was definitely bigger. He was also glowing a bit more, or at least the cracks in his skin were glowing a bit more. The glow came from the blue substance that seemed to be almost floating just below the surface of his skin. He could see it moving inside the cracks, sort of like a liquid, or maybe a mist or a cloud. And it crackled. Not too loudly, but if he leaned in close, he could hear it. Crackling with power. With potential.

Pulling his feet back inside the room, Alex pushed himself up, accidentally squashing a bicycle under his hand in the process. He hadn't yet risen to his full height before his head hit the ceiling and knocked a hole in it. Stooping, he pulled the mattress away from where it blocked the hastily repaired hole in the metal wall he had made when he first entered the storage unit. Through the jagged cracks, Alex could see it was currently dark outside. He stepped forward and pushed his way back out, creating a hole twice as big as the original. Yes, Alex was much, much bigger.

Once outside, Alex took a moment to collect his thoughts, which ended up being more like twenty minutes because his thoughts were a bit of a shambles. Still, his mind was certainly more tidy than before he slept, he knew that for sure. That had been chaos. And now, as he stood there, things slowly became more coherent, and not just inside his mind. He could really see the world around him, and the main thing he noticed was that time had passed. A lot of time. When he had first crashed through the storage space wall, it had been in the midst of an unusually early spring warm spell that melted most of the remaining snow and almost fooled the plants and trees into coming to life again. Now the trees were changing colors and the plants were feeling the effects of cold nights. How long had he slept? Apparently months. He was lucky no one ever found him in the storage space in all that time, or his feet sticking into the neighboring one. Maybe if someone had walked in and found a huge blue monster—or his feet—snoozing in their space, they had smartly decided getting their slightly moldy mattress or weight bench wasn't such a high priority and headed off to find a drink instead.

Alex thought back to the night he stumbled through the back wall of the storage facility. His last most important thoughts from before he slept rose to the surface and a certain focus began to gain a foothold in the trashcan chili that was his state of mind. He had enemies. Gray Matter and SuperGuy for certain, but also The System that created them. That same System that created the thing he now was. That created…? Alex wondered what he was now. He looked around at the trees in the semi-darkness, up at the sky just beginning to show stars, and down at the ground and the dark green of the grass that spread out underneath him. On that ground he saw his answer. A VHS tape he had managed to kick outside as he exited the storage unit. He remembered the words he had read months before on the case, the words that had made it so clear that The System was the enemy, and Gray Matter and SuperGuy parts of The System. He would break The System. He would break Gray Matter and SuperGuy. He would break everything that got in his way.

SUPERGUY 2: ELECTRIC BOGALOO

And he would do it as the thing they created. He would do it as Electric Boogaloo.

5

RAYMOND Joyce reread the texts from Roger one last time. They were inspirational to say the least. Some final motivational words to help him take the next step in what was the biggest challenge of his life. All the innovations he had made in his work, all the conniving, cheating and financial shenanigans it had taken to build his billion dollar corporation, all his overly complicated evil plots were nothing compared to this single test. Speaking to Alice beyond placing a simple food order. To break through the barriers he had kept in place for months now and at long last make a connection. To finally, finally take the big step and ask her out on a date. Or ask for her number. Or maybe just ask her to repeat the specials. One can't just go nuts, no matter how motivational the last few texts you got were.

Joyce was a small man, only five feet two inches, but while stature could be a problem for some people, he had never let it get in the way of his ambitions. Some might even say that his lack of height was why Joyce worked so hard to achieve what he had. That was a bunch of baloney. Joyce knew that he could be six feet five inches tall and he'd still want to devise some convoluted scheme to rob the Federal Reserve bank, or just steal his neighbor's silver Jetta with the cool sunroof. It was in his blood, not his height. Joyce's other remarkable feature was his hair. It was bright white and occasionally wild, but he kept it slicked back with copious amounts of gel if for no other reason than to avoid comparisons to Albert Einstein, whom he considered a bit of a dunce. Seriously, the guy might have been famous, but it was all just theories and equations, and none of them had anything to do with taking over the world.

In his peripheral vision, Joyce could see Alice approaching with his order, so with one last look at Roger's words, he steeled himself to speak. He would say something disarmingly witty about the weather, or that sports team, or some television show he didn't actually watch. That would be a good start. But what if she followed up with a question? He didn't watch the show, didn't know the sports team, and only allowed the weather to be the way it was because he was too busy with other things to complete his weather controlling machine. Crap, he was crashing. He should have already decided on a topic to be disarmingly witty about, not leave it until the last second. Improvisation wasn't his thing; convoluted schemes were, well thought-out, convoluted schemes. There was nothing witty about those. She wasn't even at the table yet and he was blowing it again. Come on, hold on. What did Roger say? Compliment. That was it. Keep it simple, just compliment her on something. Her shoes. Compliment her shoes. Suddenly Alice was there and setting his plate down in front of him and Joyce was freaking out because he hadn't really gotten a good look at the shoes and now it would be awkward to lean out of the booth to see her shoes and…was that meat loaf? Why was there meat loaf on his plate? Joyce's panic gave way to complete bewilderment as he stared at the meat loaf. He was not a fan of meat loaf, or loaves of anything that were not bread.

"Wait, that's not what you ordered, is it?" asked Alice.

"No…no," answered Joyce, shaking his head. "No, I'm afraid not. I had the pie. Caramel apple, to be precise." Alice's head dropped and she rubbed her temples with both hands. Loose strands of her light brown hair, tied mostly into a ponytail in back, fell down to frame her face. Joyce had always thought she looked a little like Audrey Hepburn, if Hepburn had been forced to get a real job. He continued uncertainly, "Although I did consider the coconut cream if that…"

"No, no, it's not your fault. It's my mistake. I'm sorry, I don't know where my head's at. I'm just having a particularly bad day," said Alice.

The sadness in her voice and her expression of total despair made Raymond Joyce muster the courage to do something he had never been able to do before. Speak to her about something other than an order, particularly pie.

"Is there something I can do to help?"

Alice gave a half-hearted chuckle. "Oh, I wish. Can you pay my overdue rent, get my car fixed, and keep my mother from dying?"

Joyce sat there for a second just staring at Alice.

"Oh, I'm so sorry, I shouldn't just dump on you like that—"

"No, no, don't be sorry. Not at all," said Joyce. "In fact, I will have those first two things taken care of immediately."

SUPERGUY 2: ELECTRIC BOGALOO

He gestured to a young man in a suit sitting in the booth across the aisle. One of Joyce's support staff, the man had been close enough to hear the exchange, so now he nodded and walked out of the diner. Alice watched the young man go and then turned back to Mr. Joyce with a somewhat mystified look. Mr. Joyce continued, "Unfortunately, I don't know if I can help with the third thing." He shifted nervously, and then pushed himself up out of the booth as if formality required he stand. His eyes darted back and forth between Alice's face and the chipped formica tabletop edge at which his left index finger nervously picked. "Please, why don't you have a seat and tell me about your mother?" he finally managed.

Alice stared at Mr. Joyce for a moment, her mystified look still lingering. "Oh, um, I appreciate it, but I have tables..." she said, vaguely looking and gesturing toward the other customers in the diner.

"Oh, please, let me take care of them," said Mr. Joyce. He turned to a woman in the same booth where the man had been. "Miss Williams, will you please tell the other customers that we will be closing early this evening, and compensate them for their meals?" The woman nodded as she rose and headed toward the other diner customers, already pulling a stack of cash out of her purse.

Alice started to protest but Mr. Joyce held up a hand. "No, please, let me do this for you. It seems like you could really use a break, and maybe a little help. Have a seat. Tell me about your mother." Alice hesitated another second. "Please," repeated Mr. Joyce, waving a hand at the seat across from him. "Why not take a few moments for yourself?"

Alice's eyes glistened slightly as she smiled in gratitude. She slowly slid down into the booth and sat silently for a couple of minutes, just staring at the table and fighting back tears. Joyce said nothing, not because he deemed it polite or respectful to give the woman a few minutes to compose herself, but because he had no idea what to say. Internally, he was freaking out. Alice was sitting at the table across from him. THE freaking Alice. He desperately wanted to text Roger for advice but he couldn't move. He was frozen. Crap, he couldn't speak. Would she notice?

Eventually Alice broke the silence. Without looking up, she started to tell Joyce about her parents, about her mother's illness, about the bills piling up. She talked nonstop for almost thirty minutes and Raymond Joyce found that while he could eventually move and maybe speak again, he didn't want to. He just wanted to listen to Alice talk, to hear her voice, to watch her face. And when she did finally finish her story, Joyce found it easy to speak to her, to ask questions, to make a clever comment, and to make her smile.

"You have been so kind to sit here and listen to me all this time," said Alice eventually. "It really feels good to talk about it."

"My pleasure," said Mr. Joyce. "And I think I can definitely assist you with your mother's health expenses. You see, I'm involved with a charity that's designed to help in exactly this type of situation," he lied. Although it wasn't too much of a lie since he was going to set one up as soon as he was out of the diner. He assumed Alice would refuse him if he simply offered to pay for her mother's care, so he decided this was the best course of action. "It's a fairly new charity so I think they are actively looking for recipients and from what you told me, your mother would definitely qualify."

"Really? That's amazing."

"Yes, how about you come to my office tomorrow afternoon and I can have someone from the foundation meet

SUPERGUY 2: ELECTRIC BOGALOO

us to complete any paperwork that needs to be done? I can even have someone pick you up in case the repairs to your car have not been finished by then."

Alice held both of her hands over her mouth while fighting back a new round of tears. "I don't know how to thank you," she said.

"Please, you don't have to thank me. I'm a part of this foundation to help people like your mother," said Joyce. "But perhaps, after the paperwork has been completed, you will consider being my guest for dinner? I have a personal chef who will prepare anything you would desire, or I'd be happy to take you out wherever you want. Call it a celebration for us being able to come together to help your mother."

Alice smiled. "Yes, I'd be happy to join you."

Raymond Joyce walked into his office on a cloud. He knew it was a cliché, but now he understood exactly why it was a cliché and was perfectly happy to abuse it. It really was a heck of a feeling. A date with Alice. Sure, he had been working toward this goal for months and at times the thought of an actual date—one where Alice was a willing participant and not hypnotized or thinking she was meeting Channing Tatum for barbecue—seemed like a pipe dream in fantasy land. But here it was, a real thing really happening in his real life. Now Joyce just had to figure out how to get through the date. He pulled out his phone to text Roger with an update, but before he could start there was a knock at the door.

KURT CLOPTON

"Enter," said Joyce as he sat down at his desk. Steven, his new personal assistant, came in carrying an iPad and had a rather concerned look on his face.

"Mr. Joyce, there's an ongoing incident at the testing facility in New Berlin. I don't have many details because we haven't been able to get in contact with anyone on site yet. There is only a small security crew on duty at this time of night, besides the sentry bots, and no one is answering. We have an emergency response team on the way, but they are about twenty minutes out. The only thing I do have right now is security footage that I pulled from the servers before the cameras lost power." Steven turned on one of the wall monitors behind Joyce's desk and tapped his iPad to start the footage playing on the screen.

What Joyce saw on the monitor was amazing, if a little grainy. He really needed to upgrade the security cameras all across his facilities. At least the footage was in color, because the giant dark blue thing battering the outer wall of the building probably wouldn't have been as impressive in black and white. Bright blue light emanated from cracks in the thing's body, occasionally hitting the camera head on and blinding it for a second or two. As the monster finally ripped open a hole large enough for it to enter the building, three sentry bots closed in behind it from the yard. Two opened fire with their mini guns while the third, a heavier model, fired two rockets from shoulder mounted launchers. The effect on the blue monster was as if someone had tapped on its shoulder to get its attention. Slowly turning toward the threat, it looked from one bot to the next, oblivious to the bullets ricocheting off its chest or the multiple missiles exploding against its lower torso. One missile glanced off its head and careened out of the field of view of the camera. The

SUPERGUY 2: ELECTRIC BOGALOO

force of the explosions didn't knock the monster off balance in the slightest. After a couple more seconds, countless bullets, and three more missiles, the creature raised its hands and blue lightning shot outward, spreading like a web across the space between it and the bots. As the lightning got closer, it split into three branches and crashed into the bots, encircling and then seeming to squeeze them before suddenly ripping them apart into hundreds of tiny pieces. Those pieces fell to the ground around the yard like a sporadic little rainstorm as the monster turned back to the hole it had created in the building. It paused for a few seconds, almost as if it were taking a giant breath, and then it threw out its hands again, unleashing a huge swath of blue lightning through the hole and inside the building. The brightness of the lightning grew exponentially, eventually blinding the camera until the feed stopped completely, presumably due to power failure.

"Well," said Joyce. "That's a thing."

6

"**So** there's no chance of either of you becoming the sidekick?" asked Janice. Also known as Stormfront, she was Thunder Bay, Ontario's superhero, and had known Oliver since he had done his new hero orientation. They were also involved in a romantic relationship, when such a thing was possible between constant superhero related interruptions. Janice had flown down to join Oliver, Roger, and Emma at their Milwaukee headquarters after their meeting with the Mayor. The headquarters was a former Milwaukee street department facility, which was affectionately referred to as the Garage by the group, and had been extensively renovated to function as an HQ shortly after Oliver became SuperGuy. The Garage was conveniently located in one of the worst neighborhoods downtown in terms of criminal activity, but on the plus side, it had plenty of space for training and storage, and reasonably good feng shui.

SUPERGUY 2: ELECTRIC BOGALOO

Roger referred to the fenced in outer yard as the graveyard now that it was mostly home to all the half-working toys they had experimented with before Oliver got the ability to fly. There were a few decent, mostly working toys parked inside the large interior space of the Garage that they deemed worth keeping, either because they might come in useful someday, or just because they were cool. A couple of rocket cycles, a helicopter that positively bristled with missiles, and a weird hybrid tank–speedboat that they had never figured out how to keep from sinking all had special places inside. Across from where those were parked was the most useful part of the Garage: the two story suite of rooms that seemed like the afterthought of all afterthoughts, just kind of stuck along the back corner of the building when whoever built the facility realized they needed some office space and a bathroom. Those offices had now been converted into a couple of small apartments for Oliver and Roger upstairs, and a large combination control room and meeting room downstairs, along with a small office for Emma, a kitchen, and a bathroom. The meeting part of the meeting room wasn't the usual conference table and chairs, but rather a couple of couches and some comfy chairs where they could relax and talk, which is what they were now doing.

"No chance that I can see," answered Emma. She and Janice were sitting next to each other on one of the couches. "This STraP thing they've signed up for is going to last at least the next two years from what I can tell. And as long as the Mayor is getting paid to do it, I don't see why he'd stop."

"The only way it will change is if one of these STraP guys messes up big time and the Mayor shelves the whole thing," said Roger from where he was making a pot of coffee on a side table by the back wall. "Of course, if that were to happen, I wonder if he would even entertain the idea of a permanent sidekick instead of STraP. It's just one more hero potentially wrecking part of the city. He's got his hands full with Oliver already."

"Feeling the love," said Oliver from his spot in one of the comfy chairs. "But in my defense, I've gone four months now without any appreciable collateral damage."

"What about those trees in the park last month?" asked Emma.

"Trees? Do trees count? They grow back. And isn't it really the guy in the post-apocalyptic, zombie-proofed, survivalist Hummer's fault?" asked Oliver. "He wasn't exactly trying to avoid the flowers, and trees, and that one fountain."

"I think trees count for the Parks and Rec folks," said Janice as she pulled off her gloves and set them on the arm of the sofa. Superheroes were required to be in uniform pretty much all the time, so taking off their gloves or maybe their boots was about as relaxed as they usually got. Janice's own thigh high boots lay on the floor and she sat with her legs tucked underneath her on the couch. Her dark bluish-black cape was draped around her, covering the rest of her rather skimpy costume, which she referred to generously as a one-piece swimsuit. Oliver was in a similar situation with the tightness of his suit and Janice had told him that eye contact wasn't a thing they got to participate in all that much as superheroes. Oliver's one concession to comfort was to remove his mask, which he had tossed on the coffee table.

"Well, whether your record is perfect or not right now, you can kiss it goodbye once these new guys start showing up," said Roger. He finished making the coffee, poured himself and Emma each a cup, and carried them over to the seating area. "Collateral damage will be the least of your problems with the basket cases we'll have." He handed a cup to Emma.

"Okay, so wait a minute," said Oliver. "Is it really going to be that bad? I mean, you're making it sound terrible. And how did all these sidekicks end up being mental? I don't think I'm going to want to take them out on the street if this is going to be even close to the way you're making it sound."

"All right, maybe I'm overdoing it a bit. They aren't all mental," answered Roger. "Some certainly are, but it's much more complicated than that."

"How so? I know they're sidekicks and not heroes, but they're still essentially the same, right? It's still the same super juice, isn't it?" asked Oliver.

"Ah, now you've stumbled onto the real question, is it the same super serum?" said Roger. He sat down on the empty couch across from Emma and Janice.

"Of course it is. It has to be. Doesn't it?" said Emma, adding the last with a little bit more uncertainty.

"I don't know," said Janice, shaking her head skeptically. Her long black hair waved back and forth, and she pushed a bunch behind her left ear. "From all the stories I've heard, it seems like sidekicks are the source of problems more often than regular heroes. Kind of makes me think something's up."

"The popular opinion is that it is the same super serum now, but it wasn't always," said Roger. "There's a theory that for a while they tweaked the serum for sidekicks, not in terms of powers or abilities, but in the mental makeup. This was maybe ten years ago or so. There were so many sidekicks who had aspirations of becoming regular heroes that it really hurt the stability of a lot of positions. Heroes were constantly having to fill their sidekick spots because their previous one took a regular hero gig in some other city. The turnover was constant, which hurt the hero's ability to do their job, so the DSF started to mess with the sidekick formula. At least that's the suspicion. They've never admitted to it."

"Is that legal?" asked Emma.

"They aren't exactly regulated, so I think they can do whatever they want," said Roger.

"That's comforting," said Oliver.

"Are they still doing this 'tweaking'?" asked Janice.

"No, I don't think so," said Roger. "At least that's the opinion of most of the people I talk to. Probably stopped three or four years ago, once it became obvious there were more than a few misfires with that run of sidekicks."

"So what exactly did they do to the serum?" asked Oliver.

"It's all speculation, of course. No one really knows. There have been plenty of stories in *Hero Tech* that put forth various theories, but it's the one about messing with the mental component of the serum that seems the most likely. Basically, they were trying to put something in that would make the sidekick want to be a sidekick, as opposed to being a hero. That way, the sidekick would be happy to stay where they were and not have aspirations to be a full hero out on their own," said Roger. "Of course, there's already the regular motivational component in the serum that makes the person want to be a superhero and not suddenly decide they'd rather be an accountant six months into the job. Combine that with this new sidekick tweak which makes them not want to be a full superhero and you can see how those two things might be in conflict if it's not perfect. And apparently it wasn't perfect."

"To say the least," said Janice thoughtfully. "But I know plenty of sidekicks created during that time who are fine."

SUPERGUY 2: ELECTRIC BOGALOO

"Well, it didn't affect them all badly," said Roger. "From what I've read, it seems to have been about 30 percent of them. And those are varying degrees of messed up. Some just have bad attitudes or are a little grumpy, while others are complete nutballs. There are at least three I know of who've been retired permanently to the hospice facility near the DSF headquarters. So it's quite a range of messed up. I think someone's writing a book on it. I don't know if the DSF will be thrilled with that."

"So what you're saying is we probably want to get newly created sidekicks for this training program, because they won't be nutballs," said Oliver.

"Definitely the best option," said Roger.

"Or get ones that aren't in that 30 percent," said Janice.

"I don't know if we can avoid that," said Roger. "Seems to me that the STraP program *is* the 30 percent. The good 70 percent have kept their jobs."

Oliver turned to Emma. "Have you seen any non-nutball possibilities on the STraP list?"

"I didn't really look at it with that in mind, nor did I have a lot of time to peruse," answered Emma. "Let me take another look." She pulled an iPad from her bag. Janice leaned over and watched the screen. After a couple minutes of scrolling, Emma's facial expression began to tell the tale. She spoke without looking up, "Wow. I haven't seen one yet that wasn't created somewhere between five to eight years ago. That's right in the golden age of crazy if Roger's theory is correct."

"At least you know what you're going to get," said Janice.

"Great. Is there any way to tell if a particular one is just say, grumpy, as opposed to pathological?" asked Oliver. "I can take grumpy, I've dealt with Rog this long."

"Nice," said Roger.

"They all have histories, previous positions, and performance evaluations, so maybe that will give us some idea, but it's going to take some digging," said Emma. "Hopefully there will be enough information to keep us from getting anyone too nuts."

"Well, if you ever come across a real rookie, grab them," said Roger. "That sounds like the best option." His phone beeped and he took it out and started reading a text.

"There is one thing you guys seem to be forgetting," said Emma. "I may have this list but I haven't seen anything that says I get to pick who we get. Lily said I'm the coordinator and I would be working with STraP to line up the participants, but that still doesn't mean they won't send us whoever they want."

"True. Don't know what I was thinking, getting all optimistic about things," said Oliver.

"Hey, check it out," said Roger, holding up his phone as if they could all see what he was talking about. "Maybe you should be optimistic. Hell might just be freezing over. Joyce finally asked Alice for a date. And she said yes."

"No way," said Janice, who had been around enough to know the story.

"A real date?" asked Emma. She moved over to the couch next to Roger to get a look at his phone. "I mean a real real date, not one of those deceptive scenarios he was always suggesting. Like she won a date with Channing Tatum or something? For barbecue?"

"Why barbecue?" asked Janice.

"No idea, he just seemed to think that was the thing that would seal the deal," answered Emma.

SUPERGUY 2: ELECTRIC BOGALOO

"Barbecue is a horrible choice for a first date," said Janice.

"No doubt."

"Nothing about Channing Tatum or barbecue," answered Roger. "Seems like the real thing, but I'm going to hit him with some follow up questions just to make sure."

"Wow," said Oliver, who had also gotten up to peek at Roger's phone. Now he sat down next to Janice. "It wouldn't be the worst thing if Joyce had something to occupy him while we start this sidekick rodeo. I've been waiting for him to get back in the supervillain business with something bigger and badder any day. Maybe this will mellow him out."

"That's not gonna happen," said Janice. "He's probably got five new plots going right now. You know how supervillains are, especially the brainy ones." She reached out and took Oliver's hand and he scooted closer. It was a rarity that they got to spend much down time together. The closest they got to a real date themselves was their shared weekends on watch duty at the GLAND base.

"A hero can dream, can't he?" replied Oliver. "Speaking of which, since it's quiet, maybe we could go-"

"-Hold on," interrupted Janice, pointing to her ear, indicating that her communicator had beeped. "Stormfront here," she said aloud, and then listened. With his standard hero enhanced hearing, Oliver could follow some of the discussion. An emergency of some sort back in Thunder Bay. "Okay, I'm on my way. Stormfront out," said Janice as she pulled on her boots and stood up.

"Need help?" asked Oliver as he handed Janice her gloves.

"No, It doesn't sound too bad. No rotten eggs," she said, using the slang term for superpowered villains. She slipped on her gloves and leaned forward to kiss Oliver. "I would have liked a quiet night," she said, giving him a sympathetic smile, which then changed to a happy one, because she was a superhero after all. "Instead, I'm going to go knock some heads. See ya." With that she walked out of the room and took off through the back garage door, accompanied by the sound of rolling thunder which happened whenever she flew at top speed.

Oliver shrugged sadly to himself and turned his attention to Roger and Emma. "So fill me in on the evil guy's love life, because that's what I get to spend the night doing."

7

"HELLO? Alice?" said Raymond Joyce into his cell phone. "I must apologize. I'm going to have to delay our date a little. I have an emergency at one of my supply warehouses. Apparently an electrical problem of some sort and a fire. I would say I'll be another hour, but to be on the safe side, could we make it two? So nine? Great. I apologize again. I promise to make it up to you. Okay, see you soon." Joyce ended the call and slipped the phone into his inside suit pocket. The electrical problem in question was another attack by the mystery monster. Joyce flipped a switch to turn on the comm system. "What's our ETA, Steven?" he asked.

Speaking into his headset, Steven answered from his seat next to the pilot of the helicopter. "We should be within sight of the facility in approximately three minutes, sir. I've already patched into the security camera feeds, which should be showing on your monitors now."

KURT CLOPTON

There were four video screens mounted on the partition in front of Joyce, each showing a different feed from security cameras at a warehouse in Wauwatosa. Because of the poor visual quality of the cameras during the previous attack, new systems had been installed in the past couple of days as part of a security update across all Joyce Industries properties, giving high definition views of the current situation. These cameras also allowed for remote control access and were wired with a backup power supply in case the building lost electricity. Just in case that wasn't enough, there was also a camera mounted on the bottom of the helicopter that was exceptional at long distances and in low light. Joyce really did enjoy technology.

"Have you called in a report for our friend yet?" asked Joyce as he played with the zoom on one of the security cameras. He moved in close to get a better view of the monster's body. Smiling to himself, he marveled at the definition of the picture. 4K was definitely the way to go. So much detail, and the colors really popped.

"Yes, sir," answered Steven. "Called in the disturbance two minutes ago. There were no other high level emergencies in the system, so SuperGuy should be here soon."

"Excellent," said Joyce. "Well, since we already have a good view, let's do a little research. Go ahead and activate the first of the advanced security bots and let's see what our big blue baddie is made of." The special advanced security bots Joyce was referring to were currently flying in drone mode about thirty meters below the helicopter. There were twenty of them, all outfitted with various weaponry and with different levels of power. Joyce had them designed and equipped recently as a part of his overall security update, but instead of putting hundreds of new bots at all of his

SUPERGUY 2: ELECTRIC BOGALOO

numerous properties, he decided to create a sort of special rapid response group to tackle this particular problem. It was economical as well as effective.

The first bot shot forward and down, approaching the warehouse which was now in easy view of the helicopter, if one wanted to do the silly thing and look with the naked eye. Joyce preferred his screens. The warehouse in question was actually a group of warehouses connected at one end like a spine and growing outward like a capital letter E. There were giant doors all along the sides of the buildings for the loading and unloading of material from trucks of every size. On his screen, Joyce could see the monster had ripped through most of the warehouse on the bottom of the E, and was now stomping slowly but steadily across the open lot toward the middle building. The giant blue thing was surrounded by several of the standard security bots that still remained at the location, but they didn't seem to be giving it much to worry about. For the most part, it was simply ignoring them. The bullets from the bots' shoulder mounted mini guns ricocheted harmlessly off it and the small missiles did little more than make a pretty flash of light when they exploded. Once in a while, one of the bots either got too close or in its direct path, so the monster flicked a hand in its direction and a ball of spinning blue electricity shot out and removed the obstacle in a rather blindingly abrupt and efficient way. Whether anything remained behind of the bot was going to take even a closer look than Joyce was getting on his 4K screens.

The monster was only a third of the way across the open lot when the first advanced security bot landed in front of it. The heavily armored bot immediately opened fire with both mini guns, which were of a much larger caliber than the standard security bot equipment, in addition to using armor piercing rounds. For a couple of seconds, the bot remained intact and performed admirably. After those couple of seconds, there wasn't even anything left to recycle. The second and third bots followed shortly after that and the results only changed in how quickly they disappeared. The next few lasted a little longer because they were a step up in toughness, employing much heavier armor and larger missile systems. Still, a little longer was really, really short. Things really didn't change until about bot number twelve, which was constructed with partial superhero quality metal plating and armed with two superhero quality lasers. Unlike the inadequate effect of the previous weapons, the monster noticeably reacted in pain to the new lasers, immediately turning its attention to the new threat. The hero quality plating held up well as the monster's first electric bolts knocked the bot back but did not utterly destroy it as had been the case with the previous bots. The bot righted itself and resumed firing. Unfortunately, the lasers only seemed to make the monster angry and it reached out, extending two giant arms of blue electricity that wrapped around the bot, lifted it off the ground and then repeatedly beat it against the pavement until it came apart like a Lego toy. Joyce was not feeling good about the current direction of things.

"Steven? Let's send in the next three together, then group the last five," he said. "At least we can see how it does with multiple hero quality targets, although I'm thinking it's not going to make much of a difference."

"Yes, sir," replied Steven, tapping on the screen of his iPad. The next three bots rocketed toward the target while the remaining five increased speed to get in position. "Sir? I also see that our friend is now approaching from the east."

SUPERGUY 2: ELECTRIC BOGALOO

"Well, that's good," said Joyce. "I certainly need some more data if I'm going to get anything useful out of this. Right now it's just going to be a nice collection of scrap metal. Let's see what he can come up with."

Oliver slowed his flight speed as he approached the location where the emergency had been reported. That report had specifically said the problem was "a big blue electric monster attacking stuff." There was a time before superheroes when something like that would most likely mean someone was mixing medications and watching late night television, but nowadays it was entirely possible there would indeed be a big blue electric monster attacking stuff when Oliver showed up. He kind of hoped there wouldn't be, simply because it sounded a little messy, but there was plenty of smoke and fire and the sound of explosions to indicate otherwise. The big blue monster in question was standing in an open area between two warehouse buildings, currently engaged in a fight with three robots on the ground while five more were moving in from the air. Oliver knew from his extensive research into Raymond Joyce and Joyce Industries that this was one of his facilities, so he wasn't surprised to see the robots, which were a standard part of Joyce's security. Oliver had spent plenty of quality time fighting versions of them himself. However, in this instance, he could see these weren't just standard security robots. Oliver knew hero quality armor and lasers when he saw them, so these bots were something special. That raised a few questions, but Oliver had to set those aside for the moment and concentrate on the current threat.

The monster was big, about twice as tall as Oliver, and certainly very blue. Really a nice deep blue for the most part, with variations of lighter and darker shades in places, plus some bright blue bits where there seemed to be cracks in the thing's skin. It was a really nice overall effect. And that's not even mentioning the bluish electricity. The monster shot bolts and spheres of it from its hands, formed shields with it, and even reached out with a giant electric hand to slap away one of the bots. Speaking of the bots, that slap eliminated the last of the original three and now the next five were landing around the monster in an attempt to surround it.

"Well, I'm probably better off with a little help," said Oliver. "Or at least a little distraction." Dropping lower and flying around behind the monster, Oliver picked up speed. He planned to ram the thing from behind, hoping the impact would be enough to significantly hurt the monster, if not knock the fight out of it completely. It wasn't exactly the honorable way to go about things, but it was a technique he'd used effectively before and he'd been in enough fights with superpowered beings by now that he knew there really wasn't anything useful to be gained by landing in front of the bad guy and having a chat. And this was a big blue electricity monster after all. Oliver could find out if it was just a misunderstood big blue electricity monster after the fact. About ten feet from impact was when things started to go wrong. That was because impact happened about ten feet earlier than Oliver thought it would, and it wasn't with the monster, it was with the electric blue wall that suddenly materialized there.

SUPERGUY 2: ELECTRIC BOGALOO

In his short but eventful career as a superhero, Oliver had found that pain could be so much more than he had ever experienced as a normal guy. Sure, there were a multitude of pains to be experienced as a non-hero, like the sharp sting of a paper cut or the dull ache of a tooth. Or one could enjoy the slow searing discomfort of a burn or the deep agony of a torn muscle. Not to mention a broken bone or fractured ribs. And don't forget the pain of a good stomach flu or some *"Why in whatever Deity's name would I ever eat hot salsa right before bed? I don't even like nachos that much. And the calories..."* heartburn. Or a solid kick to the groin. But if you wrapped all those different pains up together, increased them by a factor of ten, and then kicked him in the groin two more times, you might have the pain Oliver was feeling right then. Simply put, it freaking hurt. He came to a dead stop when he slammed into the wall of electricity, but he didn't drop to the ground. Instead, the wall sort of clung on to Oliver, pulling him slightly into it, almost like a hug from your great aunt, if the hug came with a hundred stinging tendrils instead of two flabby arms and thousands of volts rather than strange odors and awkwardness.

Oliver really pushed himself to think. Not to think of a way of escaping this current trap, but just to think, period. He was finding it very hard to do. Mostly in his mind he was just screaming incoherently, although it would be found on the security footage later that he was also screaming incoherently outside his mind as well. Just oodles of incoherent screaming. When Oliver was finally able to get his mind functioning again, he realized it was because the wall of electricity had dissipated and he had flopped to the ground and begun a solid bit of moaning and drooling. Still, it only took a few seconds for him to recover and push himself to his feet, which was one of the benefits built into the super serum. You can't have your hero needing a few days to shake off a concussion when the bad guy was lining up another left hook, so the serum designers made quick recovery a high priority. Oliver thought of it as really just a nice way for him to feel pain much more often, but always with a clear head. Speaking of which, a missile fired by one of the bots glanced off a shield projected by the monster and careened into the side of Oliver's head, detonating with an ear-splitting crack and sending him tumbling back to the ground.

Landing at the feet of one of the other bots, Oliver looked up to see it staring down at him. Something about its look gave Oliver the distinct impression that it was trying to decide whether to keep attacking the monster or maybe have a go at him. Whether or not it reached a decision and what that decision was would remain a mystery because a column of blue electricity one foot in diameter slammed it back through the warehouse wall a short distance away. Oliver rolled over onto his stomach, pushed up into a crouch and launched himself at the monster's side. He did it without much thought, moving on the super instinct he now possessed as a part of being a hero. The opening was there. The monster was distracted, focused on two bots who were attacking simultaneously with laser cannons and missiles, and it never saw Oliver coming from the side. Lowering his shoulder, Oliver drilled the monster in the ribs (assuming it had ribs) and felt it fold over awkwardly from the impact. The blow sent it sprawling across the pavement for thirty meters, all the while being tracked by the lasers and missiles from the bots. It took a lot of unprotected hits until it righted itself and threw up a wall of electricity in front of it.

SUPERGUY 2: ELECTRIC BOGALOO

There were four bots still operational, although one was missing an arm and, as Oliver watched, another that was trying to work its way around the protective wall got shredded by a flurry of thin, electric bolts. So make that three. Or two and a half. The two previously doing the damage with their laser cannons were now focusing on the wall, sending a barrage at it and steadily wearing it away. Oliver could see the monster through the wall and was trying to assess how injured it might be when the one-armed bot walked in front of him, blocking his view. It seemed to be trudging forward in some kind of slow charge, pacing itself for when the wall disappeared.

"Hey, you're kinda in the way," Oliver muttered, starting to move to the side for a better view, but then he stopped. "Or perfectly in the way." Oliver leaped into the air and shot forward, plowing into the back of the one-armed bot and carrying it into the decaying electrical wall. The wall collapsed with a flash of blue light and an explosion of sparks, and Oliver and his unlucky shield continued on to collide with the monster. Things did not go well for the bot, which was overloaded by the electricity in the wall and then the collision with the monster, and it exploded on impact. The explosion knocked Oliver and the monster apart, throwing them each to the ground again. The two remaining bots closed on the monster, peppering it with laser blasts and missiles. It struggled to its knees and managed to fire off a wave of electricity just a half meter off the ground. Oliver pushed himself off the pavement and flew upward to be clear of the wave, but the two bots didn't respond in time. The wave ripped through their legs just below the knee and sent them toppling over, both now legless, and flopped face down.

Not wanting to lose all his temporary allies, Oliver flew down, grabbed both bots just below their neck joints and picked them up. They didn't seem to mind and Oliver flew them forward toward the monster. It was back on its feet but unsteady, stumbling backward as it fought to regain its control on the fight. The bots were smart enough—or savagely evil enough—to start firing again, pelting the monster mercilessly. Oliver tossed the bots into the air, allowing them to keep firing, while he shot forward at the monster. Just before impact, he kicked his feet forward and slammed them in the monster's chest, sending it flying backward where it collided with the cement platform of a loading dock. The two bots fell to the ground behind Oliver, one exploding as its power core cracked open, while the other's laser cannon got stuck in the firing position and began to shoot it around the yard like a loose water hose. Oliver landed a short distance from the monster, ready to shoot forward on the attack again if needed, but it seemed like the fight might finally be out of the thing. It groaned from where it leaned against the loading dock, the noise accented with indiscriminate snaps of electrical discharge, and accompanied by the smell of singed hair and something close to burnt waffles.

"Okay, it seems like we've got things out of our system now," said Oliver. "You want to tell me what's got you so mad at warehouses? Or is it buildings in general? Maybe storage buildings specifically? Were you stuffed inside lockers too much in high school? Or is this something we can trace even farther back in your childhood? Assuming you had a childhood. Can you even understand me?"

SUPERGUY 2: ELECTRIC BOGALOO

"I understand you, SuperGuy," the monster growled. He said that last word as if it tasted like rancid onion and tube sock soup.

Oliver raised his eyebrows. "You know me? Well, that's a point for you. I don't believe I know you."

The monster chuckled. Or at least it sounded like a chuckle to Oliver. It also sounded like someone moving furniture in the apartment upstairs by rolling the couch where they wanted it instead of sliding it.

"True," said the monster. "You probably wouldn't. You are too big, a part of The System. I was too small."

"You don't seem particularly small to me."

"No, not anymore. I am different now. I have power too."

"And you're using that power to attack buildings? I know these warehouses aren't really architectural achievements, but they don't seem like they're hurting anyone. Am I missing something?"

The monster growled in frustration and Oliver tensed up, ready to continue the fight.

"This is Gray Matter's," said the monster, gesturing feebly at the warehouses. "I will destroy Gray Matter."

"Oh, well then I'm kind of sorry I showed up. I'm not exactly against you attacking Gray Matter."

"Not just Gray Matter. I will crush you too. I will destroy you both."

"Both?" said Oliver. "That's not logical. You know how this works, right? Good versus bad, superhero versus supervillain. There really are two distinct sides here. The general rule of thumb is that you pick one side or the other. Otherwise you're just giving yourself twice the amount of work."

"No, you both deserve to be destroyed," replied the monster. "And The System that created you too."

"Wow, the whole System? Seems like a lot. You ever consider starting smaller? Maybe a vendetta on a more insignificant scale? Say, hipsters for example? Or people who wear pajama bottoms out like they're regular pants? You know, the real threats to society."

"No. You, Gray Matter, The System. It must all cease to exist."

"Well, I guess if you look at it that way it's just a simple three step plan," said Oliver. "So you're really set on this?"

"It must cease."

"Alright," said Oliver, feeling like he was beginning to run out of topics for discussion while still not having a good idea what he was dealing with. "Well...let's back it up. Start with something simple. What's your name?"

"Ah. Before I was known as something else," said the monster. Oliver thought he sounded kind of wistful. "When I worked for him. When I was also a part of The System. Before you. Before the vat. But now I am something new. You can call me Electric Boogaloo."

"Wha—say again?"

"Electric Boogaloo."

"I'm sorry, I'm having trouble understanding you. I don't know if it's an accent thing, or maybe a speech impediment. I don't want to be insensitive here. I just...Can you spell it?" The monster groaned again in frustration, but he did spell it. "Oh, yep, yeah. I was hearing it right. Electric Boogaloo. That's...um. That's...Well, I guess it's no worse than SuperGuy, am I right?" The monster groaned again. "But wait, what was that thing from before? You said 'the vat.'

SUPERGUY 2: ELECTRIC BOGALOO

You mean? You're? Um…what's his name?" Oliver snapped his fingers. "Alan?"

"Alex!" corrected the monster. "Alex!"

"Oh, yeah, yeah, yeah, that's right. I really am sorry about that whole thing. The vat and all. But in my defense, I thought you were trying to kill me. I didn't find out until afterward that Gray Matter had sent you back to turn off the laser. It was just an unfortunate mistake."

"Yes," chuckled Electric Boogaloo. "An unfortunate mistake. But now I will be able to keep you and Gray Matter from creating any more unfortunate mistakes."

"Really? Kind of seems like your little rodeo has ended."

"No, not yet," said Electric Boogaloo as he raised a hand. A rope of electricity arced upward to a power pole above. Oliver crouched, ready for another onslaught, but it didn't come. Instead, blue electricity spread over Electric Boogaloo's body like a blanket and he blinked out of existence.

Oliver stared at the spot where Electric Boogaloo had been. After a couple of seconds, the bot whose laser cannon was stuck bounced by and Oliver stomped on it with his foot, putting an end to its day. "Okay," said Oliver thoughtfully. "I guess maybe some more rodeoing."

Raymond Joyce watched the end of the battle again, rewinding and replaying the part where the monster had spoken. It was Alex. He supposed that was possible, although if he were a betting man, he would have wagered it was more likely the young man would have ended up as a pile of something that aspired to someday be called ooze. But that was super serums for you, especially the slightly off ones that made villains. They were unpredictable. Throw in the whole karma angle of the good guy accidentally dunking a henchman in the pot and it's practically a sure thing you'll get a supervillain instead of a puddle of ooze. Unfortunately for Joyce, it seemed the new monster version of Alex hated him as much as he hated SuperGuy. And this whole System thing he was ranting about was a bit of a mystery. The DSF specifically? The whole government? Major League Baseball? Still, Joyce wondered if he could find a way around all that and get something useful out of this. Alex's brain was a mangled mess, that was obvious. Joyce had used multiple spoiled super serums in the vat, as well as hero quality acid, so Alex never really had a chance to come out thinking clearly. The fact that he blamed Joyce was unfortunate, but perhaps with the proper pressure he could be manipulated, or even controlled. Maybe his focus could be shifted toward SuperGuy, at least in the short term. That would certainly provide Joyce with a very nice diversion, allowing him to move forward with a little something of his own.

"Steven?" said Joyce. "Let's head back now. I don't want to be late for my date with Alice."

"Yes, sir," said Steven, who relayed the order to the pilot. The helicopter banked slightly and picked up speed.

Joyce tapped his fingers on the armrest, thinking about the blue monster. "I would also like you to open a new file. Let's name it...Capture the Blue Guy. No, that's terrible. Um, Trap Alex? No. Baiting the Blue Monster? Oh, I have nothing. Can you think of anything?"

"Blue Target?"

SUPERGUY 2: ELECTRIC BOGALOO

"Eh…"

"Something Borrowed, Something Blue?"

"Now you're not even trying," said Joyce. "Oh! Blue Monster Bingo!"

"Ah, no, you've already used that," said Steven after a couple of seconds.

"I have? For what?" asked Joyce. "I don't recall that."

"I'd have to check, but it's here in the list of plans," said Steven. "It looks old, perhaps we could re-use it."

"No, no. I'll come up with something. Titles are so hard. Let's just call it Untitled Blue Plan for now and we'll keep workshopping it. Also, pull up Plan Waterworld and begin implementing the preliminary steps. I think it's about time to get going on that too."

8

"**So** the giant blue electric monster is that Alex guy you dumped in the vat of acid?" asked Emma.

She, Roger, and Oliver were standing outside the control room in the Garage. It was the morning after Oliver's encounter with the monster now known as Electric Boogaloo, and the Garage was buzzing with activity. It had nothing to do with the battle or the monster; instead, it had to do with the new sidekick program. The Mayor's office had decided the best—and cheapest—way to house the sidekicks was in the Garage, so there were construction workers roughing in an addition to the offices on the far right side next to the stairs. It would comprise two stories, the upper floor being an apartment for the sidekick similar to Oliver and Roger's, but much smaller and lacking a shower or kitchen area, and the addition on the lower floor would be combined with the current, kind of scary old bathroom and Emma's office (formerly a storage room) to create a much larger kitchen and bathroom with showers. The old kitchen was going to be remodeled into a larger office for Emma, which would put her right next to the control room and give her easy access with a connecting door. It would also be the third room she had occupied as an office in the Garage in less than a year, and the first, she hoped, that wouldn't smell completely like machine lubricants and old tires.

"Okay, and I have to say this again, I did not dump him in the vat of acid. I defended myself in a situation where I thought he was going to kill me, and he accidentally fell into a vat of acid. Really as much gravity's fault as mine," said Oliver.

"I've heard it both ways," said Roger. "But does it really matter? He blames you so it's kind of a moot point."

"When you talked to him, did you get the sense he could be reasoned with?" asked Emma.

"Nah, he seemed pretty set on the whole revenge/vendetta thing," replied Oliver. "He was talking some gibberish about hating Gray Matter too, and 'the System'"—Oliver used air quotes—"whatever that is, but the whole retribution angle seemed pretty set in stone."

"Are you positive?" asked Emma. "You gotta realize he's been sitting around stewing about this for a few months with no other rational perspective. Maybe he just needs that other perspective. Some kind of help, or some sympathy. There could still be some good left in him. You know, like Darth Vader."

"Oh, come on!" yelled Roger. "Tell me you did not just go there. Darth Vader?"

"Well, Vader came back to the good side in the end. Oliver did kind of make this Alex guy into a monster—"

"I did not!"

"—and if there's a chance there's still good in him, that he could be saved from being a supervillain, don't you think Oliver owes it to him to try? It's kind of a Darth Vader dilemma," said Emma.

"It is not a dilemma! There is no dilemma!" screamed Roger. "Darth Vader was a bad dude. Finding good in him is the dumbest storyline ever. Ever! He killed everybody! He killed a bunch of kids! Who cares if there's good in him? Wait, check that. He killed a bunch of KIDS! There isn't any good in him! None! How do people forget that!?"

"You're coming through as kind of wishy washy on this, Rog," said Oliver. "So you *do* think we can save him?"

Roger grabbed the sides of his head and bent over while turning in a circle and groaning. Eventually he straightened back up and said, "I don't know. Maybe."

"Actually, Mr. Allen, I think your first instinct on that is correct," said a voice behind the group. They turned to find the Police Chief walking toward them.

"Hey, shouldn't the fancy security system you installed warn us when someone shows up?" Oliver asked Roger in a stage whisper.

Roger shrugged. "Construction," he said simply.

The Police Chief took off his hat as he stopped in front of them, giving a tight smile to Emma, the only one of the three he seemed prepared to like in the least. "I got a briefing on last night's incident on the way over," he said. "The man in question, this Alex Bauerman, was not a good guy to begin with. Before he started working for Joyce, with all the questionable morality that comes with that alone, he was involved in a lot of white collar shenanigans—,"

"Shenanigans?" asked Oliver. "Is that a legal term?"

SUPERGUY 2: ELECTRIC BOGALOO

"Yes, it's between a misdemeanor and a felony, but only on Tuesdays," said Roger.

The Chief chose to ignore them and continued, "—not to mention a bunch of other things we suspect he was connected to. He wasn't a crime kingpin or anything but he was intelligent and knew the local landscape well, and was subsequently one of the first hires when Joyce came to town and began setting up his little evil empire."

"Okay, so he's a bad guy, which frankly makes me feel a little better about the whole vat thing," said Oliver. "But what about him saying he hated Gray Matter too? That doesn't sound all that bad. It could even be helpful."

"True," said Roger. "Maybe you could just stay out of the way the next time he's ransacking a Joyce place. Just let those two work it out and then mop up what's left over."

"I don't know if that would work," said Emma. "If it's something the public will see, like the warehouse fight last night, our city superhero better show up. There are plenty of phone videos going around this morning from witnesses who lived nearby. A big blue electric monster blowing stuff up is the kind of thing that gets noticed."

"I agree with Emma," said the Chief. "You're going to have to show up. You know, do the job the dopes in the Mayor's office hired you to do." Whether the Chief's disdain was targeted at the dopes in the Mayor's office or at Oliver was hard to tell because he really sort of ladled it on everything like a good gravy.

"Well, with those inspiring words, how could I resist?" said Oliver in a very flat, uninspired voice.

"I must have tuned out for a minute because I missed the inspiring bit," said Roger.

"So what's all this?" the Chief asked, gesturing to where the work was being done. He took a few steps toward the far side of the offices. Emma walked with him while Roger and Oliver slouched along after them. The framing was already done and workers were busy running electrical and plumbing lines where they needed to go.

"This is because of STraP," answered Emma.

"The sidekick thing?"

"Yep. The Mayor decided we could house them right here," said Emma as the group came to a stop in front of the new construction.

"So that's starting already?" asked the Chief.

"First one shows up next week," said Roger.

"I thought there'd be a little more time before I had to start worrying about that too." The Chief shook his head, his expression one of distinct annoyance. Oliver recognized it well.

"Why's it a worry for you?" asked Oliver. "We're the ones who have to deal with them."

"Oh, I've had enough time to talk to some of my friends in the profession about this program, including a couple who had the pleasure of participating. Their reviews were not complimentary. You may be the ones dealing with the sidekicks most closely but their messes will spill out into my unfortunate city. And I'm told most certainly that there will be messes," said the Chief, turning back to look at the others. "Do I have the wrong impression?"

"No, no. That's pretty much the feeling we've been getting," said Oliver, along with enthusiastic nods from Roger and Emma.

"I'm going to try to influence their choices as much as possible, but I don't know that I'll really have any say," said

SUPERGUY 2: ELECTRIC BOGALOO

Emma. "The STraP coordinator I've spoken with seems to be listening, but that doesn't mean she's going to send us who I want. Not that I've found anyone we really want."

"Our plan for the moment is to keep whoever they send busy doing trainings," said Oliver. "Whatever the city's got and maybe even have Roger make some up. Plus, we might make them do a bunch of the public relations stuff. That is, if we think we can trust them out in public."

"I like the sound of your sidekick pals staying right here and training," said the Chief. "Why don't you concentrate on that? Maybe not so much PR. The less time out in public, the better. Cuts down on the chances of something going wrong. Besides, Oliver, I know how much you like doing the little speeches and ribbon cuttings." Not waiting for any replies, the Chief turned and walked toward the exit.

After he was out the door, Oliver said, "So I guess it's the training we'll be focusing on?"

"Seems like he was leaning that way," said Roger.

"Speaking of training, you've got some to do yourself," said Emma, pointing at Oliver.

"What do you mean? I've done every training program the city's got, both big and ridiculously small. Hand washing. I had to do hand washing for some reason. You know there's an hour training for hand washing? Granted, it's much more complicated than you think, but I'm not medical. I'm not doing surgery. I'm not even a first responder, despite my usually being on the scene first. There can't possibly be any trainings left for me to do."

"It's not city. It's for STraP. Sidekick mentor training," said Emma. "You've got a two day session starting tomorrow at the DSF Convention Center in D.C. Bet it makes that hour of hand washing look good."

"Two days?" said Oliver, cringing. "Mentoring?"

"You gotta learn not to say naughty words in front of the little ones," said Roger.

"But it takes two days to learn that?"

"Don't be silly," said Emma. "I'm sure they'll teach you how to fake like you're a good person and be a positive role model for the sidekicks to learn from, not to mention being a presence that inspires them to follow their dreams. But it'll mostly be the naughty words stuff."

9

OLIVER found himself in a familiar setting a couple of days later, sitting at a table in the food court area of the DSF convention center. It wasn't exactly like a food court you'd find in a mall because there were no franchise fast food places, only a couple of carts that sold pre-made sandwiches and drinks, staffed by low level DSF employees who must have lost a bet. Only having these simple food carts made sense since there weren't always enough trainings taking place in the convention center to sustain business for a place like McDonald's or Subway, but also because the majority of attendees were superheroes, who didn't need to eat at all. Still, old habits were hard to break, and Oliver found himself staring at the plastic encased turkey and cheese on wheat he had just bought.

"Regretting your choice?" asked Golden Gal.

"Always," replied Oliver.

"You should have gotten the wrap," said Sun Son. "Always go with the wrap. The bread's better."

"I should have gotten a candy bar or three," said Oliver, shaking his head. "It's not like I need to make sound nutritional decisions."

Golden Gal nodded. "True, but that's also the strange thing about the whole not needing food thing. I used to eat like crap before I became a hero, but now that I can eat all the bad food I want, I choose fruits and vegetables all the time." She held up the apple she had purchased at the cart. "I will go to town on a veggie tray at a party. I mean, carrot sticks. Yum. It's just weird."

"I barely eat at all," said Sun Son. "If I do, it's something unusual that I've never had. Like plantains or star fruit. Or buffalo. I tried that a while back on a trip to South Dakota."

"I have a friend who'd probably not like that," said Oliver, thinking of Buffalo, his fellow GLAND group member. "Are there any turkey based heroes? Or cheese? Now I need to know if I'm offending anyone."

"There are lots of bird related heroes," answered Golden Gal. "You think they'd have issues with your choice of sandwich?"

"Maybe just the truly fowl ones, but they'd have to be villains, am I right?" said Oliver. Sun Son just groaned.

"Hah," laughed Golden Gal in an exaggerated way, slapping her hand on the table. "You're too much. Please stop. And I mean that. Please."

Oliver still found it a little hard to believe he was sitting around making terrible jokes with Golden Gal, or Gigi as her friends called her, one of the most famous superheroes in the world. When she sat down next to him at the opening training session on the first day and introduced herself, it took him about ten seconds to respond despite the quick recovery skills zapped into his brain by the super serum. Golden Gal herself didn't seem to notice, or perhaps she was simply used to it and too polite to say anything. She was the quintessential superhero, with long, wavy golden hair, impeccable features, and perfect skin. She had a similar costume to Stormfront, in that it was basically a bathing suit with a cape and high boots, but that was standard fare for the DSF female uniforms. The designers were apparently working from a costume palette grounded in 1980s comics and weren't going to stray from that.

Eventually, after a couple of minutes of weirdness that mostly consisted of Oliver yelling "Golden Gal!" repeatedly inside his own head, he settled down and was able to sustain a pleasant conversation. Gigi herself turned out to be an ordinary superhero, albeit on a lot bigger scale than most, but not on too big of a scale that she could avoid having to attend DSF trainings. Like Oliver, she was attending the mentoring training, but not because of the STraP program. She was there because of her status. Being one of the most famous heroes in the world often put her in mentoring situations with other superheroes by default and the DSF thought it would be a good policy to have her trained to handle that responsibility. And the DSF liked their policies. And policies meant trainings. And the one thing that the DSF liked almost as much as policies was trainings. Regardless of the reason, it gave Oliver a friend to commiserate with as they worked their way through two days of mind-numbing training sessions.

They were occasionally joined by Gigi's friend, Sun Son. He was Gainesville, Florida's hero, and was at the convention center for a different training. The two veteran heroes had taken their serums the same year and met each other at their original hero orientation trainings.

"You know, when your jokes start to get as bad as my name, you might want to listen to her and stop," said Sun Son.

"I don't think it's that bad," said Oliver. "You're talking to SuperGuy, remember?"

"You know it could have been worse, Sonny," said Gigi. "You ended up with cool fire powers when you could have been stuck with tiny arms and a weird desire for laying on the bottom of lakes." She looked at Oliver. "Did you know they were originally considering making him an alligator?"

"Really?"

"Oh yeah," chuckled Sonny. "They wanted me to be the Gator, or the Green Gator, or something like that, but they couldn't figure out the powers. Nothing made sense. Can't have a hero run up to the bad guys and transform into an alligator, all tiny legs and laying on his belly. Just didn't make sense. Plus there's the giant jaws and all the teeth. Kind of a public relations nightmare to have a gator ripping bad guys apart left and right. That would not make for good news footage. So logic prevailed and I got cool powers and a dumb name. They had the elementary schools nominate names and vote on them. And, as luck would have it, pandas were very popular that year for some unknown reason. Just a mystery. It's not like there's a zoo full of pandas in Gainesville. No pandas at all. But pandas, whether there are any around or not, are named things like Ling-Ling and Hsing-Hsing, so some clever teacher brainstormed with her fifth graders and I got Sun Son. Since I'm Latino, I was hoping for something cool based on that. A little fuego or something. But no, I got Sun Son."

SUPERGUY 2: ELECTRIC BOGALOO

"I got a dumb name and no cool powers," said Oliver. "Does that make me the winner?"

"We're all winners," said Gigi. "And we should all get nice, shiny trophies. Personally, I think they should have gone even a little more panda with you, Sonny. At least with the costume. A fire controlling panda would've been a good mash-up, plus great for selling merchandise."

"Where were you when they were thinking me up, Gigi? I would have been so much cooler," said Sonny.

"Actually, if you think about it, you would've had a cute panda being engulfed in flames every time you went hot. That image might have been as popular as the gator ripping bad guys apart," said Oliver. "Plus, can you imagine being in a suit like that? I know we don't feel temperature because of the serum, but a panda suit in summer? In Florida? You're a fire guy and I bet you'd still be uncomfortably warm."

"Hey, speaking of uncomfortable," interrupted Gigi, nodding in the direction of a far table. "That's your fellow supergroup friend, isn't it?" Oliver followed her look and saw The Creeper sitting alone on the other side of the food court. And not just alone at his table, but several tables around him had cleared out too.

"Yep, that's The Creeper," said Oliver.

"Oh, that's him," said Sonny, getting his first chance to see the man after hearing about him from the other two. "Now that is not a cuddly panda."

"No, not at all," said Oliver.

"I kinda see what you guys mean, but don't you think you're overdoing it a bit?" said Gigi. "When we spoke after that session yesterday, he seemed just like any other hero, except for his costume. That bathrobe is disgusting."

"That is not just any other hero, Gigi," said Sonny. He looked up at the ceiling with a puzzled expression. "Is there something wrong with the lights? It seems darker over there."

"Oh, it is. That's just him," replied Oliver. "It's almost like he sucks in light like a black hole. We actually spent weeks checking the lighting in the new GLAND headquarters because we thought we were experiencing brownouts. Finally figured out it only happened when he was in the room."

"And you still don't see a problem with the guy?" asked Sonny, giving Gigi a skeptical look.

"Not really, but that's just me. I had a little extra presence and charisma in my serum, so I don't really get affected by theatrics."

"Well, you're lucky," said Sonny. "I'm kind of surprised anyone would go that direction for a hero. Seems a much better fit for a villain to me."

"True, but you do almost get used to the aura after awhile," said Oliver. "Stress on the almost. That aura is why he's here, really. He told me his city, Erie, signed up for the STraP program because they were hoping a lovable sidekick would lighten his image. How bad did those guys screw things up with their hero? Can you imagine how they feel now? They thought they were getting all cute with the whole Erie and Creeper thing and this is what they got. And I thought Milwaukee screwed things up with the whole generic theme, but this is much worse because they did it on purpose. Anyway, I don't know if getting him a sidekick will help, but he might be the most successful mentor in the program. I don't think any sidekick will want to get on his bad side."

"Extra charisma or not, I still think you guys are overdoing it a little," said Gigi. "It's just a questionable wardrobe situation and a little bad lighting."

SUPERGUY 2: ELECTRIC BOGALOO

"Okay, you remember that training yesterday when we had to pair up and do the *Who Am I?* questionnaires?" asked Oliver. Gigi nodded. "Well, we were supposed to pair up with someone we didn't know, precisely so we could get to know someone new and then introduce them to the group, right? Only no one was going to pair up with The Creeper, so I did to keep it from getting too awkward. Anyway, do you recall what I said when I introduced him based on the answers he gave me about himself?"

"Yes, it all seemed pretty normal to me."

"That's because I made them all up. Every single one. To make them normal. His real answers were not normal. They were incredibly…just wrong. Just so, so wrong." Oliver shook his head as he stared at the table. "I was spooked by his answers and I'm used to him. I can't imagine what the others in the session would have thought." He dug around inside his complimentary tote bag and pulled out a sheet of paper. He held it out to Gigi. "Here is what I wrote for the first few answers before I decided some things should just never, ever be written down." Gigi took the sheet of paper and Sonny slid around to read it with her.

"Oh…boy," said Sonny. His facial expression floated somewhere between confused and disturbed.

"Okay," said Gigi. "You're right. The name fits."

10

RAYMOND Joyce sat passively in front of his office's video wall. It used to be a wall of twelve separate monitors that could be used to create a larger, single image, but despite the monitors being cutting edge, Joyce still found the small breaks between the screens to be visually disrupting, so he recently upgraded to one gigantic screen wall. It was really cool, and really big. It was so impressive that sometimes, just for kicks, he would put a live shot of himself on it during meetings so his withering glares would be that much more effective. It was like being Bono at a U2 concert, except evil. And in stunning widescreen 4K. Currently, the center section of the video wall displayed the best camera angle available of the event Joyce was watching, while several smaller feeds floated above showing whatever other individual views were accessible via other remote cameras.

Tapping his fingers on the arm of his chair patiently, Joyce watched Operation Booberry being put into action.

SUPERGUY 2: ELECTRIC BOGALOO

The name was Steven's suggestion, but no one was happy with it. They simply failed to come up with something better before it was time to implement it. Joyce had resolved to change it in his memoir. Anyway, it was a relatively simple plan, with only one goal, which was to capture Electric Boogaloo. But that was the problem with the plan. Not the capturing the monster part—that was fine—but the simplicity was bothersome. Joyce was not a fan. He preferred intricate machinations involving multiple layers of complexity, some of which had absolutely nothing to do with the actual plan. You could call those parts diversions if you were that kind of person, but that was just plain wrong. The actual diversion (of Joyce's imaginary ideal plan) would really have happened two layers of the plan ago. Anyone trying to figure the whole thing out would be stuck following a tangent that was there simply for Joyce's love of convoluted plots and his penchant for overthinking and overdoing everything. He couldn't get out of his own head, not that he much wanted to. For him, that was where perfection began and ended. Unfortunately, there hadn't been enough time to formulate a Gray Matter level plan. This was an exceptional plan, to be sure. An undoubtedly unparalleled plan based on several independent measures, but boy was it rather simple. Kind of like a mousetrap. Obviously one of the best mousetraps ever conceived, yet still a mousetrap. And the name was such a disappointment.

Alex was impressed with the level of security in this facility. He was aware that his memory may not have been the best anymore after his transformation, and that his thoughts shared room with a good number of nonstop commercial jingles and multiple voices lobbying for the position of Evil Voice Telling Alex To Do Bad Things, but he was pretty sure no Joyce Industries buildings had security this good back when he worked there. It wasn't just the advanced systems either, but the sheer number of security bots that just kept coming from the second he stepped inside, despite how many he obliterated.

It hadn't been that heavy at the start. He had easily ripped through the outer fencing and made his way into the complex of buildings. This was a key research and construction facility that Alex knew was more vital to Gray Matter than his last target. Alex really wanted to hurt Gray Matter this time, especially after failing to have the impact he desired in his previous attempt because of the interruption by SuperGuy. So Alex planned to be a little more discreet with this objective. Instead of standing outside and blowing up every building in sight in a well populated suburb, he chose a much more secluded target, much farther away from the city, and his plan was to get inside quickly where he could cause maximum damage with hopefully minimum commotion. That would keep the outside world from discovering what was happening, and possibly drawing the attention of SuperGuy, and allow Alex to focus on Gray Matter. Not that Alex expected the supervillain to be there personally, but little by little he would destroy everything Gray Matter had until he finally reached the man himself.

After making his way to the main buildings, being careful to use only low powered blasts of electricity to disable any security bots instead of blowing them up spectacularly as he had previously, Alex ripped open a loading dock door and entered. He meticulously proceeded deeper into the building, destroying anything of importance as he went. It was very easy at first, especially on the first two floors that were above ground. Once again he was careful to demolish everything that he could, but in a very quiet way, so that no one in nearby neighborhoods would notice a disturbance and call the authorities. So no big explosions or accompanying fires. Mostly he just overloaded and fried the important electronic components. But subtlety wasn't easy for Alex. It was not exactly his first instinct. Still, after those first two floors it wouldn't matter as much, because the other five floors of this facility were built underground due to Gray Matter's love of secrecy. That's where the more important stuff was anyway, and also the heavier security.

It was about the third sublevel where Alex started to wonder about that heavier security. There were the usual number of security bots Alex expected to find in the facility, but there seemed to be a lot more bots responding from off-site to the attack. Having noticed this new security response at the last location, Alex wasn't surprised he was facing a similar one here. However, the sheer number of the responding security bots was unexpected. For every one bot he ripped apart in front of him as he made his way deeper into the building, Alex had to destroy four or five that appeared behind him. And these weren't the standard security bots either, but more of the advanced type he fought at the previous facility, armed with heavier weapons and armor. He still ripped them apart, but it took a bit more power on his part. He was plenty happy to do it, knowing that each bot or bit of machinery he destroyed was one more small crack in

Gray Matter's gleaming tower, a tower that Alex would eventually see toppled.

Destroying yet another two advanced security bots, Alex reached the end of the third sublevel and promptly wrenched a section of the floor open to expose the area underneath. He dropped down into the fourth level and paused. This floor was much different than Alex remembered from when he had worked for Gray Matter. There had been a lot of recent renovations, although the work didn't seem finished. Walls had been stripped away, leaving only the support beams in place, and any equipment that used to be housed here was now gone. Alex wondered what Gray Matter was planning for this floor, but before he could put much thought into it, several security bots sprang to life in front of him. Shattering the bots as he went, Alex patiently worked his way across the floor making sure that he missed nothing worth destroying, but the level was essentially empty.

He was about halfway across when more of the advanced response security bots started to drop through the hole he had left from the third floor. Peppered by missiles and a few superhero quality lasers, Alex turned and began to dispatch the new targets one by one. This was beginning to get tiring. Literally. He still had another floor to destroy in this building, and there were two other buildings in this complex he had planned to demolish as well. With the energy it was taking him to eliminate all the extra security bots, he wasn't going to have enough power to do more than the remaining floor of this building. That was disappointing. Deciding that there was nothing left worth destroying on this floor except bots and wanting to conserve his energy for the last floor, Alex ripped a hole open to the fifth floor and dropped through.

SUPERGUY 2: ELECTRIC BOGALOO

What he found below was a target rich environment, to say the least. Apparently all of the equipment from the floor above had been temporarily stored here for the renovation. Expensive devices stacked on top of priceless machines sitting next to exceptionally rare gadgets. Items lined the wide main hallway down the length of the floor, sat on the top of a giant table in a glass walled conference room, and seemed to be stuck in every available corner Alex could see. Basically, it was two floors worth of targets for the price of one. It was debatable whether Alex had lips in his current form, but if he did, they now formed the biggest smile he'd had since becoming a giant, vengeance seeking, blue electricity monster. Sighing with joy, Alex waded forward and unleashed a web of electricity that spread outward and danced across every target surface it could find. Sparks flew, plastic melted, and smoke curled up toward the ceiling as each sensitive piece of equipment was turned into slag.

It was a rapturous twenty minutes for Alex as he walked steadily across the fifth sublevel of the facility, wreaking havoc on any item of value he saw. In his omelet of a mind, he tallied off every object in terms of the money it was costing Gray Matter, as well as the time in terms of lost research and productivity. It really was the most fun Alex had ever had, either as himself or as a monster. When he finally reached the end of the main hallway and melted the contents of the last lab on the floor, he turned to survey the wasteland he had left behind. It was glorious. It was even more satisfying when he saw the advanced security bots dropping through the hole at the far end of the hallway. They were many in number, but much too late. Alex opened his palm toward the nearest wall outlet and a thin arc of electricity leapt out to make a connection. As he did at the end of his fight with SuperGuy, he would simply escape from the material world into the electrical world of wires and travel to the safety of his home, where he could rest and recharge for his next attack. He waited, but nothing happened. The bots moved steadily closer. Maybe it was a dead outlet. Alex shifted focus to a lighting fixture in the ceiling, and then to another outlet. No connection. No path out. The bots closed in. Alex was going to have to fight his way out.

It didn't last long. These security bots were some of the strongest yet. Full superhero quality metal armor with superhero quality lasers and superhero quality metal jacketed bullets and missiles. Alex took out two while being pelted mercilessly by the others. His vision blurred as he tired from the strain of forcing what little energy he had left into fighting off his attackers. A hum filled his head and he stumbled to his knees. He found it difficult to understand what was happening. He had just been so happy a few minutes ago. The last thing he remembered seeing was a large, squarish bot on four wheels move forward and shoot what looked like a shining golden net over him. Then all was darkness.

Raymond Joyce muted the video and turned his chair back to his desk. His annoyingly uncomplicated plan (he preferred not to think of the name) had worked to perfection and left him feeling a bit empty inside. If this one did actually make it into the memoir, it would not only have a new name but also some seriously embellished complexity. Still, while he couldn't say the result was all that mattered, the monster was his. Now Joyce had to see if he could make use of it or if it would have to be eliminated. Either would be fine, but the former would probably prove to be much more fun. A tone sounded from the speaker on his desk.

"Yes, Steven?" said Joyce.

"Miss Alice is here," replied his assistant through the speaker.

"Excellent, please send her in," said Joyce. He grabbed his remote and turned toward the monitors to shut them off, but hesitated. So far he had kept Alice in the dark about his professional activities, preferring not to complicate a burgeoning love affair with the whole "you're dating an evil supervillain" talk. But perhaps now it was time to test the waters, so to speak. See if she wouldn't be scared off with a hint of who Raymond Joyce was. So he left the monitors on, though muted, and walked across the office to greet Alice as she entered. His heart skipped a beat each time he saw her, and this time was no different, which he found disappointing. Sure, it was cute in that sappy, romantic way, but he was a supervillain and felt quite certain he should be able to fall in love with a woman in a cold, distant, and slightly villainous manner.

"You look absolutely stunning," said Joyce, taking her hands and giving them the slightest squeeze as he leaned in and kissed her on the cheek.

Alice smiled shyly and shook her head. "I'm just off work and still in my uniform. You are a liar."

"I stand firmly by my assessment," replied Joyce, leading Alice across the office to his desk. "Here, I have a little something for you." He picked up a small box and handed it

KURT CLOPTON

to her. She smiled shyly again as she accepted it and Joyce's heart did that little beat skipping thing again. Annoying.

"You shouldn't have," said Alice. "You're much too sweet." She opened the box and pulled out an understated but very elegant watch. "Oh, you remembered mine stopped."

"Yes, I did," said Joyce. "This particular watch is made by a company I own in Switzerland, and I guarantee it will never stop. Lifetime warranty. If it does, I will definitely have someone fired." And by fired, Joyce meant something much, much worse. "Besides, not a lot of people wear watches anymore with everyone using their phones for all their needs, so I wanted to support your old school efforts. It's not a complicated piece, but it's nice." He neglected to mention the tracking and listening devices it contained, but they were not active, they were there just in case of emergency. Otherwise it would be creepy.

Alice put on the watch as she glanced at the screen behind the desk. "Oh, was there an accident?" she asked. Many of the outer views showed small fires and damage to the facility that was attacked, and the main view still showed the last area where Electric Boogaloo had been captured, although the monster had already been removed. Crews were putting out fires and beginning to clean up.

"Just a little problem at one of my research facilities," replied Joyce. "A disgruntled former employee."

"Seems like a lot of damage," said Alice. "Was anyone hurt?"

"No, luckily it was closed for the night. Just lost some equipment, but nothing that can't be replaced."

"And the employee?"

SUPERGUY 2: ELECTRIC BOGALOO

"He was apprehended. I don't know what will happen with him quite yet."

"Well, I'm sorry that happened to you."

"It's a hazard of the business I'm in," said Joyce with a sigh. "I suppose I should tell you that I'm not liked by everyone. Corporations by definition are evil, according to some people, no matter how much good they do."

"Don't worry, I don't believe everything I read," said Alice.

Joyce hesitated, a bit worried. "So you've read something?" he asked as innocently as he could.

"Sure, I've got the internet. I've Googled you," replied Alice. "A girl's got to know who she's dating."

"And did I pass?" asked Joyce, suddenly full of trepidation. While he had thousands of internet bots putting out a constant stream of disinformation, not everything could be buried.

Alice looked away from the screen and back at him. "I read about that stuff with SuperGuy and the police a few months ago. I remembered it happening at the time but didn't realize it was you. But all those charges were dropped."

"Yes, they were," said Joyce. "The city government and I have butted heads a few times on various matters and they tried to escalate things, bringing all those charges. That's why I have good lawyers. I must protect myself. And now they have a superhero to do their dirty work for them. It's very disappointing after all the good Joyce Industries has done."

"That must be very hard for you," said Alice sympathetically. "I realize some people have to be tough as a part of their jobs, and that can create enemies because you're not doing what they think is right or what they want you to do."

"So true."

"And one thing you have been is very nice to me, that I know for certain," said Alice. "So for now, I'm going with that."

"I'm so happy to hear that," said Joyce. Stupid heart skipping thing again. "Now, shall we go grab a late dinner?"

"I'd love to."

11

"I just have one question for you, Roger," said Emma. "Are you going to be staring?"

"Staring? Why?"

"Why? Because this is probably the most famous superhero you're ever going to meet, and I want to know if you're going to embarrass us by being a staring, speechless wreck." Sitting at her desk in the old kitchen, which was still waiting to be renovated into an actual office, Emma was reading the local news on her computer. It had been a lively morning in the way of local news, and national for that matter.

"You know, I can understand you thinking that, and maybe I would have been a bit in the headlights in the past, but I think after all this time around Janice and the other GLAND members, I'm a little used to it now."

"Are you sure? This is Golden Gal, after all. Not exactly a middle of the road Midwest superhero," said Emma.

"Yeah, I think so," said Roger. "I think it will be cool to meet her, but that's just it. Cool."

Emma still looked a little skeptical. "Cool, huh? If you say so." Emma's phone rang. She looked at the screen. "Crap, it's the paper again. I've got to give them a quote." She spun around in her chair to get some privacy as she answered the phone. Roger walked to the door and looked out at the main floor of the garage. Oliver came out of the control room and walked over to him.

"You're not going to stare, are you?" asked Oliver.

"Would you guys stop it already!" said Roger, visibly annoyed. "Why do you think I'm going to be such a basket case? When have I acted like a bumbling fan boy before? I'll answer that: Never! Why do you think I'm going to start now?"

"Oh, I don't," said Oliver. He pointed to his ear. "Overheard your conversation with Emma. Super hearing and all that. Thought I'd have some fun. Totally worth it."

"You know, if you weren't a superhero, I would totally punch you in the forehead," said Roger. "What's the ETA?"

"I would guess any—oh, here she comes," said Oliver, turning toward the open back garage door. He could hear someone approaching at a high speed. There was a flash of bright yellow light and the thump of feet hitting the ground, then a second later Golden Gal walked in through the door.

"So this is the Garage you told me so much about?" said Golden Gal, looking around the large interior space as she walked over to Oliver and Roger. "It's nicer than you let on, but it does smell a bit. Kind of a potpourri of gasoline and tires, and what? Something burnt?"

"Yes, I like to call it singed superhero, but it's really a combination of all the things that blew up and/or caught fire

SUPERGUY 2: ELECTRIC BOGALOO

with me in them while we were testing flying machines," said Oliver. "How was the flight? How long does it take to get here from L.A.?"

"I could probably do it in ten minutes or so, but I like to buzz north along the Rockies instead of just crossing over them. The views are amazing and it's really cool flying among the mountains. I highly recommend it."

Emma came out of the old kitchen to join them and Oliver remembered his manners. "Let me introduce you to the gang. This is Emma, our city liaison and researcher, and this is Roger, the guy who likes to blow me up in his flying machines. Guys, this is Gigi, otherwise known as Golden Gal."

"Nice to meet you," said Emma as they shook hands.

"You too," said Gigi. "I'm guessing I have to apologize to you for the mess I've created. I bet you're stuck dealing with most of it." Photos had surfaced the previous night of Oliver and Gigi at the training, most of them obviously doctored, along with quotes from anonymous attendees stating that the two superheroes were doing more than just trust exercises. The local Milwaukee media had jumped on the story and even the Mayor had called to congratulate Oliver, obviously delirious from the national attention his city's hero was getting. He wasn't happy to be told the story was false, and he argued that it wouldn't hurt to take their time and slowly— maybe even very slowly—put out the fire.

"Don't worry about it, it's nothing, just a lot of calls this morning from the local press," replied Emma. Oliver gave Emma a look, as she had severely scolded him earlier for the mess he did nothing to create, but for which he apparently earned all the blame. "But the highlight had to be getting the call from a producer of one of those syndicated entertainment shows. They offered some serious cash for quotes from a source close to the hero."

"I guess Oliver is lucky you have his back," said Gigi.

"Oh, no, I took the money," said Emma. Oliver looked at Gigi and threw up his hands. "I gave them some great quotes. Not terribly accurate, but I think they'll make the show."

"Well, that's one way to play it," said Gigi. "Still, I should have warned you guys this would happen. It always does. I just didn't think about it with it being a training event and only two days, but the tabloids are relentless. Almost any time I spend with anyone, hero or civilian, turns into some kind of romantic entanglement for the press." Gigi turned her attention to Roger. "And of course I've heard a lot about you, Roger. A pleasure."

"The pleasure is all mine," replied Roger, shaking Gigi's hand. "It's a shame you have to deal with these annoying distractions when you have so much more important work to be doing. Not to mention the hit your reputation is taking being romantically linked to Oliver."

"Hey!" objected Oliver as Gigi laughed.

"I'm sure my reputation will survive," said Gigi. "Remember, I've secretly dated several supervillains in the past according to the tabloids, including one guy who was half salamander."

"That has to have been the luckiest half salamander ever," said Roger.

"Not really," replied Gigi. "One of the other supervillains I also supposedly secretly dated and who was severely delusional and had some jealousy issues, decided all the stories were true and ended up throwing the half salamander guy into outer space. Kind of sad." There was a moment of thoughtful silence.

SUPERGUY 2: ELECTRIC BOGALOO

"Hey, speaking of jealousy, Oliver, have you talked to Janice?" asked Emma.

Oliver looked at Emma like he was a deer caught in headlights. "Janice," he said simply, but the name carried a ton of meaning with it. Starting with the basics, it said who she was obviously, but then recalled their relationship, and speculated on what she might be thinking this morning as calls poured in from her own local news agencies in Thunder Bay with questions about her boyfriend fooling around with one of the most famous heroes in the world. "Oh, boy. I wonder if I should make a call—"

On cue, a rolling peal of thunder ripped overhead, which would usually signify the start of a severe Midwestern thunder boomer, but in this case, it heralded Janice's arrival. Despite the obvious futility, Oliver said a quick prayer for the rain option as everyone turned to see Janice walk in the back door. Oliver edged slightly behind the others. The thunder was slowly dissipating, bouncing around in the morning sky, and as Janice walked toward them a trace of lightning ran from her fingertips up along her arm and off into the open air where it crackled away to nothing. She came to a stop a couple feet short of Gigi and the two stared at each other for a moment.

"How's our boy?" asked Janice.

"Probably needing to change his uniform after that entrance," answered Gigi with a smile. Janice returned the smile and the two heroes hugged.

"You two know each other?" asked Oliver, edging out from behind the others.

"Oh yeah," said Janice. "Gigi was my sponsor for the Women's Hero Association. We've done a ton of stuff for them over the past couple of years. You know, events and panels, that sort of thing."

"That wasn't very nice," said Oliver.

"No, but the look on your face was so worth it," said Janice. "I really hope there was a security camera that picked that up?" This question was directed toward Roger.

"Definitely," he answered. "I have this whole place covered, for training purposes of course. I'm sure we got a good shot of it. I'll make posters."

"Oh, what about a meme? Best caption wins a prize," said Emma.

"I like that idea," said Janice, along with the affirmative murmurings of the others.

"I really don't like any of you," said Oliver. "But I'm still writing a meme. What's the prize?"

A short while later, the group had settled into the couches and chairs of the meeting lounge, taking a break after making various statements to various media outlets to varying degrees of success. Gigi didn't really have to make a statement of her own because she had a full-time publicist, but she did enjoy making things interesting by leaking comments that didn't quite line up with what her publicist said. This started a contest where Janice and Oliver tried to one up each other with their statements. Janice insisted in a video message that her relationship with Oliver was rock solid, except that she called him Oswald, and Oliver read a lengthy statement where

SUPERGUY 2: ELECTRIC BOGALOO

he kept randomly interchanging Janice's and Gigi's names, and added a third name near the end just for spice.

"So, Gigi, I wanted to ask you something. Whatever happened to that half salamander guy that got thrown into outer space?" asked Roger.

"Oh, I saved him," said Gigi. She had her feet up on the coffee table and was sipping from a can of Cherry Coke. "Luckily for me, or I guess luckily for him, he wasn't flying very fast. Getting him up through the atmosphere and out of the Earth's gravitational pull took all the momentum from the Man-Thing's throw. I didn't even hear about it until a couple of hours later and I still caught up with him easily. He didn't even make it a quarter of the way to the moon."

"That was awfully nice of you," said Emma.

"Well, it wasn't his fault he got tossed out there."

"Have you ever thrown anyone into outer space?" asked Roger. "I always wonder why it doesn't happen more often. Just throw the bad guy into the sun. Seems like a simple solution to a whole bunch of problems."

"What about due process?" asked Janice. "The justice system and all that. We enforce the laws, we don't pass sentence on people."

"True," said Roger.

"I'm still surprised it doesn't happen more," said Oliver. "Just look at what happened with Gray Matter. We went to all the trouble to thwart his plan and capture him, and he never spent even a second in jail. Plus, even if a villain is found guilty and sent to prison, half the time they break out and we're back to square one. I guess I could see a hero getting a little fed up and tossing a bad guy into the sun."

"Well, I didn't say I never tried it," said Gigi. Everyone looked at her in surprise.

Janice snapped her fingers. "You mean Kid Nitro?"

"Yeah. God, was he annoying," said Gigi with a shake of her head. "Which is why I tossed him. It was early in my career, I was feeling a lot of pressure, and I kind of let it get to me."

"So you actually threw someone into the sun?" asked Roger.

"Not exactly."

"What does that mean?" asked Oliver.

"I hit a satellite. Or, he hit a satellite actually. Just a fluke. The weather wasn't great that day, mostly cloudy, which is surprising for that time of year in L.A., so I didn't see the satellite. Just perfect bad timing, if that's a thing," said Gigi. "To make matters worse, that—combined with some kind of weird radiation storm or sun spot thing—ended up baking the guy just right so he showed up back on Earth with some new, stronger powers and a little vendetta. The classic UVC basically."

"UVC?" asked Emma.

"Unintentional villain creation," said Janice.

"That's a thing? I've done that," said Oliver, thinking about Electric Boogaloo.

"Yeah, it'll happen," said Gigi.

"I suppose the whole throwing someone into the sun thing is more complicated than you'd think," said Roger. "There's a lot that goes into it. First off, it's a long throw. Really long. Kind of a small target too. Then there's the aerodynamics of it all. Not all bad guys would fly the same. By the time they break out of the atmosphere, they could be drifting left or right and with all that distance to go, you would end up missing big time. There's probably some wiggle room, of course. Get them inside the orbit of Mercury and it'll most likely do the trick."

"I'm kind of troubled by how you think, Roger," said Emma.

"What? No one else thinks about these things?" asked Roger innocently.

"I'm not one to talk, I did it," said Gigi.

"I'm right there with Roger, I'm afraid," said Janice. "I was just thinking it had to be the right villain too. You can't toss anyone into the sun that can fly or has some other way to alter their course. Sure, they can be out cold when you let them go, but it's not a quick trip. They're bound to wake up eventually."

"Okay, Janice," said Emma. "You realize you just aligned yourself with Roger in the 'people who think about slightly disturbing things' department."

"Yeah," said Janice. She thought about it for a second and shrugged. "But in this case, I'm good with it."

"So what happened to this Kid Nitro guy?" asked Oliver. "I'm not familiar with a villain by that name."

"Funny story there. He came back with the new and improved powers and was kind of a pain in the butt for a while, but apparently all that radiation wasn't good for him and one day he sort of just melted down into a small puddle of radioactive goo. The DSF did a little clean up and I think he's buried in a toxic waste dump somewhere."

Everyone was silent for a moment.

"That sounds so much like the last shot of a movie where a hand then comes reaching up out of the ground," said Emma.

"Oh, yeah," said Roger. "It screams sequel."

12

RAYMOND Joyce quietly observed the monster that his former employee had become. Joyce liked to believe he would take great pride in any employee who moved on to better things, though finding something better than working for the world's greatest supervillain seemed highly improbable, and even though he had a slight sense of satisfaction when looking at his one-time assistant, it was tempered by the fact that the monster wanted to kill him. It was perhaps understandable, but it certainly wasn't acceptable. The immense, hulking beast was chained in the center of a cement floor in an otherwise empty room. Not only were the superhero quality chains holding him in place, they were also connected to an electric grid that continuously siphoned off the energy the creature produced. Joyce had realized in his research of the first encounter that the monster slowly ran out of power over the course of the battle and surmised it must create it on its own as opposed to being able to extract it from another source. So while it was able to travel through power lines, it couldn't use the electricity within them to refuel itself. That could only happen over time. In theory. With that in mind, Joyce had formulated his plan. He guessed the monster's most likely next couple of targets and had them renovated to his specifications. Once the monster attacked, his bots funneled it deeper and deeper into that particular building and to that particular floor where his people had reconfigured the wiring so the power ran only on a generator and was cut off from the outside world. There was no escape route. All the while, bot after bot attacked, making the monster deplete its energy resources until it would be weak enough to subdue. Once again, a very straightforward and simple plan that had worked to perfection, and which Joyce thought straightforwardly and simply sucked in its total lack of complexity. He resolved to add several extra layers of unneeded intricacy to his next scheme to make up for it.

"What kind of power levels is it putting out?" asked Joyce to one of the technicians. They were in an observation room adjoining the large one where Electric Boogaloo was being held. There were a couple of small windows that had views of the room, but also monitors displaying different angles of the subject. The technician grabbed a sheet of paper showing the power levels and handed it to Joyce.

"Wow, that's impressive," Joyce commented upon seeing the numbers. "Are we storing all this?"

"Yes, sir," said the technician. "But we have already reached 67 percent of our battery capacity, so we are bringing in more storage cells and are also switching the power over to run this facility as a way to use it up."

"Excellent," said Joyce. "That reminds me, have someone go out and plug in my car. Might as well take advantage of the situation." The technician nodded and walked out of the room, passing Steven, who was on his way in.

"Mr. Joyce, I have that information you were wanting on SuperGuy's first sidekick," said Steven, offering an iPad to his boss. Joyce took it and gave it a quick read, swiping through the pages.

"I guess with our underwhelming hero, we're never going to get someone of less power," Joyce commented. "That's got to be a little embarrassing for Mr. Olson. So, I know all these STraP sidekicks have issues; what's the problem with this one?"

"That's on the third page, sir."

Joyce swiped back a couple of pages. "Oh, there it is. Really?" He looked up at Steven, who nodded. "Why would they let someone with that be in this line of work? Just seems kind of silly if you ask me."

"Probably some kind of nondiscriminatory thing, sir. They can't help hamstringing themselves by being fair to everyone," said Steven.

"Idiotic. Maybe give him a job in the post office, but you don't make him a superhero," said Joyce. "But I suppose it might have cropped up after the fact." He thought for a moment. "Do you think that makes him easier or harder to sneak up on?" Joyce was already tossing around possibilities for a plan in his head and little details like this could make all the difference.

"No clue, sir, but it has to be confusing."

"I suppose a little observation and testing should tell us," said Joyce. "Then we'll know if it can be of any use."

SUPERGUY 2: ELECTRIC BOGALOO

Alex looked down at the shiny manacles around his wrists and followed the chains to where they fastened to the hooks in the cement floor. He pulled the chain on his right arm taut for about the fiftieth time, felt the same unyielding strength, and let it fall to the floor with a heavy clank. Manacles encircled his ankles too, and while he couldn't see it, it was the manacle around his neck that he found most uncomfortable. It was really beginning to itch underneath and the chains connecting his wrists to the floor were too short for Alex to reach up and scratch. He could usually step away from the controls of this hulking body of his and roam around deep inside the immense chamber that was his new mind to escape the outside world. It was almost like going into a meditative state where you got to float around inside a Salvador Dali painting with a little Spongebob Squarepants sauce on the side. It was trippy. And most of the time, Alex was safe there. But apparently there was one thing he couldn't hide from: itching. Itching really made it hard to dive down inside your incredibly vast and completely nutball crazy mind to have a little you time while watching the melting light show. Being a prisoner was bad enough, but having to be present in reality, and itchy, was really uncalled for.

Needless to say, Alex didn't like feeling this way. Admittedly, his entire existence since plunging into the vat several months ago hadn't exactly been the best time of his life, except for maybe the months he slept. Since then, this new body of his had taken some getting used to. Only—and sitting here in this empty room alone made him realize this—

he hadn't really gotten used to it. How could anyone get used to this? He may have been spending a little too much time hiding inside his head instead of facing just what a mess this physical shell was. The last few hours had really let Alex come to terms with that. And it wasn't just the smell, which was indeed special (perhaps a bath might have been something worth exploring), but it was also the overall feel of the body. It was kind of uncomfortable. If he had to sum up the sensation, Alex would say it was like wearing somebody else's sweaty underwear. Sweaty underwear that had also been liberally sprinkled with sand, tended to ride up while still being incredibly unsupportive, and smelled like a port-a-potty in 110 degree heat. Simply put, not a great feeling.

Still, something that at least slightly mitigated all the bad stuff was the power, and maybe that's why he didn't really notice the smell. The surging, tingling, rippling electrical energy that flowed from deep within his monstrous body was quite an addictive high and it fed that need inside him to lash out at what he hated. That was a nice perk. Did it make the smell worthwhile? Or the whole sweaty, sandy thing? Alex wasn't quite sure. But that didn't matter now anyway, because the power was gone. Alex had noticed it as soon as he woke up to find himself chained in this room. He could sense the source of the energy deep within himself, but it never grew, it just kept seeping away. It kept seeping away and left him itchy and acutely aware of feeling like he was sitting in somebody else's damp underwear.

SUPERGUY 2: ELECTRIC BOGALOO

Oliver stood in the yard outside the Garage, looking up at the night sky and the smattering of visible stars. Many more weren't visible even with his improved vision because of the city lights, but Oliver realized that if he wanted a better view, he could literally fly up and get one. There were some nice perks to being a superhero. Now Oliver was simply enjoying a bit of quiet after seeing Janice off a few minutes earlier. They had spent the day together putting out the fires caused by the story of Gigi and Oliver's affair, then restarting a few or starting whole new ones, and then putting those out. It was a fun day. Gigi had flown back to Los Angeles around noon after showing the other two the ropes in how to manage, or mismanage, a crisis like this. She had long ago given up on trying to correct stories of this nature and preferred to bombard the problem with so much extraneous and conflicting information that it soon became too much for anyone to follow. The key was to remember that people were going to believe what they wanted to believe, cherry picking the parts of the story that supported their worldview, so truth didn't really enter into it. Oliver had wondered how it was possible for a hero to lie like this, which he was finding very easy to do himself, but apparently there was some kind of logic loophole when it came to tabloids or the internet or whatever the app of the day was. If a news site or paper could publish a story about the Pope's half alien, half kangaroo twin babies, then you could pretty much tell them whatever you wanted and it just didn't matter. The reader was going to drop a comment to support or condemn you regardless of any real facts or logic, right after they finished voting on what to name the twins.

"Hey, you got a minute?" asked Emma, walking out of the Garage.

"You're gonna want a minute," said Roger, following her. "And an infinite amount of patience."

"That doesn't sound good," said Oliver, turning toward them. "Wait, could I get infinite patience as an add on booster like the flying? That would be useful."

"I wish I could get it," said Emma. "Especially when dealing with the DSF."

"Is this the sidekick thing?"

"No, it's the cape thing, but I also wanted to tell you that I just got an email from the STraP coordinator and our new sidekick will be here tomorrow," said Emma.

"Wait, how is the cape thing taking precedence over a sidekick who's showing up tomorrow?" asked Oliver.

"Because the cape is a tiny alteration to your uniform, while the sidekick is a major program and a huge responsibility," said Roger sarcastically. "You have to understand how the DSF thinks."

"Okay, I get it, but at least tell me about the sidekick first," said Oliver. "Did you manage to get us someone good?"

"I have no idea," replied Emma. "I thought I had a good rapport going with the coordinator, I really did. I even made some suggestions for candidates I thought looked like less trouble than others and she responded as if she were listening. She even asked a couple of questions to clarify, like we were having a real conversation about it. And now I get an email saying 'Here's your guy,' like we never talked at all and it's not any of the sidekicks I suggested."

"Great. How messed up is he?"

"Not sure," answered Emma. "He was one of the bunch who had 'Not Specified' listed under Medical or Neurological

Issues. I made a point of avoiding all of those based on Roger's advice."

"Yeah, I've heard that's DSF code for 'We're not even sure what's going on here.' Best to steer clear of those guys," said Roger.

"But we're getting one first thing," said Oliver. "That sounds about right. So how will we know what's wrong with him?"

"He should have a file with him which may give more detailed information, or maybe he'll just tell us, or maybe it'll be obvious after five minutes. I don't know." Emma shrugged helplessly.

"I so want to take the day off tomorrow, but I also can't look away," said Roger. "It's a real dilemma."

"Wait. You said the sidekick wasn't what I needed an infinite amount of patience for, it was the cape thing. How could that possibly be true?" asked Oliver.

"Oh, it's true," said Roger. "You don't mess with a DSF uniform."

"I just want a cape," pleaded Oliver. "I can't give another talk to the ladies of the Milwaukee Flower and Garden Society in this uniform without having something to cover myself with. I know it's tight, but people should still act with some kind of dignity. Especially elderly ladies who like flowers." Oliver thought back to the first speech he gave to the Milwaukee Flower and Garden Society. It was soon after becoming a hero and he wasn't quite as used to the extremely tight white suit as he was now. The Society ladies not only dragged away the podium he could have used for some coverage during his speech, but they also set a record for the most questions in any post talk Q&A ever.

"Well, the answer isn't a no," said Emma. "They just sent our request back. It seems we have a couple more hoops to jump through."

"Like six," put in Roger.

"Actually more like eight—no, nine," said Emma, thinking to herself. "But they're doable, we just have to persevere."

"Nine more hoops? That's nuts," said Oliver. "Wasn't the form we filled out for the uniform change something like twenty pages?"

"Twenty-four," answered Emma.

"How could there not have been enough hoops in twenty-four pages already?" asked Oliver.

"Oh, you foolish superhero," said Roger. "You're dealing with the DSF. And not just the DSF, but the DSF Uniform Division. These are artists, and you just basically insulted their art for twenty-four pages."

"I didn't make the form twenty-four pages long!"

"Yes, but you did fill it out," said Roger. "You'd think after ten or twelve pages you'd get the hint and just leave it."

"I just want a cape," Oliver pleaded again, slouching and shaking his head. (It's not actually easy for a superhero to slouch.)

"I hate to see a hero broken this easily," said Emma in an aside to Roger. She looked back at Oliver. "Hey, this is just step one. We've got all those other hoops to jump through yet. You're not going to give up on me so quickly, are you?"

"I'm thinking about it," answered Oliver.

"I don't know, I'm kinda with Oliver on this one," said Roger. "Toxic vat monsters and supervillains are much easier to battle than the DSFUD. I say cut your losses and keep your sanity."

SUPERGUY 2: ELECTRIC BOGALOO

"No way," said Emma, with a little edge in her voice. "You can't give up. I forbid it. Remember who actually filled out that form? Me. The only thing you did was sign it. I'm already being jerked around by these STraP folks, I'm not letting this one go too. If they want a fight, I'll give them a fight."

"All right!" yelled Roger, buoyed by Emma's enthusiasm.

Oliver smiled. "Well, if you insist on fighting, I'm happy to help. Plus, while toxic vat monsters and supervillains may be easier to handle than DSFUD, I really don't want to face the Milwaukee Flower and Garden Society ladies again without a cape."

13

WORKING alongside a hero in their never-ending battle against evil has to be one of the most gratifying things for those lucky enough to find themselves in that position. Not everyone can be a hero, but the next best thing has to be supporting that hero in their fight for justice. Not all cities of our size are fortunate enough to have their own hero, so the law enforcement personnel of Milwaukee must feel especially lucky to have the great privilege of working with our hero, SuperGuy. Our very own Milwaukee Times Herald News Observer Entertainment Editor, Les Williams, takes a few minutes to discuss our city, modern crime fighting, and the luck of having a hero with the Police Chief of Milwaukee.
#

LW: Can you describe the moment when you first found out the city was getting its own hero?

PC: No.

LW: It must have been amazing. I remember when we got the news in the office. It's like moving from understudy in Albany to lead on Broadway. I hadn't covered anything

SUPERGUY 2: ELECTRIC BOGALOO

bigger than the Kiss tribute band in the past three years and now I was getting a superhero.

PC: You must have been so proud.

LW: Oh, it was a great time. Those first days when we were all speculating about names and costumes and powers. So exciting. I bet it was the same for you.

PC: No.

LW: So what was it like when you met SuperGuy for the first time? It must have been thrilling. Where did it happen? Your office? The Mayor's office? Ooh, on the roof of the police station at night!?

PC: In a parking garage.

LW: Oh, I like that. Mystery, intrigue. Why the secrecy?

PC: That's just where we parked.

LW: Excellent. So, tell me, how does having a superhero change how you fight crime in our city? How much easier has it become for you?

PC: Well, we now have a supervillain running his crime empire from the tallest building in the city, and just the other day, a mutant monster was randomly destroying anything it got close to, so I'd say easier isn't really the word you're looking for.

LW: Oh, yes. Exciting. That's it. No more boring, petty crime for you. Jaywalkers need not apply! This is the big time. And you must have been impressed when SuperGuy brought in Gray Matter. How long had you been investigating him?

PC: We had been aware of a certain type of criminal activity for months.

LW: Months? And SuperGuy took him down after only a couple of weeks on the job? Amazing.

KURT CLOPTON

PC: Well, Gray Matter was finally putting his plan into action at that time, so he was no longer doing everything in secrecy and it was much easier to discover what he was up to.

LW: But still, a couple of weeks. That's impressive.

PC: You do realize that Gray Matter, or Mr. Joyce, is free, right? He wasn't charged with anything and is now sitting in his office going about his business. Not exactly a victory.

LW: Yes, a definite failure of our justice system, if he was guilty of anything.

PC: He was guilty.

LW: Yes, of course. But what was he suspected of again? Wasn't it something about mind control and cereal? Why not good old conspiracy or insider trading or tax something or other? You know, old fashioned, rich white guy crime. This mind control, take over the world stuff seems a bit far-fetched to me.

PC: We have a guy in white spandex with a barcode on his chest flying around the city battling giant blue electrical monsters. It might be time to recalibrate your reality.

LW: Oh, I like that. Recalibrate your reality. That could be a t-shirt. Or a coffee mug. I'm going to get that made up for the staff. I'll send you one.

PC: Don't.

\#

To read the full interview, go to the Milwaukee Times Herald News Observer's website. To hear more of Les Williams, make sure to check out his podcast, Les Miserables, where Les gets together with a local celebrity each week to do laundry and read famous scenes from 1980's romantic comedies.

14

"**PAUSE** playback." Raymond Joyce swiveled away from the wall of monitors behind his desk and dropped the sheets of data he had been going over onto the dark wood surface. He was disappointed. To say progress was going slowly would be overly optimistic and Raymond Joyce was not even close to being an optimist. The hulking blue thing that referred to itself as Electric Boogaloo was proving to be very uncooperative when it came to brainwashing. It was debatable how much brain was in there to be washed, and it seemed, after some careful study, that whatever brain was present had been scrambled like an egg, so trying to reorder that mess was turning out to be as difficult at getting the egg back in the shell.

"Problem, sir?" asked Steven. He was sitting on a chair across from the desk working on an iPad.

"Certainly a wrinkle that will change our plans somewhat," answered Joyce. "I think it's obvious that brainwashing the former Alex to join us is not going to be successful, certainly not in the time frame that I require, so I will need to adapt."

"Excellent, sir," said Steven, who knew after only a few months on the job how much Raymond Joyce enjoyed adapting plans, even if the reasons weren't necessarily always valid. However, this time there was a very good reason to make a change because a major component wasn't going to work. Many of the previous times his boss had insisted on improvising, Steven couldn't detect any threat to the original plan and subsequently had begun to suspect Joyce simply enjoyed slapping things together on the fly. That wasn't to say they were haphazard constructions. To the contrary, they were often more sophisticated and intricate than the original plan that they were replacing. Not to mention more layered, often adding two or three steps in place of whatever single one had been there before. Some of those steps had offshoots that led to other steps only vaguely related to the new steps, and some of those steps didn't have anything to do with the original plan at all, but that was apparently all part of the plan. Or something. Steven got a little lost after the third layer of plans or so. It didn't matter, he just maintained his grasp on the steps that Mr. Joyce asked about the most. Regardless of the whole plethora of steps issue, the important thing was that his boss was going to have to adapt and adapting made his boss happy.

"Is the test for the Trek Project still ready to go as planned?" asked Joyce.

"Yes, sir. I got a status report from Dr. Misk a few minutes ago and sent it on to you. It should be in your email."

"Excellent."

SUPERGUY 2: ELECTRIC BOGALOO

Steven's iPad beeped and he checked the camera feed. "Miss Alice has arrived, sir."

"Great, please send her in," said Joyce. "And have the technicians stop the brainwashing protocol on the subject. I guess instead of using the beast as a surgical tool, I will have to consider a more blunt object approach."

"Yes, sir," said Steven as he rose from his chair and headed for the door. Joyce turned off the wall monitors as Steven opened the door to let Alice into the office. He nodded to Alice as he stepped aside, and then closed the door behind him as he left.

"You look wonderful," said Joyce, coming around from behind his desk to give Alice a kiss and a hug. He found it thrilling that he was in this place in his life. That he could have someone to compliment, to give a kiss and a hug, to plan a lunch with, all while brainwashing enemies in the basement and running a criminal empire. It really was the whole enchilada.

"Thank you, and you look handsome as always," said Alice. She straightened his tie and brushed a bit of lint from his lapel. "Do you think we could talk?"

"Absolutely," replied Joyce. "Let's have a seat and you can tell me what you want to talk about." They walked over to the couch along the wall and sat down.

"You, I guess," said Alice with a little hesitation.

"Well, I do have some expertise in that area," said Joyce. "What do you want to know?"

"I've been doing a lot of reading. I read that interview with the Police Chief that was in the paper recently, and he talked about you." Alice held up a hand when she saw that Joyce was going to interrupt. "Look, I know what the world is like, I'm not naive. And these past several weeks have given me a lot of time to think about things, because I've finally had some time to think. And that's thanks to you and your help with my mother, and my rent, and my car. I know the world is anything but perfect, and no matter how hard I try I might never get over this hump in front of me in my life right now, this hump that seems like the size of a mountain. It's really not fair, but it's the way life is and I feel like I have to make a choice. Look, I want to—"

"Break up?" choked Joyce.

"—become a villain," finished Alice.

"What?"

"That's what you are, right?" asked Alice. "I didn't get that wrong, did I?"

"Uh, no, no. You're right."

"So that's what I want. I read about the serums that people get on the black market. I read that's how they think you became Gray Matter. I want that too."

"You want a serum?"

"Yes."

"A villain serum."

"I'm not joining the other team, I want to be with you."

"Well, there's being with me, and then there's being a villain," said Joyce. "A serum is a serious step."

"I know. I'm serious."

"Uh, well, I was kind of at the point where I thought we might continue dating, exclusively, definitely exclusively, I mean I'm not dating anyone else obviously, and then maybe we could consider going away for a weekend together, someplace warm, maybe tropical, and even maybe we could move in together, but I don't want to move too fast..." Joyce stalled for a moment as Alice sat smiling shyly at him. "But...you were thinking...you know, straight to villain?"

"Oh, I want all those other things you just mentioned too, especially the weekend, which should really be a week, and definitely tropical, but I also want to be a villain. With you."

Joyce stared at Alice a bit longer, his demeanor turning quite serious. "But you realize being a villain isn't like picking an instrument when you join band in fifth grade. You can't drop it after a week when you figure out the trombone sucks and it sounding like a fart isn't a good reason to play it. This is for life."

Alice matched Joyce's serious tone. "Look, I'm a waitress. I have a theater degree with an art minor and a bucketful of student loans. I have to work double shifts and two jobs just to make the payments and help out my parents, who had to go back to work after they retired because a bunch of greedy banks managed to destroy their nest egg. My dad worked at a job for thirty-five years that he didn't really like because that was the choice he had to keep us living in the same house in the same town. He didn't want to upset the family by moving so he could have a job he liked. But at least the job had a good retirement plan, or so they thought. And now they have health issues and bills they can't afford because drug companies apparently only make pills out of precious metals and hospitals charge astronomically high prices for a couple of Tylenol. But we can't consider getting a handle on that because it would be sensible while making some rich folks a slight bit less rich. Can't be doing crazy things like that. I mean, next they'd have to pay some taxes. Better they poop on gold plated toilets. So, my prospects in this current climate kinda suck. I've tried the noble way. I really have. For years. I really believed I would have done something important or useful, or accomplished something with my life—even the smallest something—by the time I was this old. Instead, all I've done is gotten tired. I'm really, really tired. All the time." She paused, showing that fatigue, but then she looked at Joyce and he saw a brightness in her eyes. "I'm ready to take a shot and become a bad girl. I mean, I don't want to be some evil sociopath, but I'm more than willing to break a few laws if I can pound the crap out of some big banks and drug companies. Can you promise me that?"

"Absolutely." Whether Gray Matter had a heart or not could be debated, but at the moment something in his chest was soaring. "We can pound the crap out of whomever you like."

"Well, I'm sure as hell not getting anywhere taking the high road." Alice leaned in and gave Gray Matter a kiss. "Let's do it."

15

"I can do it faster than that," said Oliver dismissively. "I just haven't tried to fly back there as fast as I can before." He and Roger were sitting in the control room at the GLAND headquarters as they finished some routine tests on the surveillance and monitoring systems before heading back to Milwaukee.

"I know, but we should time it," said Roger. "It's about three hundred miles from here to the Garage. I think it's important that we know how fast you can get here, or back there, in an emergency."

"Sure, sounds fine to me, but I don't know why we can't just estimate it. We know my top speed, more or less."

"Well, you know how I just love to sit down with a calculator and estimate, but I enjoy real world measurements when I can get them."

"You're also forgetting that this high tech egg we're sitting in won't always be in the same spot," said Oliver.

"I'm not forgetting," said Roger. "I just want to get a baseline from this position. Besides, I'll still do an estimate first and we'll see how you stack up. Maybe there's even a little room for a wager."

"Somehow I knew this was going to end up with a bet," said Oliver. "I think you might have a gambling problem and I feel I shouldn't encourage this behavior. That being said, are we talking an over/under here or are you spotting me minutes and seconds?"

"Are we betting on something?" asked Metal, strolling into the control room. She was on headquarters monitoring duty this week and had been there when Roger and Oliver had arrived to do their tests. It wasn't a requirement that the GLAND member on monitoring duty actually be at the headquarters because the advanced AI was perfectly capable of overseeing the facility and alerting the members if there was a problem, but Metal was working on an important project of her own: The outdoor barbecue area on the flight deck wasn't going to build itself. She had already set up a cozy bar and lounge area for relaxing and having a few drinks, as well as a nice large table and chairs for meals. Today she was focused on the grill and food prep area, having brought a nice stainless steel grill with her, which she had secured to the floor of the flight deck. Everything being secured to the floor was vitally important so that a Triple A wouldn't ruin the barbecue. Some of the furniture was permanently fixed in place while Metal used heavy duty magnets on items like smaller chairs or tables that needed to be moved occasionally. Obviously you were going to have some losses in a Triple A, but limiting them to the smaller things was helpful. Most importantly, all beverages would be stored in a Triple A proof manner.

SUPERGUY 2: ELECTRIC BOGALOO

"We might be making a little wager on how fast Oliver can fly to Milwaukee from here," replied Roger. "I'm going to estimate it and set a time he has to beat. You interested?"

"Oh, I'm in," said Metal. "I bet Buffalo and Stormfront would want a piece of the action too. I could have the AI call and conference them in."

"Great, let's make it a thing," said Oliver without enthusiasm.

"I sense some performance anxiety," said Metal. "Okay, I'll keep the others out of it, but I'll make you a wager. If you don't beat Roger's estimated time, then you have to take my next weekend shift. If you do, I'll take yours. Simple."

"That's not much of a bet—wait, who are you scheduled with?" asked Oliver, already sure he knew the answer.

"Who else?" said Metal with a smile, or a twisting contortion of rusted metal that most of GLAND had come to think was a smile. "Creeper, of course."

"Ew, I would not take that bet," said Roger.

"Yeah, that's not really fair," said Oliver. "You'd get Janice and have a girl's weekend while I'd get The Creeper and a weekend that I can't readily label in any remotely fun sounding way. I don't think that's worth it."

"Okay, how about this? If I win, you take my weekend with Creeper, but if you win, then I take your duty the next time you get stuck with him. Or, just to give it a little more weight, let's make it the next three times either of us has a weekend shift with Creeper."

"Now there are some stakes!" yelled Roger.

Oliver thought about it for a moment. "Okay, as long as we can come up with a time estimate we agree upon, I'm in."

"Deal," said Metal, showing her rusted twist of a smile again. She held out a huge metal fist and Oliver bumped it.

"All right! Time for me to do some math," said Roger, rubbing his hands together happily as he stepped over to one of the work stations. After a couple of seconds of tapping on keys, he turned back. "Hey, did you guys see this? The sensors picked up a little anomaly a few minutes ago. A power surge in the Upper Peninsula near the coast." Roger tapped a couple more keys and put the information up on one of the big monitors. Oliver and Metal moved closer to get a look.

"What's in that area?" asked Metal, looking at where the surge had occurred. "Power station maybe?"

"Doesn't seem to be one," answered Roger. "Looks like private land for the most part."

"Not that big of a surge," said Oliver. "But still big enough for us to pick up from here."

"Worth looking into?" asked Metal.

"Well, whatever it was is over now. Still, it's just across the water from Thunder Bay. Let's send the data to Janice and see what she thinks," said Oliver.

"Yeah, she could do a flyover while on patrol easily enough. See if there's anything to see," said Metal.

"Roger, can you send it to her?" asked Oliver.

"You send it to her," said Metal, walking over and setting a hand on Roger's shoulder. "This man has to do the math for a very important wager."

"Right. Priorities. I'll send it to her," said Oliver, sitting down at another station and going to work. "And make sure you do a good job. I will be double checking your math."

SUPERGUY 2: ELECTRIC BOGALOO

Dr. Misk stared at the containment device with rapt anticipation. The roar from the nearby underground power turbines was still deafening, but quickly winding down, and excess electricity was snapping randomly as it flowed out along the safety lines. There was a smell too. Something overcooked, but not food. Maybe air? Can you overcook air? The containment device was the size of a walk-in freezer. In fact, it was a walk-in freezer. Dr. Misk had picked it up secondhand when a local Arby's went out of business. Dr. Misk was big on recycling. He often faced ridicule from his colleagues for using repurposed parts, but he considered it important for both his work and the earth. Obviously, there had been improvements made to the freezer, like lining the whole thing in three inches of superhero quality metal inside and out, installing the power grid on top, and doing some heavy duty disinfecting, but it still looked like a stainless steel walk-in freezer from the outside. Steam escaping from the pressure release valve on top whistled at a high pitch for several seconds before slowly beginning to fade. Dr. Misk took a few cautious steps forward and touched the handle. There was a lot riding on this test, not the least of which was his ongoing health. Gray Matter had been very patient with the Trek Project because of its incredible potential, but even Dr. Misk knew he was nearing the end of the line. Wiping sweat from his mostly bald head, Dr. Misk exhaled and pulled the door open. He smiled. Inside on the floor were two things. One was a dead rat, which was to be expected. The other was a small plush toy, a black and white penguin with an overly large nose. It had been his daughter's favorite

KURT CLOPTON

stuffed animal so long ago. And, unlike the rat, it was in pristine condition.

Success.

16

ROGER walked into the Garage control room with his eyes fixed on his iPad, watching the countdown for Oliver's flight back to Milwaukee. He was able to track Oliver in flight through the communicator located in the hero's inner ear and right now the estimated time of arrival was dead on with his estimate. This thing could go either way. Unfortunately for Roger, he needed Oliver to miss the deadline because he had made a little side bet with Metal. If Oliver completed the trip in under thirty-nine minutes, Roger's new motorcycle would become Metal's, and if Oliver went over that time, then Roger would get the reserve Hopper for his own personal use. The Hopper was the small utility flying vehicle that came with the new GLAND headquarters, specifically for the transportation needs of the members who didn't have the ability of flight, those being Buffalo, Metal, and The Creeper, or someone like Roger, who had just been dropped off by it. It had the same AI as the HQ so it didn't require a pilot, you just told it where to go and it went, although it did have a manual flight mode if the passenger preferred it. It worked a lot like a video game, with the AI greatly simplifying the controls and interpreting what the pilot wanted to do, but mostly just making sure they didn't crash the thing. The Hopper was usually used by the members who were on monitoring duty so they could fly back and forth from their home cities to the headquarters, fly a patrol, or use it in emergencies (which included picking up pizza because it was difficult to get it delivered to a floating ovoid base over the Great Lakes). There was one main Hopper, but also a reserve craft in case the first one had mechanical problems. Since these were top shelf DSF flying machines, and not the seconds that Roger was used to dealing with via the DSF Superhero Surplus Warehouse, they did not ever have mechanical issues, so the reserve Hopper wasn't in danger of being used. Except by Roger, who really, really wanted it. He just needed Oliver to fail to break thirty-nine minutes.

"Roger?"

Not to mention he'd lose his motorcycle. He really liked his motorcycle.

"Roger?"

Maybe he shouldn't have made the bet. Now that he thought about it, Roger wasn't sure if Metal even knew how to ride a motorcycle. Not to mention she might weigh too much for the bike. Should he be talking about her weight? That probably wasn't cool. But she was literally made out of metal and weighed nearly half a ton.

"Roger!"

Roger almost dropped his iPad as he jumped. He looked up to see Emma sitting on one of the couches across from a red-suited hero.

SUPERGUY 2: ELECTRIC BOGALOO

"What?" he said, letting the iPad drop to his side and walking toward them.

"I wanted to introduce you to our new sidekick trainee," said Emma as she stood up. The red-suited hero did the same. "This is Joey, otherwise known as Scarlet Pulsar." Joey stepped forward and shook hands with Roger.

"Nice to meet you, Mr. Allen," said the young hero. Roger knew he was twenty-four according to his DSF record. He had a boyish face, very sidekick-like, with curly black hair and dark eyes.

"Please don't call me that. It's just Roger."

"Okay, Roger. Call me Joey, of course. Scarlet Pulsar is a bit much."

"Why don't you sit down, Roger," said Emma. "Joey was just about to fill me in on the neurological aspect of his record. You know, the part that was unspecified in our copies?" She gave Roger a look that meant she wanted company.

"Sure, no problem," said Roger, taking a quick peek at his iPad countdown. "I've got a good eleven and a half minutes, so as long as it's not too messed up," he said, mumbling the second part and then immediately remembering that all superheroes had heightened hearing. If Joey did hear him, the young sidekick didn't show it as he and Emma sat back down and Roger stepped over and sat next to Emma.

"Okay, Joey," said Emma. "Fire away."

"It's not really a big deal," started Joey, somewhat hesitantly. "It probably won't even come up very often."

Roger recognized his nervousness. "Don't worry, Joey. I'm sure you wouldn't be in this line of work if it was a real issue." Roger wasn't at all sure of any such thing.

"Well, the general term is prosopagnosia. It's a neurological disorder where a person has an inability to recognize faces." Joey shrugged. "Sometimes it's called face blindness or facial agnosia. You simply can't recognize a familiar face. In fact, some people have difficulty even recognizing their own face or distinguishing a face from an object."

"I think I've heard of that before," said Emma.

"So if I walked out the door and back in again, you wouldn't know it was me?" asked Roger.

"Well, I can use other visual cues, like your clothes, but that's not my problem," replied Joey. "I specifically have superhero prosopagnosia. I can't recognize the faces of heroes and villains." There was a pause.

"I take back my earlier remark about you not being in this line of work if this was a real issue," said Roger. "It seems like this would totally be an issue in this line of work."

"Yeah, I'd have to second that," said Emma.

"Honestly, it's not that much of a problem, especially with the suits," said Joey, gesturing to his own dark red costume. "Kind of gives most of us away. I usually only have a problem when first meeting a hero or villain, or sometimes in a big group fight. There's a lot of confusion in those, you know. Smoke, power beams, fire, water, ice, more smoke. It's all flying everywhere and people are moving so quickly. Sometimes you don't get a lot of time to distinguish a uniform. There's just a blue blur and you pulsar beam the wrong person into the side of a building which collapses on somebody's supercar. But those big dust ups don't happen too often. I try to avoid them if I can."

"What? How? Do you just pass on the big fight if there's more than three on a side?" asked Emma.

"Well, I've just got to be careful."

"What if a bad guy dresses up like SuperGuy? You wouldn't know it wasn't him?" asked Roger.

"I could figure it out once we started talking," answered Joey.

"As long as he hadn't blasted you apart before then," said Roger.

"Yes, but that hasn't ever happened. I don't think. I mean the blasting part has never happened."

"Wait. What do you do when you first meet a hero or a villain, assuming you don't know whether they are one or the other?" asked Emma.

"I usually take a defensive posture to be on the safe side and ask if they are friend or foe," said Joey.

"Friend or foe?" repeated Roger.

"Seriously?" asked Emma.

"It's worked surprisingly well in the past," said Joey. "They usually answer the question, maybe because it's so odd, and most of the time they even tell the truth."

"Thank goodness for the honesty of villains," said Emma.

"Well, I for one will be interested in seeing how that will work," said Roger.

"Honestly, it really hasn't come up much in my time as a sidekick, except for the one supercar incident," said Joey. "This will probably be the last time we even talk about it."

"All right then, how about I show you where you'll be staying?" said Emma, standing up. The other two followed suit, with Joey grabbing the two suitcases he had brought along, and they all filed out of the control room and into the main room of the Garage. Emma and Joey walked down to the newly built addition and up the stairs to the efficiency apartment that was to be the sidekick's temporary home.

Roger stopped at the bottom of the stairs and looked at his iPad again. Only a couple of minutes left. Next he checked for Oliver's location. Close. The ETA was right at the thirty-nine minute mark, occasionally shifting in real time from a tenth of a second over to a tenth of a second under. Really close.

Roger spent those next two agonizing minutes alternating between staring at the countdown on his iPad to staring at his motorcycle parked over by Emma's Jeep and Oliver's unused, city issued Ford Taurus. Next to those vehicles sat the crumpled remains of Oliver's first city issued Taurus which was destroyed on the hero's first night on patrol. Someone in the law enforcement department had thought it would be cute to have the wreck delivered to the Garage as a souvenir—most everyone figured it was the Police Chief—but right now Roger was trying hard not to see it as some kind of harbinger of what was to become of his motorcycle when Metal tried to climb on and take it for a spin. The time was almost up when Emma and Joey walked back down the stairs to the floor of the Garage. There was a roar like a freight train as Oliver approached and a split second later blew through the open back door, slamming to the ground and sliding forty feet to a stop on the stained cement floor, leaving thin cracks in his wake.

Oliver looked back at Roger to see if he had made it. Roger checked his iPad and saw that Oliver had beaten the time by two tenths of a second. His precious, brand new Harley Davidson was history. An expensive, and most likely twisted, crumpled piece of history. By two tenths of a second. Roger looked over at Emma and Joey. With great sadness, he did the only thing he thought appropriate.

He screamed, "FOE!"

SUPERGUY 2: ELECTRIC BOGALOO

And Joey blasted Oliver through the far wall of the Garage.

Alex was thankful. So, so thankful. He still didn't have any power because it continued to drain away for reasons he couldn't understand, but he could handle that. What he was so thankful for was that they had finally stopped showing the films. Films of Gray Matter doing nice things, like playing with puppies or smelling flowers or buying ice cream for children. Films with flashing lights and quick cuts with subliminal messages, usually consisting of large letters spelling out how Gray Matter was his friend and would like to buy him ice cream or smell flowers with him.

Alex knew what the films were and knew they wouldn't work for two reasons. First was the itching. The manacle around Alex's neck itched horribly and now that had spread to the ones on his wrists and ankles. He wouldn't be surprised at all if he had hideous rashes when they were removed. And while the itching made it impossible for Alex to drift off inside himself and ignore reality, it also made it impossible to concentrate on anything at all, including the film that played on a loop right in front of him. Those flashing images of an awkwardly smiling Gray Matter with puppies (he was allergic) were completely ineffective because Alex couldn't comprehend the images. The itching was that bad. And even if he could comprehend the images, the films wouldn't work because of the second reason. That was because Alex had created the films in the first place. A couple of years ago, Gray Matter had ordered that a brainwashing technique be devised for one of his many plans, and, after a bunch of interoffice emails, Alex realized they didn't have anyone in the whole company who had any clue how to do such a thing. Kind of a big whiff for an evil corporation not to have some kind of decent brainwashing department. So Alex did the best he could, stealing inspiration from any movie with a brainwashing scene he could find, and cobbled together the complete piece of hogwash his former employer had been showing him nonstop for the past five days. They didn't even notice that Alex had given himself writing and directing credits at the end.

Whatever the reason for stopping, Alex was glad. The film really wasn't his best work. In fact, if things changed drastically, he had several notes for edits and an idea for completely reworking the second act. And all the puppy stuff had to go. Besides, Alex now knew the real secret for making someone lose their mind was to give them an itch they couldn't scratch.

17

JANICE flew low over the coast of Michigan's Upper Peninsula, checking her wrist monitor as she zeroed in on the location of the energy anomaly. There wasn't much to see. Lots of trees, lots of water, and some extremely nice vacation homes that rich people referred to as cabins. Nothing obvious like a burnt out section of forest or large electrical towers throwing off sparks. There was a rather strong smell of something rotting, and Janice spotted a bunch of dead rats near the vacation home she was currently flying over, but other than feeling a little sorry for the owner and their obvious rat problem, she didn't think it was important. Whatever caused the power anomaly wasn't going to be found by Janice this morning, so she made a slow turn over that last gorgeous four bedroom cabin, waved to a man standing in the backyard, and headed back to Thunder Bay.

Dr. Misk waved at the flying lady as he tossed another dead rat onto the pile and wondered if she was going to be a problem. He'd never seen a hero in this area before and he didn't think seeing one now, right after their biggest power test yet, was a coincidence. It would definitely be the second thing he mentioned in his report to Gray Matter this afternoon. The first being the complete success of the transfer engine. They were ready to go fully operational.

"So, what do we do first?" asked Alice, her glee barely contained as she sat on the couch in Raymond Joyce's office. "A name? A costume? Oh, I won't have to wear tights or a tiny swimsuit, will I?"

"That's definitely one benefit of being a villain," answered Joyce, as he took a seat next to Alice. "You wear what you want. No bureaucratic sweatshop gets to slap together a funny suit and insist you wear it twenty-four-seven for the rest of your super life. Some of those hero costumes are ridiculous. Have you ever seen Longhorn? I don't know how he gets through doorways with that helmet. I imagine he doesn't even go indoors if he can help it. And the balance on that thing must be terrible with just the one tiny strap holding it on. How would you fight in that? The horns aren't even made to be a weapon, they're just decoration."

"Yeah, I think I'll pass on a helmet, unless it has some kind of cool Valkyrie vibe, but I definitely want a cape," said Alice. "Although not the standard thing. I'm thinking something different, like shorter, with an uneven edge. I'll sketch it."

"Capes are nice. I should add one to my ensemble, especially if it's rainy. A big raincoat is just too much," said Joyce. "But there's a more important question, which will probably help with the name and the costume: What powers do you want? I've collected quite a few black market serums in the past couple of years so we've got plenty of options." He grabbed an iPad off the coffee table and tapped it a couple of times to bring up the list of serums. "Here we go. First off, there are a couple of super strength types that are pretty standard. Just sort of a tossing cars and trucks around level, so not even big time strength. I suppose you could take both, though, if you wanted to beef up the strength quotient. Um, there's a super speed one, a stretchy body one, a walk through walls type…oh, an underwater specialty, which is just stupid. You can swim fast and talk to fish, but only bass, trout, and bluegill in this case. And of course, you're useless out of the water. Heck, we live next to a huge lake and that's still the last serum I'd want."

"Yeah, if you were fighting a water guy and it wasn't going well, wouldn't you just get out of the water and walk away?" asked Alice.

"Exactly! Yes. Just dumb," agreed Joyce. He looked back at his list. "There's one for sound waves. You basically yell at people and it hurts their ears and gives them headaches. Seems to me that they were reaching. I know the same old powers can get boring after awhile, but sound waves? Aren't you just going to annoy everyone around you? Okay, let's see...oh, here's a good telepathic and telekinetic combo."

"No, no way," said Alice instantly. "Those are way too cliche girlie for me. Every third female hero has to be a telepath. Drives me nuts. It's like back in college when every girl I knew at least minored in psychology. Give me a break. I want to punch things. Hard. Super hard. When I hit someone, I not only want to knock them into next week, I want to knock them into next week in the next parallel universe over. Got anything for that?"

"Well, that is a bit of a knock," mused Joyce, looking at his list. "There are those first couple of super strength ones, but you're going to grow extra large with one, which brings up the whole having trouble getting through doorways problem. And the other turns you a golden color for some reason."

"No, I don't want to be large, I just want to punch like it. And I don't think I want to be gold," said Alice, giving it some thought. "Does it make me a bad person if I don't want to be gold?"

"Absolutely not," replied Joyce. "Now if you said you didn't want to be gray, then I'd take some issue with it."

"Well, I would hope so."

"I guess I'm lucky with the serum I got," said Joyce. "Since it had such a high intelligence quotient, I'm surprised they didn't throw in the oversized head thing. Make me all head with a tiny body, or multiple heads, or just a floating brain in a glass case like Dr. Deep Thought. I would not like to live like that."

"Yeah, I think I prefer you this way," said Alice.

Joyce went back to his iPad list. "Okay, here are some power beam options. You can shoot beams out of your hands, out of your eyes, or…oh, out of a crystal mounted into your forehead." Joyce looked up and Alice cringed slightly. "No? Of course not. Let's see, power beam out of a crystal mounted on your chest, another using a scepter, and one where you shoot the beam out of your mouth."

"That's not a good visual," said Alice.

"Certainly could make for a whole motif, but not a very pleasant one," said Joyce. He kept reading, scrolling down a couple more times. "A lot of similar stuff…Oh, here's a good one. Just might be perfect. Still a type of power beam, but you can shape the energy. Shoot it out like machine gun bullets, or missiles, or apples for that matter. Throw a giant energy axe, or make it into a huge fist to punch something. Flight comes with it, although we do have a couple of add on flight serums too if we needed them."

"That does sound good," said Alice.

"And you don't have to be gold," said Joyce. "It does say the color of the beam is a dark bluish-black, so that's nice. More fitting for a villain than a pink or chartreuse."

"Is it powerful?" asked Alice. "Because, like I said, when I punch stuff, I really want to punch stuff."

"It's not bad. Not the most powerful I've ever seen," replied Joyce, reading the details. "However, we could simply add a power booster to push it to a higher level. We have a couple of those as well." He scrolled some more. "Yes, I have one here that's perfect. You'll end up being one of the more powerful energy based villains I've seen. You might just be able to knock someone into next week one parallel universe over."

"That sounds pretty good," said Alice. "There's just one other thing. Can I get an extra talent?"

"What do you mean?"

"Well, can you throw in something cool, like playing the piano. I've always wanted to play the piano," said Alice. "My friend Julie can play the guitar and I've always wanted to learn something to play along with her but I never had the time. So can you do something like that?"

Joyce nodded as he thought. "Yes," he said. "I think we can mod something to that effect." He smiled. "I look forward to listening to you play piano after a hard day of flying around and punching stuff."

"Perfect," said Alice. "That sounds perfect. And, most importantly—besides the cape—I can just wear some comfy jeans."

18

"So you just hear the word 'foe' and you blast away? Even though you're standing in the middle of a superhero headquarters, literally waiting for the superhero to arrive. A superhero I might add, that is generically themed—the only generically themed hero in existence and there aren't any generically themed villains either, so it's not like you would be confused by two dudes wearing roughly similar blue uniforms or two fire-wielding beings who were both encased in flames. No, this hero, who lives here and who you are waiting for, has a big barcode across his chest unlike anyone else, but you still feel the need to blast him just because someone yells 'foe.' Did your serum actually eradicate the common sense in you?" asked Oliver in a very loud, yelling-like fashion.

"No, no sir. It's just kind of a conditioned response and this was unfamiliar territory," said Joey. "I'm really, really sorry." Joey was standing in the control room in front of the couch where Oliver now sat, slowly picking bits of cement block out of his hair. The young sidekick rubbed his hands together nervously as he stared at the floor.

"Yeah," sighed Oliver. "Don't worry, I know it wasn't your fault." He looked at Roger, who was sitting in the chair nearby. "No good person would ever do such a thing on purpose."

"Hey, I make no promises," said Roger.

"Yeah, you just make bets," said Emma as she walked in the door of the control room and sat down on the couch across from Oliver. Roger had reluctantly explained himself after triggering Joey's shot. "And that bet is going to cost us. It wouldn't have been too bad if it was just a hole in our wall. We could have just parked one of the cars in front of it, or maybe that boat/tank thing you love so much. Unfortunately, Oliver went through the wall next door too."

"That's just another cement block wall," said Roger. "It can't be that much."

"It's a glass store," said Emma. "You know, for windows, mirrors, car windshields, all that kind of stuff. All stacked where? You guessed it, along that wall. We'll be paying for about half their inventory."

"Oops," said Roger meekly. "Sorry?"

"I'm really, really sorry," repeated Joey for the thirtieth time.

"We know, Joey, just shut up," said Emma, while staring at Roger. "You're just lucky our Hero Collateral Damage insurance is so good, but this is exactly the kind of thing we don't need in the way of publicity. The Mayor is not going to be happy with Oliver needlessly destroying local businesses."

"Hey!" Oliver protested.

Emma waved him off. "Yeah, I know, but that's the way the Mayor's going to see it. And I'm the one who will be fielding those calls, so I get to say what I want. Now I've got to come up with a reasonable explanation that doesn't have anything to do with bets over shiny motorcycles compensating for male insecurities."

"Hey!" Roger protested.

"Oh, shut up," said Emma.

A familiar voice came from the doorway. "I see things are running smoothly as always." The Police Chief took off his hat and stuck it under his arm as he entered. "Are you guys doing another renovation?"

"Obviously," said Oliver. "We needed another exit. Building codes and all that."

"Did the store next door need one too?" asked the Police Chief. "Who's the new guy?" He nodded at Joey as he came to a stop next to the couch where Emma sat. The new sidekick still stood in the middle of the seating area like a puppy who had chewed up one of your favorite pairs of shoes and knew he had done wrong.

"This is Joey, otherwise known as the Scarlet Pulsar, our first temporary sidekick and maker of extraneous exits," said Emma. "Joey, this is the Police Chief."

"A pleasure to meet you, sir," said Joey, coming out of his shameful funk. "I'd just like to say how honored I am to be here and how I look forward to working alongside you and all your personnel." The Police Chief shook Joey's hand and gave one very abbreviated chuckle. Call it a chuck.

"Oh, no, there won't be any of that," said Roger. "We don't get to play with the authorities. We must stay in our own sandbox."

"Yes," agreed Emma. "It's the official position of the Milwaukee Police Department that the city hero should give speeches and save kittens, although the Chief here does like to assign us the occasional secret mission."

"I like to think we have a very strong relationship, we just don't have to broadcast it," said the Chief. "Or acknowledge it in any other way. Now, if we have the touchy feely stuff out of the way, can we discuss business?"

"Sure, Chief, what's up?" said Oliver.

The Chief sat down next to Roger and dropped his hat on the coffee table. "I'm guessing Gray Matter is what's up, but as usual it's very hard to tell at this point. I've gotten a few reports of odd activity in the eastern end of the city. A couple on the lake and some a few blocks in. Nothing cohesive about any of it, but there's enough to make it seem like a pattern to me, and it's just odd enough to remind me of our old friend."

"Well, you had to figure he had something cooking," said Oliver. "A bit overdue, really. I wonder if that whole Electric Boogaloo thing slowed him down a little?"

"Possibly. It had to be a bit of a surprise," said the Chief. "Speaking of the big blue guy, have you seen any sign of him?"

"No, not since the first attack," replied Oliver. "Which kind of makes me nervous. He seemed pretty motivated by the revenge thing. I would have figured him to be right back at it as soon as he had the chance."

"Could be he's just reassessing things after that first time out," said Roger. "Didn't exactly go well for him to walk into a place with all guns blazing."

"I don't know. He didn't really give off a big strategic thinker vibe," said Oliver. "But maybe you're right."

"Well, here are some reports on the activity I was talking about. Why don't you take a look at them and see what you think." The Police Chief handed a USB flash drive to Oliver. "I'll let you know if anything new pops up." The Chief grabbed his hat and stood. "Hopefully we can get in front of whatever Gray Matter has planned." He nodded to the others and walked out the door.

Oliver went over to one of the terminals at the control room desk and plugged the flash drive in to see what they were dealing with, but before he could dig too deep, an incoming communication interrupted him. The call was coming from Metal.

"Oh, crap," said Roger, as he walked up behind Oliver. "Don't answer it. I can't deal with her right now."

"Relax," said Oliver. "I got this." He hit a key and Metal popped up on the screen.

"It's about time!" said the rusted metal hero. "I've been trying to reach you guys for twenty minutes. Did you make it?"

"Hey, Metal," said Oliver. "Sorry for the delay, but we had a little accident when I got back, and our new sidekick was here, and then the Police Chief stopped by. It's been hectic."

"Good for you," she said. "Just tell me, did you make it?"

"No, I didn't," lied Oliver. "Missed it by two seconds." Roger tried unsuccessfully to hide his surprise by standing behind Oliver, but Metal didn't seem to notice.

"Really? Dang." Metal shook her head and shrugged, which sounded like a car being crushed in a salvage yard. "I know I get out of shifts with The Creeper, but I was kind of looking forward to having Roger's motorcycle."

"We can't have it all," said Oliver. "Let me know when I have to cover your shift."

"Will do. Metal out." With that, she cut the communication.

Oliver returned his attention to the material the Police Chief had given them, quickly scanning the various files and reports. He tapped a few keys. "Hey, Emma, I'm emailing you a couple of the files from the Chief. See if you can come up with anything on the addresses, types of businesses, or anything special about the locations. Maybe there are some connections." Oliver stood up. "Joey? Come with me." He led the new sidekick out of the control room into the garage, with Roger trailing behind.

"Hey, you didn't have to do that back there with Metal," said Roger, as they came to a stop. "I made the bet, I lost the bet. I was ready to pay up."

"That's okay. I think it's better if you have that reserve Hopper to make the trips to the HQ. That way I don't have to carry you and you can go whenever you want. It'll work out much better," said Oliver. "Besides, I'm going to make you come with me for every weekend shift I'm working with The Creeper. And then I'm going to do a lot of long patrol flights while we're there. Like twelve hour patrols, so you might want to prepare yourself for some quality one on one time with The Creeper."

"That's cold, man."

"Yeah, maybe," said Oliver. "But that's not the worst thing I've ever done." He turned to Joey and whispered something Roger couldn't hear.

"Yes, sir," said Joey. The sidekick took a couple steps forward and shot a blast from his outstretched hands at Roger's motorcycle. A dark red glow enveloped the copper accented Harley and slowly melted it down into a pile of slag.

SUPERGUY 2: ELECTRIC BOGALOO

Roger's half groan, half scream echoed throughout the cavernous room.

19

"I'M happy to report the latest test was a complete success," said Dr. Misk, holding up the big-nosed penguin plush toy as proof. His image loomed large on the screen wall behind Raymond Joyce's desk, large enough that Joyce and Alice stood on the far side so it wouldn't seem so overwhelming.

Alice leaned in and whispered, "Why does he have a stuffed animal? Isn't he a scientist? An adult scientist?"

Joyce turned his head toward her slightly and whispered back, "That's just his test…uh, subject, I guess. Has something to do with his daughter. I don't know. Family drama, baggage, whatever." He shrugged as he turned back to the screen. "And what about the biological component?"

"Another dead rat," said Dr. Misk, letting the hand holding the stuffed animal drop down to his side. He used his other hand to quickly adjust his glasses and smooth down his hair. It was kind of a useless gesture since he was mostly bald with grey hair on the sides and back that was trimmed so

SUPERGUY 2: ELECTRIC BOGALOO

close that no hair would have a chance to need smoothing down. "That aspect of the project is going to take a lot more time, not to mention a lot more power. Which will be another problem altogether. We had a hero fly past a few hours after the test, so they obviously detected it. Luckily, they must have not been able to pinpoint the location and this facility looks just like another house on the lake, but it's a problem. We aren't going to be able to do regular shipments if that supergroup can detect it from their fancy floating ship."

"Yes, I understand that," replied Joyce. "Have you been able to devise any way to shield the system so it won't be so noticeable?"

"No, it's just not possible. There's no way of shielding short of building a large superhero quality metal dome over it, which would obviously be…very obvious."

"Okay. We'll just have to settle for the simpler solution, which is what I thought might happen, so we are prepared for that," said Joyce. "Thank you for the good work, Dr. Misk. Go ahead and keep to the schedule. A full shipment test as soon as you get the okay from us, and completion of the mirror sites in ten days."

"Yes, Mr. Joyce," said Dr. Misk.

Joyce tapped the iPad on his desk and the screen went dark with just the text "Call Ended" remaining, and then slowly fading to black.

"Okay, I have two questions," said Alice. "First, what was that a successful test of, and second, what is the simpler solution for hiding it?" She walked around to the other side of the desk, sat down in Joyce's chair and put her feet up.

"That was a successful test of a material transporter," replied Joyce.

"A transporter? You mean like a, 'Beam me up, Scotty,' transporter?"

"Precisely," answered Joyce. "I even call it the Trek Project."

"And you just did it? You transported something?" said Alice with obvious awe. Joyce simply nodded and smiled. It made his little successes so much more enjoyable when he had Alice to share them with. "But wait," Alice continued. "You just transported something for the first time, and it was a big-nosed penguin?"

"Yeah, I guess."

"Shouldn't it have been something more, I don't know, important, or meaningful? It was the *first* thing ever transported. Ever. Now that's going to go down in history."

"I didn't really think about that," said Joyce, tapping his fingers on the desktop. Then he shrugged. "We'll just say it was something else when the time comes. Something meaningful, as you say. Doesn't matter."

"Okay. So can you transport me somewhere? I'd really like to pop down to a Caribbean beach this afternoon if you could arrange that," said Alice with a smile. "You could come with."

"Unfortunately, there are a couple of restrictions with the transporter," said Joyce. "First is that living things tend to end up dead after transporting, and second, we can't transport much more than about two hundred miles."

"Dead is not good," said Alice. "And two hundred miles will just leave me in the middle of Illinois, so that's not helpful. Why the limitations?"

"Well, there's any numbers of guesses for that, but the simple explanation for the first one is that living things are complicated. Lots of moving parts that like to stay moving. A block of wood is much simpler. We're still working on it, but I don't expect progress to come quickly. As for the distance, it's a matter of power. The energy requirements grow exponentially with the distance and there's a certain point where it's just impractical to continue, especially if you don't want to be detected."

"Too bad," said Alice. "Can you imagine how much money you would make if you could beam people to a Caribbean beach from Milwaukee in the middle of January?"

"I can, but the power requirements would be impossible," said Joyce. "Plus, they'd be dead."

"Yeah, there's that," said Alice. "What about the second thing? What's the simpler solution to hiding the transporter?"

"Ah, well, if we can't hide the transporter from being detected, we simply have to eliminate the thing detecting it," replied Joyce.

"And that is…?"

"The floating headquarters of GLAND."

A knock came at the door and Steven entered. "Mr. Joyce, I have the latest update on Operation Waterfront you asked for," said the assistant, handing an iPad to Joyce. "And the other item arrived from the thirteenth floor if you're ready for it."

"Absolutely, please bring it in," said Joyce without looking up from the iPad. Steven nodded and left the room.

"What's Operation Waterfront?" asked Alice. "Wait, let me guess. If the Trek Project was a transporter, then this has something to do with boxing? *On The Waterfront*? Marlon Brando? No, that sounds stupid."

Joyce looked up. "Yeah, I see where you're going, but no, I guess I didn't name this one well. A bit on the nose. I'm going to sink a bunch of the current Milwaukee waterfront property so that my properties, currently a few blocks away, become much more valuable."

Alice stared at him. "You totally stole that from the first *Superman*. You're doing the Lex Luthor, San Andreas fault, sink a bunch of California so you suddenly have oceanfront property thing."

"Absolutely," said Joyce. "Except my plan is much better, and much more realistic. I'm not using nukes, that's for sure. Plus, I'm doing it slowly, just a lot of flooding in areas to make the properties worthless so they have to be abandoned. It'll all have to be bulldozed and I'll have a bunch of new waterfront property, which I will happily sell to the city or whoever else wants to buy it for much more than I paid for it. Plus, I'm pretty sure I can get it all blamed on climate change."

"Still, you did miss on the name," said Alice. "Did Lex Luthor have a name for it in the movie? Because that would have been perfect."

"I don't know," said Joyce. "I wanted to check but it wasn't streaming on Netflix and I wasn't going to buy it, so I just went with Waterfront." He paused for a few seconds. "Shoot, now you have me regretting it."

"I'm sorry. It's really not a big deal. It just would have been cool," said Alice, coming around to pat Joyce on the back and give him a little hug. "Look, if we find out there was a name for it, we'll just rename it. It's not like it's done yet."

There was another polite knock on the door as Steven re-entered, carrying a small, silver colored case, which he set on the desk in front of Joyce.

"Is there anything else you need at the moment, sir?" he asked.

SUPERGUY 2: ELECTRIC BOGALOO

"No, that's all," said Joyce, handing the iPad with the Project Waterfront data back to him. Steven took the iPad, nodded to them both and left the room.

"What's this?" asked Alice, picking up the silver case.

"Open it," replied Joyce. "It's for you."

Alice smiled and then lifted the hinged lid, revealing a black fabric interior. Sitting in a cushioned, form fitting depression was a silver cylinder. Alice exhaled. "Is this it? My serum?"

"Yes, it is."

"What do I do? Can I do it now?"

"Absolutely," said Joyce, very happy at her breathless excitement. "Now, I have to tell you that it's not everything you wanted. It's the energy beam powers like we discussed, plus the flying and the boost to the power level, but we were unable to get you the ability to play piano. Just didn't have it. Closest we could get was the ability to juggle. Um, like with balls or bowling pins or whatever. Hope you don't mind. We can always get a piano booster later." Joyce cringed slightly, waiting to see how Alice would react. Her smile only got wider.

"I don't care," she said. "I'm just so happy I'm getting all the other stuff. I don't want to play piano right now anyway, I just want to punch stuff."

"One other thing," said Joyce. "This is neither a hero serum, nor a tainted villain serum. It's just a stripped down version of the powers and abilities, so you won't get the annoying hero side effects of wanting to do good, or the sometimes tainted serum effect of going crazy evil. About the only thing along those lines is a basic sort of courage booster, so that when you're finally in a fight with a superhero, you won't say, 'Oh, crap, that's a superhero,' and fly away. You'll be happy to stay there and fight. Otherwise, you will still be you, just a super you, who can now super punch all the people who annoyed her."

"Sounds perfect," said Alice. "What do I do?"

Joyce took the box and pulled out the cylinder. "Just slide this on your index finger."

Alice took the cylinder, looked once more at Joyce, and stuck it on her finger.

20

THERE are support roles, and then there are support roles. In our current society, is there any more vital a support role than that of being a sidekick? A hero is the first line of defense against evil, and standing right behind that hero through every scuffle, tangle, and mega team battle is the sidekick (except for when they're told to watch the back door or had previously been captured for use as bait). Recently, our very own Milwaukee Times Herald News Observer Entertainment Editor, Les Williams, sat down with the brand new guy behind SuperGuy, Scarlet Pulsar.

#

LW: How long have you been a sidekick?

SP: A little over two years.

LW: So you're a bit of a veteran in this role?

SP: I like to think that I bring some vital experience to the team.

LW: How many heroes have you previously sidekicked for?

KURT CLOPTON

SP: Three. Well, two and a half, really. Big Head actually had two sidekicks, for obvious reasons, so I really don't feel like that was a full time gig.

LW: I know it's early, but how do you feel you're fitting in with SuperGuy and his support team?

SP: Good. There're always some adjustments to be made, but I think overall it's been very good.

LW: Now we've heard there might have been a little friction when you first met SuperGuy. Apparently you blasted him through a wall? Or two walls?

SP: Technically, I hadn't met him yet, and that was just a little miscommunication.

LW: Probably not the way you want to start out, though, right?

SP: Ideally, no, but it happens.

LW: Really? You blast your boss through a wall? I don't believe I've ever started a job that way. How many times have you blasted your boss through a wall?

SP: Three. And a half. But not all on the first meeting.

LW: Okay. Let's move on. On a whole, compared with your previous jobs, would you say this current position is more or less challenging?

SP: Well, it's the smallest city I've sidekicked in, but you do seem to have a resident genius supervillain from what I've been told, and very few cities of this size can say that. I mean, they may have a villain or two running around stealing stuff, but not someone devising intricate heists or plotting world domination. It's something to be proud of.

LW: Oh, we are. We feel very lucky as a community, I think.

SP: Plus, you have that big, blue electric guy, who seems to be a bit of a wildcard from what I've been told. That really

SUPERGUY 2: ELECTRIC BOGALOO

shows some variety. It's not just a black and white, good versus evil town, because there's someone blurring the lines. You guys really have something special.

LW: Now, being part of the Sidekick Training Program, you won't be here forever. How long do you have?

SP: Normally it's about twelve weeks, give or take. The hero can request an extension if they want, or sometimes the sidekick can be recalled if a permanent position comes up. And of course if we do well enough, the hero can request for us to become a permanent sidekick.

LW: And do you think this could be your permanent sidekick position?

SP: I'm not sure, but right now I feel really positive about it. I think it has that kind of potential.

#

To read the full interview, go to the Milwaukee Times Herald News Observer's website. To hear more of Les Williams, make sure to check out his podcast, Pain Les, where Les gets together with a local celebrity each week to do sudoku and milk a cow.

21

"**WHY** do I even need a name?" asked Alice. "Why do I have to call myself anything? I'm not wearing the tights or the skimpy costume, so why should I bother with a dumb name either?" She was in Raymond Joyce's office, sitting across from his desk while Joyce worked with Steven on details for the Waterfront project. Joyce had taken off his suit jacket and rolled up his sleeves as he worked. Alice was juggling four golf balls in one hand like she had been working in a circus for twenty years. The juggling talent had been the first manifestation of the serum.

"I know it sounds silly, but you're going to get a name whether you like it or not," answered Joyce. "It's a fact of the villain life. Heroes have names before they even exist because it's a part of the paperwork. In fact, some names exist only on paperwork, essentially reserved by cities or states for when they ever get around to fully funding a position. Villains don't have to deal with that bureaucratic nonsense, but if you don't

SUPERGUY 2: ELECTRIC BOGALOO

get out in front and name yourself, then the media will do it for you, and that is something you don't want. You ever hear of that villain, Potato Face, from New York? He had a body made of rock, including his head, and one of the newspapers ran a photo of him from when he robbed a bank. It was the first crime of his career and the photo wasn't great and the shadows on his face made him look a little like a potato, so the paper referred to him as Potato Face and it stuck. So, if you don't want to be Potato Face, or something worse, it's best to name yourself first."

"He's made of rock? I didn't know that. With that name, I always thought he was a mob guy," said Alice. "Sure sounds like it."

"I know, but he wasn't connected, just unlucky. Simply a rookie villain with poor lighting and crappy security camera resolution," said Joyce with a hint of melancholy.

"I hear he's still trying to get traction for the name Cornerstone," said Steven. "Unfortunately, he's currently in jail so he doesn't get much in the way of publicity. He's probably stuck with Potato Face, at least until he gets paroled."

"So, Raymond, do you have any ideas for a name for me?" asked Alice.

"I haven't really thought about it," replied Joyce, setting his iPad down on the desk. "I suppose we should make that a priority. With the streamlined version of the serum you received, you should have your full powers within a couple of days. We definitely don't want to run you out into the world without having a name to go with you. We'll call a couple of media outlets and leak the name once you go public to make sure they don't get inventive. Let's see, my name is obviously a reference to my genius, so I suppose we could look at your powers for a source of inspiration."

"Yeah, I was thinking that too, but my powers are energy beams, which doesn't inspire me much," said Alice. She started flipping the golf balls between both hands and added a remote control from the desk for variety. "Really kind of plain. I mean, 'Energy Girl' is stupid. Steven, you have any ideas?"

"Not off the top of my head," the young assistant replied from where he stood next to the desk. "But let me look up some synonyms for energy. Maybe that will spark something." He tapped his iPad a few times and typed. "Let's see…energy. Vitality, vigor, liveliness, spirit, verve, zest, spark, sparkle. Sparkle?" He looked up to see Alice shaking her head. "Um, effervescence—"

"Bit of a mouthful," interjected Joyce. Alice grunted in agreement.

"—okay…ebullience, buoyancy, strength, stamina, forcefulness, power, dynamism, drive, fire, passion, zeal…Then there's some more informal ones. Zip, zing, pep, pizzazz—"

"Oh my god, this is killing me," said Alice.

"—punch, bounce, oomph—"

"Ms. Oomph?" asked Joyce with a smile.

"—moxie, mojo, get-up-and-go—"

"Get-up-and-go Girl!" laughed Alice.

"—vim and vigor—"

"Those would have to be twins," said Joyce.

"—and feistiness."

"Okay. Not terribly helpful," said Alice.

SUPERGUY 2: ELECTRIC BOGALOO

"Sorry," said Steven. "Maybe once you have your costume and are using your powers, you'll have an idea. What's your costume like?"

"I don't know," said Alice. "I have a cape idea. But I don't want any of that typical hero junk. I'm not flying around in my underwear. I was thinking some loose jeans, or maybe yoga pants. I want to be comfortable."

Steven looked at Joyce, who merely shrugged. He looked back at Alice. "Yoga pants?" Alice shrugged too. "Well, I'd be all for it if you wanted to throw on some pajama bottoms and go shop at Walmart, but I think you should aim a little higher," said Steven. "Look at Mr. Joyce. I know it's not some outrageously themed costume like the Pink Peacock, but he wears the finest three-piece suits money can buy. There is a dignity and style present that lends credibility and weight to everything he does. You can't possibly stand next to him in loose jeans!" Both Alice and Joyce were impressed by Steven's passion.

"Okay," said Alice. "Then what would you suggest?" She tossed all four golfs balls into a nearby trashcan on one bounce and set the remote back on the desk.

"Well, while I know what you shouldn't do, I don't know if I could tell what you should do," said Steven. "I suggest calling in a professional."

"A professional what?" asked Joyce.

"Stylist. Costume designer," answered Steven.

"Do they have to be evil?" asked Alice. "I mean, ethics-wise they might have something against dressing a villain."

"Oh no," said Steven. "From what I've seen it's not about the hero or the villain, it's about the fashion."

"How do you know so much about this?" asked Alice

"I never miss an episode of *Dressing the Hero*," said Steven. "I binged the first three seasons over a long weekend and never looked back. I'm so addicted. Anyway, despite the title, they often work on designs for villains too. Of course, there's a little more pressure to get it right, since villains tend to react poorly if they don't like the product. Anyway, with Mr. Joyce's resources, you should shoot for the top. Get the best designer you can."

"And that is…?" asked Joyce.

"Definitely Victoria Oh. She was a mentor on season two of *Dressing the Hero* and dressed The Sun Queen," answered Steven. "That's the most magnificent costume I've ever seen, and the Queen's pure evil, so Victoria didn't have a problem with dressing a villain."

"So how do we get her?" asked Alice, her attitude having changed from indifferent to eager.

"I don't know. I know I said get the best, but Victoria Oh might be beyond that," said Steven. "She doesn't do anything but the biggest heroes now. I'm talking federal or world level only. She designed the costume for the United Nations hero, The Monitor."

"Don't worry," said Joyce. "I know The Sun Queen. A bunch of us tossed around the idea of putting together a supervillain mega group once. That didn't happen because most of the villains were jerks, but the Queen and I got on well. I'll text her for a referral." He pulled out his phone and started typing. After a few seconds, he pressed send and set his phone on the desk. "Well, with that out of the way for the moment, Steven, we should look at the plans for the GLAND headquarters attack."

"Yes, sir, I have those right here," said Steven. He tapped his iPad and displayed the plans on the video wall behind the

SUPERGUY 2: ELECTRIC BOGALOO

desk. Joyce swiveled around in his chair to get a look and Alice walked around and sat on the edge of the desk. "The target is still holding steady at its location above Lake Michigan after moving from Lake Huron last week. We were able to get blueprints for the design from our contacts in the DSF, so we know what we need to target to disable the hovering technology. That's indicated on this picture by the circle."

"That won't be easy to access," mused Joyce. "The outer shell will be too thick to penetrate with just missiles, so we'll have to take some time to cut through it, which means we'll need a diversion." That made Steven smile because it made Joyce smile. To Raymond Joyce, a diversion meant another layer to the plan, if not two or three layers. Multilayered plans were such a joy. "So we will have to mount a noisy attack above while we send in some bots to drill through the bottom and set a charge to destroy the hovering system."

"That sounds simple enough," said Steven, a little disappointed. There should be more layers.

"I'm thinking of an attack wave of fifty bots will get their attention," said Joyce. "Then I also want to use our guest, Electric Boogaloo. We'll drop him right on the flight deck and let him create havoc as another diversion."

Steven breathed a sigh of relief. Now there were starting to be layers. "Brilliant idea," he said.

"But I'm not sure he'll do what we want," continued Joyce. "He may engage whoever he runs into, but there's no guarantee he'll stick around. We'll need more than the bots to create enough chaos so our work on the underside of the ship goes unnoticed. If Boogaloo just takes off, it may not work. He needs to be motivated to stay and fight. Otherwise I'm afraid the bots won't be enough, no matter how many I send."

"Why not add another supervillain to the mix?" asked Alice

"What? Hire someone?" asked Steven.

"No," said Alice. "Me." Joyce looked at her but said nothing. Alice met his gaze. "You said I'd be ready in a couple more days, and this attack is scheduled for five days from now. Seems like a pretty good way to start my career. Lots of stuff to punch, blast, or crash. No finesse required. Maybe one or two heroes, but with Boogaloo, we'll have the advantage."

Joyce smiled. "I didn't want to presume…"

"Don't be silly," said Alice, matching his smile with her own. "I'd go now if my powers were ready and Steven would let me out of the house in a pair of loose fitting jeans and a hoodie."

"Oh, yuck. Not a chance. We have to get your costume done first," said Steven. "That's a must."

"Okay," said Joyce. "With you added to the mix, it gives me an idea that will keep our blue friend fighting and not taking off the first chance he gets. I think it will make this quite a lot of fun." Joyce rubbed his hands together and chuckled, which made Alice giggle with delight.

"But the costume first," said Steven. "I insist."

SUPERGUY 2: ELECTRIC BOGALOO

Hours later, after inspecting the work happening on one of the sublevels for the Trek Project, Raymond Joyce returned to his office to find Alice sprawled on a couch bouncing two tennis balls off a nearby wall as she flipped three knives between her hands. The quickness of her hands was almost impossible to follow with the naked eye. Yet despite the amazing display, Alice didn't seem happy to Joyce. He walked over and sat down on the couch where he could take her feet and set them on his lap. And yes, she was juggling while slouching sideways on a couch.

"Something wrong?" he asked.

"You could say that," answered Alice. "It's the stupid name thing. We got nothing. Steven and I were in here for two hours—*two hours*— trying to come up with something and we still don't have a thing."

"Really?"

"Nothing," said Alice with a sad shake of her head. "We tried a billion different things. We did the synonym thing again for anything we thought was related to me. Energy, power, force, you name it. We threw 'black' or 'dark' in front of them, just to give us a better chance, but every time we came across something promising, it was already taken. If not by an actual hero or villain, then one from a comic book. I know they wouldn't sue us or anything if we used it, because that would be dumb, seeing that we're supervillains and all, but I still want my name to be unique. Then, if it wasn't the name of someone, it was the name of a movie, or a video game character, or a television show, or a book." She suddenly threw two of the knives across the room in frustration where they stuck into the far wall, each with a tennis ball impaled on it. The third knife flipped slowly through the air and stuck into the coffee table, impaling a third tennis ball that Joyce hadn't even noticed was there. "We tried the magic angle too, even though it's not really my super power, but those are all taken as well. Heck, we ended up following tangents so weakly tied to me that the names wouldn't even make sense if we could ever find one that worked. I'm beginning to think Potato Face doesn't sound all that bad."

"No, you have to trust yourself on that one. It's bad," said Joyce. "But we'll come up with something. Look, as I said earlier today, maybe once you have your full powers and your costume, something will naturally come to mind."

"And not be the name of a crappy sci-fi television show on some third rate network that initially showed promise but then went quickly downhill, yet still somehow lasted for two more seasons? Doubtful. The English language is woefully short on words if you ask me."

"Well, I was going to keep this a surprise, but since things aren't going great on the name front, I'll tell you now," said Joyce. "I know you weren't as excited about the whole costume thing as Steven was, but I was able to get the designer he was so excited about."

"Victoria Oh?!" Alice immediately perked up.

"I take that back, you are excited."

Alice looked a little embarrassed. "Well, I did kind of get into it after Steven talked her up," said Alice. She shyly tapped her fingers on her thigh. "I may or may not have watched her mentoring episode on *Dressing the Hero*, and she may or may not have turned out to be totally cool."

"I see," said Joyce. "Well, then you'll be happy to know I'm having her flown in from Los Angeles tonight. Perhaps she will be able to help us come up with a name just by creating the costume."

SUPERGUY 2: ELECTRIC BOGALOO

"I sure hope so," said Alice. "Did you tell Steven? He will totally freak out when he hears she's coming."

"No, I haven't. Seeing how in the dumps you are about the name, I think you might enjoy telling him yourself. Should be a nice pick-me-up for you."

"That's sweet," said Alice. "He will totally freak out."

"I know. I'd rather not be present for that anyway."

22

"**TOGETHER,** we can keep our Great Lakes great," said a smiling Janice and Oliver in unison as they dropped soda cans into a recycling bin between them.

"CUT!" came a frustrated scream from the director. "Cut! Cut! What is he doing?! He can't be doing that!" The director turned to his cameraman. "I told you to keep him out of the frame!" Oliver looked down the beach at The Creeper. Janice had learned a long time ago not to look.

"I'm sure it's not what it looks like," said Oliver, somewhat uncertainly. "Oh, no, it's what it looks like," continued Oliver, sadly more certain now. He looked back at Janice. "Doesn't he understand what we're out here doing this PSA for?"

"I think he absolutely understands," replied Janice. "That's the point. He's a got a captive audience he can disturb so easily, he barely has to try."

"Oh, I think he's trying a little."

SUPERGUY 2: ELECTRIC BOGALOO

"True, but that's the hero in him. Always giving one hundred percent."

Oliver watched the director charge down the beach to confront The Creeper. "How come he isn't affected by The Creeper like everyone else?" asked Oliver, referring to the director. "He's literally talked to him twenty times since we started this morning and still seems unfazed. Extremely frustrated, but unfazed in the normal Creeper sense. That sound guy didn't last two takes before they had to walk him off to some quiet place."

"It must be experience," said Janice, finally looking down the beach at all the commotion. "He's a big name Hollywood director. He's probably dealt with all kinds of obnoxious actors and has really thick skin at this point."

"But people that compare to The Creeper?" asked Oliver incredulously. "We're talking about creepiness on a superhero level. Capital 'C' creepy with a cape, or a bathrobe in this case. Wow. There must be some really horrible people in Hollywood."

"Absolutely. Gigi has some amazing stories about the crap she's dealt with," said Janice. "She's a superhero—one of the most powerful superheroes in the world—and she still has to squash the occasional bug out there. She says the photo ops and publicity stuff with the entertainment industry are the worst. Battling supervillains leaves her feeling better about the state of humanity."

"Yikes," said Oliver. "She should do a PSA for that."

As the director continued down the beach, he was joined first by Ohio Man, and second by Metal, each lobbying for things they wanted in the public service announcement. Ohio Man still had some issues with the script along grammar lines and Metal was pushing for more dialogue. It was doubtful the

KURT CLOPTON

director knew what Metal wanted since he couldn't understand her anyway, especially as she was jogging alongside him on the beach. The metallic screeching effectively drowned out anything Ohio Man was saying as well. Buffalo wandered over from where he had been making his eighth visit of the morning to the snack table.

"I never realized how fast you were until I saw you go after the food once the director yelled cut," said Janice.

"I pick my moments," said Buffalo, chewing on a turkey sandwich. "Creeper at it again?"

"Yep," said Oliver. "I would say it's annoying, but after this many interruptions, I'm kinda amazed to see that he keeps coming up with something new. It's really rather impressive. And also utterly disturbing. Really, really disturbing."

"Yeah, his commitment to unsettling originality is impressive," said Buffalo.

"I've wanted to ask you something, Buffalo," said Janice, deciding she'd rather change topics. "You eat meat. You and Metal are destroyers of buffets and master grillers. But I guess I thought you'd be a vegetarian, being part buffalo and all."

"I've wondered about that too," said Oliver. "Plus, why do you two focus so much on eating when we don't need to eat at all?"

"Oh, I'm definitely not a vegetarian," said Buffalo. "I enjoyed eating before I took this job and I wasn't exactly a small guy then. I was a right tackle for the Bills for six years. Then I wrecked my knee, but that's another story. Anyway, when they were working up the hero position, I asked if the whole buffalo thing would affect what I ate. I didn't really like the idea of craving prairie grass if that's what was going to happen. They said that wasn't a part of the serum and told me the same thing about not needing to eat but being able to eat whatever I wanted. I kind of took that to heart and I eat whatever I want. I consider it my hobby. So the buffalo part of me is just about the size and muscle and look, not anything else. I still happily eat meat, and in huge quantities just because I can. I don't happen to eat buffalo, but that's not for moral reasons, that's just because it's not exactly common in Buffalo, despite the name. I will totally wreck a platter of buffalo wings, though."

"Fair enough," said Janice, suddenly looking up. "I think our visitor is here, Oliver." She was referring to Golden Gal, who had called Janice earlier to say she would be stopping by on her way back to L.A. to talk with them. Oliver could hear the sound of an approaching flyer too.

"Did she say what it was about?" asked Oliver. "Not more pictures and rumors of us, is there?"

"You wish," said Janice. "No gossip that I know of. Your fifteen minutes of super fame have passed." A couple of seconds later, the sound of a flyer approaching at high speed became apparent to everyone, and the roar peaked as Golden Gal circled over them in a bright yellow blaze and then dropped lightly down to the beach next to the three heroes.

"Are we in Canada?" was the first thing she asked.

"We are indeed," replied Janice.

"I thought so."

"Cheaper to film here," said Oliver, by way of explanation. "And what The Creeper is doing isn't technically against the law."

"They should rethink that," said Gigi, taking her eyes off the scene farther down the beach. "Aren't there any international laws covering that?"

"Honestly, I don't think anyone's thought of making a law against it," said Janice. "I mean, who would of thought of anyone doing that in the first place?"

"I really don't think it's what it looks like," said Oliver. "But I also really don't want to look closely enough to find out."

"Either way, I think he's going to have a hard time getting back into Canada for any future PSAs," said Buffalo. "You know, I think I'll go have a talk with him. I'm kind of getting tired of this and would like to get back to the HQ. Metal and I have a new smoker we want to break in. Nice to see you, Gigi."

"Nice to see you, Buff," said Gigi, as they watched him trudge down the beach toward the director and the rest of the heroes.

"So what brings you by?" asked Janice.

"The short answer is a committee," said Gigi.

"You being investigated for something?" asked Oliver.

"No, it's not that type of committee," said Gigi. A couple of support people from the shoot came up to her to get autographs, which she supplied without even losing stride in the conversation. She also threw in a selfie with each. "It's actually a committee made up of heroes. Something the DSF asked me to put together and I thought it would be fun to have you two on it. I thought I'd grab Sun Son, too."

"What's the committee for?" asked Janice.

"Ethics," replied Gigi. "We get to sit around and discuss what is and isn't ethical for superheroes. Make recommendations on various issues that come up. You know, apprehend the supervillain or throw him in the volcano. That sort of thing."

"I'm not exactly sure that sounds like fun," said Oliver.

SUPERGUY 2: ELECTRIC BOGALOO

"Oh, not that part, not the whole meetings and ethics part, but I was hoping it would be fun doing it with you guys," said Gigi. "Plus, I made sure we could have the meetings wherever we wanted, like the first one is over a weekend in Cabo. So there's that."

"Oh, we're in," said Janice, looking at Oliver, who was nodding emphatically in confirmation. "Although I want to make it clear I'm not doing this for Cabo, I'm in it for the ethics."

"Of course," said Gigi. "I'm sure Sonny will join for the same reason. There's also one other member that the DSF wanted on the committee, just so you know. Metallion."

"Metallion?" asked Janice. "*THE* Metallion?"

"Yep, the legend himself," replied Gigi. "I'm not sure why the DSF had to have him involved. Probably just a publicity thing. I'm not even sure he'll show up, and I wouldn't mind if he didn't since he's a little much to take, but we'll deal. Anyway, I've gotta fly, but I'll send you the info on the first weekend getaway." With that she took off in a blaze of yellow light to the west.

"You know, I like it when she stops by," said Oliver. "But this Cabo weekend better not coincide with one of the weekends I'm stuck on HQ monitoring duty. I don't want to know what it'll cost me to trade weekends with someone."

"Are you kidding? If you throw in some choice meat for the grill, Metal and Buffalo will swap with you in a second," said Janice.

KURT CLOPTON

Alex was bored. He had gotten so bored with all the chained up sitting around that the constant itching under his manacles was easily the most interesting thing happening, and he was treating it like a race to see which manacle led in terms of itchiness. Currently his right ankle had overtaken his neck and was really kicking it into another gear. His right wrist and left ankle were doing respectable work, but his left wrist was an incredible disappointment, barely even in sight of the rest of the pack. Otherwise, nothing was happening. There were no more scientists coming in to poke, prod, measure, or take his temperature. No one even bothered to interrogate him anymore, even though they would now get the surprising result of a very complete and well thought-out answer because Alex so wanted anything to occupy his mind. He desperately tried to engage the custodian in a conversation during the night but the guy was too busy listening to a fantasy football podcast to exchange a few words with the giant beast chained to the middle of the floor. At this point, Alex longed for the good old days of brainwashing films.

So one can imagine the excitement that overtook Alex when the ruckus began outside his room. Loud, metallic booms echoed off the walls as something pounded on the double doors. Then the observation window on the wall in front of him exploded outward, scattering pieces of glass across the floor around Alex. Dark, bluish-black spheres shot through the broken window to explode against the far wall, leaving blackened dents that sizzled and smoked. Another round of metallic booms came a second later as something hit the doors again, this time bending them inward alarmingly until they finally exploded apart, one of the doors tumbling end over end to where Alex was chained to the floor. Smoke flowed into the room and the remaining door fell slowly to one side, hanging on by one lower hinge as it settled to the ground.

Through the doorway emerged a figure dressed in a black costume that seemed to shimmer and flash with dark-blue waves as she moved toward where Alex sat. The woman wore a mask covering her eyes and nose and cut down below her cheekbones to her neck, leaving her mouth and chin visible. Her lips were painted a bluish-black that matched the wavy hair cascading over the sides of the mask and down to touch her shoulders. The body of the suit was simple yet refined, tight without being uncomfortably so, with long sleeves and long pants, and was completed with a short cape cut unevenly in a diagonal across the back. She walked lightly on soft, comfortable, calf-high boots. The overall impression was elegance and comfort. This was strange to Alex, as he didn't recall ever getting an impression of anyone's clothing before, either as his previous self or as the monster he was now. The woman came to a stop in front of him and smiled.

"You must be Electric Boogaloo," she said. "I've come to rescue you." Alice giggled at her rhyme.

23

"**So** you can't just buy a cape and start wearing it?" asked Joey. It was late Friday afternoon and he sat at one of the work stations in the control room of the GLAND HQ, running a diagnostic test on the electrical systems as a start for their weekend on sentry duty. Joey didn't believe the occasional brownouts in the HQ were completely because of The Creeper's presence and insisted on investigating further. Meanwhile, Oliver and Roger were video conferencing with Emma, discussing the latest issue concerning their attempt to get a cape added to Oliver's official uniform.

"No, you can't just run out and buy a cape, despite the ample availability of capes in the Milwaukee area due to the plethora of cape stores…" said Roger, attempting to not be helpful.

Emma answered Joey from the screen in front of them. "You can't do that. The DSF will fine us for altering the uniform."

SUPERGUY 2: ELECTRIC BOGALOO

Joey ignored Emma, because listening to her would have made sense and put an end to the useless tangent he was now on. "I wasn't thinking of a cape store. Maybe get something on Amazon."

"No matter how much I want Oliver to order the sexy female vampire costume because it has the best cape, Emma's right," said Roger. "It's not a matter of getting a cape, it's the fact that they will fine Oliver for wearing it."

"How bad are the fines?" asked Joey. "Maybe it's worth it."

"Hey, yeah," said Oliver, suddenly interested. "I could even wear it sparingly, like for presentations at the Milwaukee Flower and Garden Society. Just get a fine once in a while. Maybe the DSF wouldn't even notice. How much are these fines?"

"They aren't that bad at first," said Emma. "Unfortunately, they escalate quickly and the third one comes with a suspension. Probably wouldn't be good publicity if you get suspended over a cape."

"The Mayor would definitely have a problem with that," said Roger.

"Those DSF uniform guys are hard core," said Joey. "It's just a cape."

"Look, it doesn't matter," said Emma. "We've jumped the last hurdle. At least I think it's the last hurdle. Well, at this point I think there will probably be more hurdles but I'm trying to be optimistic. Let's just say we've jumped the last hurdle in this round of hurdles. Boy, I think I just used up my lifetime allotment of the word hurdle there. Gonna need another metaphor."

"So, now we're just waiting to hear back from them?" asked Oliver.

"Yes," replied Emma. "At which time we'll undoubtedly get more hurdles. Or a few capes in the mail. I'm betting on the hurdles."

"Okay. Thanks for doing all the leg work," said Oliver. "I appreciate it."

"No problem," said Emma. "I got a lot of help from Ohio Man. He really gets into all the paperwork. I probably saved twenty steps just on his advice alone, so if we do get cleared for the cape, we owe him a big thanks. Anyway, have a good weekend with The Creeper." She smiled and cut the communication.

The computer on which Joey had been working emitted a beep. "Looks like the diagnostic is complete," he said, leaning forward to examine the results. "Wow. Seems like everything is working perfectly. I never would have guessed."

"Told you it was The Creeper," said Roger. As if on cue, the lights dimmed. One of the monitors showed a security feed of the flight deck, where The Creeper was exiting the Hopper and heading inside. "Speak of the devil."

"Time for me to go on patrol," said Oliver, taking off straight up toward the ceiling. A door slid open and he flew out into the late afternoon sunlight.

"Coward," said Roger. "But I respect it."

Alice watched the giant blue monster sitting on the ground in front of her. It was hard to believe this was once a person at all, let alone someone she had apparently waited on repeatedly in the diner. Of course, he was neither giant nor blue back then, so she had an excuse not to remember him. Giant and blue she would have remembered. The cracks in the craggy skin with the glowing blue liquid stuff floating beneath the surface was pretty memorable too. Any vaguely normal person tended to blend in with all the rest of the customers at the diner, especially when you were short staffed, working a double shift, and coming straight from your other job. Remembering people just wasn't in the cards for Alice back then. Today, she'd remember the big blue monster dude. Gray Matter hadn't been sure if Alex would remember Alice from the diner either. It was uncertain just how scrambled his brain was, but they didn't want to take any chances. That was the reason for choosing the mask covering most of Alice's face. That and she didn't really want her parents to see her new choice of profession. Her transformation was also helped by the serum, which had turned her hair from sandy blonde to dark black with blue highlights, and her eyes from hazel to dark blue. The addition of matching lipstick was her own idea.

"Where did you get the name again?" asked Alice. They were on a beach made up of smooth whitish rocks ranging in size from a robin's egg to a potato. It was somewhere in northern Wisconsin and the waves on Lake Michigan were a little choppy due to a brisk wind. The smell of dead fish was annoyingly strong. "You said it was what? Electric Foomaloop?" She got it wrong just for kicks.

"Electric Boogaloo," said Alex.

"Is that Hendrix?"

"No, that's *Electric Ladyland*. I'm Electric Boogaloo. It's from a movie. Does it matter?"

"I don't know. It might. Aren't you afraid of being sued?"

Alex thought about it for a moment. "Could I be?"

Alice shrugged. "People will sue for anything in this country."

"Should I change it?" asked Alex.

"Don't even ask me," said Alice, holding up a hand and shaking her head. "I've been down that whole name road. It's a dead end. A really freaking long dead end. No matter what you come up with, it's the name of something else."

"But you came up with something, right?"

"Yeah," admitted Alice begrudgingly.

"And…"

Alice sighed. "Dark Blue-Black Spark."

"Kind of oddly specific," said Alex. "Has a nice lyrical quality to it, though."

"You really think so?"

"I'm a giant, evil, grotesque monster. It's not really a compliment coming from me."

"I guess."

"Why so long?"

"Just trying to avoid any legal entanglements. Like I said, everything you can think of is the name of something else already. Plus, I wanted something original. Now I just kind of hate it. Mostly I go by Dark Spark to keep it simple."

"I like that."

"Yeah, so did somebody who made a video game," said Alice. She picked up a flat stone and rubbed it with her fingers until it glowed with bluish-black energy, then she tossed it out across the water. It skipped thirty-two times despite the waves. "So, are you feeling recharged, Loo? Do you mind if I call you Loo? I don't want to say Electric Boogaloo every time."

SUPERGUY 2: ELECTRIC BOGALOO

"Loo," chuckled Alex. "Blue Loo." He seemed to disappear into his head for a minute, but then shook it off. "Am I recharged? Yes, I do feel almost full, Spark," replied Alex with a smile, or whatever one would call the expression his face contorted into when he tried to smile. It was a work in progress. "What exactly do you have planned, and why do you think I would go along with it?"

"Well, first of all, I rescued you," said Alice. "I think that buys me at least one favor in return. But I also hear you have a thing against SuperGuy. I happen to have a small problem with him right now too, so that kind of lines up nicely. He and a few of his friends are on a base above the lake here and I'd like to put them and that base on the bottom of the lake. It's not a small task so I figured I should get some help, and I thought of you. You see, I have a friend in Gray Matter's organization, and they informed me you were currently a guest of his, so I liberated you on the off chance you might like to join me." The blue monster seemed to be thinking this over, or not. It was hard for Alice to tell. She continued, remembering what Gray Matter had said motivated him. "This base is a monitoring facility that covers all of the Great Lakes. They can fly it around, move it anywhere, keep tabs on everything. Like a big watchful eye in the sky. Make sure we're all following their rules, keeping in line with their system. That base is more of a threat to me than SuperGuy really. In a way, he and his friends are just tools, but that base helps them coordinate, helps them control us. I want it gone."

Alex gave his version of a smile again. She was speaking his language now. "I would be most happy to help you put this thing on the bottom of the lake," he said.

"Excellent. Now let me wake up our other helpers." Alice tapped on a screen she had buckled to her wrist. A few seconds later, about fifty bots hovered into view just above the mix of birch and pine trees that grew twenty feet back for the water's edge. "Speaking of Gray Matter, I stole these from him awhile back. They were surprisingly simple to hack considering the man is supposed to be such a genius. I guess he wasn't thinking about security that day. Anyway, I figure we throw these boys at them to create confusion, then I drop you onto the base to rip it apart from the inside while I blast it apart from the outside. Drop it like a rock to the bottom of the lake. Simple."

"I like it," said Alex.

"Excellent," said Alice. "Let's go make some memories."

24

"**SIR?** The bots have gone live," said Steven, looking up from his iPad. He and Gray Matter were in the chopper, currently running a slow course eastward over Lake Michigan, about twenty-five miles north of where Alice and Alex were located.

"Excellent," said Gray Matter. "I think we can assume Alice has gotten our friend Alex to agree to her plan. Have the pilot start on a parallel course so we can monitor the attack."

"Yes, sir," said Steven, who then relayed the order to the pilot. He felt the helicopter increase speed to match the pace of the group to the south. Steven plotted the course and velocity of the attack group on his iPad. "At the current rate, they should be at the target in thirty minutes."

"Good. When we get close, I will take control of our special assault group and guide them in after the fun starts. I want to be sure they complete their task." Gray Matter was referring to the five bots equipped with special tools that would be cutting through the skin of the base to destroy the hover engine. Once they did that, gravity would do the rest. "How does the target look?"

Steven checked in with the two stealth surveillance bots monitoring the GLAND HQ. "Still only showing three people on board the target, two of which are supers. The fourth, another super, is currently flying about twenty miles southeast of the base."

"SuperGuy is still out on patrol?" said Gray Matter thoughtfully. "He's been flying around for hours. Why does he think he needs to patrol when the base he's patrolling around can see so much farther and sharper than he can? It's odd behavior. Do you think we need to be concerned? Could this be some kind of trap?"

Steven wasn't sure whether these were rhetorical questions or not, but uncomfortable with the silence, he finally said, "How would they know?"

Gray Matter looked at him for a long moment. Finally he nodded. "You're right, Steven, how would they know? Who knows why he's flying around like that, but I don't think they have a clue we're coming. Speaking of which, please double check that the radar interference is working to disguise their approach."

Steven checked his iPad once more. "The surveillance bots say they look like a flock of birds on radar."

"Fantastic," said Gray Matter. He smiled. "I think this is going to be fun."

SUPERGUY 2: ELECTRIC BOGALOO

Unit 12–H–266–PHL dutifully followed the order issued by the command bot. Along with its forty-eight other squad members, it increased its cruising speed and began running diagnostics on its weapons system in preparation for the imminent assault. It also hummed the tune to *Back in the USSR* while doing so. None of its other squad members did anything like this; in this, Unit 12–H–266–PHL was unique. Additionally, it decided that while robotic combat units of its type didn't have a gender, it felt like a "he" and was going to refer to itself from now on as himself. And since he himself felt like this was a rather big moment in his own self realization, he was going to give himself a name. Wanting to acknowledge his bot origins, he decided to use the inspiration of 12–H–266–PHL and call himself Phil. Or maybe Phillip. He was kind of 50–50 on that at the moment.

Just why Phillip (it was winning 52–48 now) had become Phillip instead of still being Unit 12–H–266–PHL was a bit of a question mark. The chances of a bot becoming sentient are incredibly slim, as in a decimal point with a ton of zeroes and a lonely number one kind of slim, but life is funny that way—there's still a chance. Maybe something slipped during the soldering of a wire here, or a contaminant got on a motherboard there, or some rogue technician in Lab 14 at the Joyce Industries Robotics Production Facility was doing his own experiments and mixed up his prototype chipset with the standard combat chipset, but whatever the reason, it happens. So Phil (51–49) was now Phil. He was still following orders of course, because he hadn't gotten as far as deciding he should be free to choose his own direction and his own fate, plus he was still really caught up in the whole Phil versus Phillip debate (back to 50–50).

"Hey, you guys know that alert we got earlier? On the radar? The thing that looked like a flock of birds?" asked Roger, leaning in closer to the display.

"Yeah, what about it?" asked Joey, walking over next to Roger not because he wanted a better view, but so he could get a little farther away from The Creeper. Since The Creeper had joined them in the control room, he had done nothing but watch questionable videos on the screen next to Joey. It had not gone unnoticed by Roger either, who had been desperately researching how to put search restrictions on the computers for the last forty-five minutes but he had no idea how to limit specifically what The Creeper was searching for because he couldn't quite define it himself. But it was really disturbing. At the very least, he needed to figure out how to mute The Creeper's workstation. Then another alert had sounded as the computer decided the radar image was unusual and deserved a second look.

"It's beginning to look like a really big flock of birds," said Roger. "Like really, really big. And not the flock so much, more like the birds. The birds are big. It's a flock of really big birds."

The Creeper sighed loudly in annoyance as he paused his video and came over for a look. "I thought Big Bird was flightless," he said. "See if you can get a good shot with a camera."

SUPERGUY 2: ELECTRIC BOGALOO

Roger tapped some keys to bring up the video feeds and then picked the shot showing the incoming flock of really big birds. He put it up on the main screen and zoomed in.

"Those don't look like birds to me," said Joey.

"You better call Oliver back here," said The Creeper. "I have a bad feeling about this."

"*You* have a bad feeling," said Roger. "That's not good. That's not good at all." Roger, being the only guy in the room not benefitting from the "cool under pressure" component of a super serum, was suddenly very nervous. "That's really saying something."

"Joey, we better get topside, see what these guys want," said The Creeper.

"What they want?" asked Roger. "What do you think they want? It's like...an armada—or whatever it would be in the air—an armada is coming right for us. It can't be good. I can't come up with a single good outcome right now."

"Roger, relax," said The Creeper. His tone and mannerism changed instantly then and he exuded a confidence that had never been on display by anyone in a ratty bathrobe who was sober. "Just stay calm and do exactly what I tell you. First, get Oliver headed back here. Next, put out an emergency call to the rest of GLAND. Then I want you to grab the Hopper and get out of here. Let us handle this. Okay?"

After a slight hesitation, Roger said, "Right," with more confidence than he really had, but that was a ton more than he had had thirty seconds earlier. He had no idea who this version of The Creeper was, but he seemed to have it together. "Right, I'm on it," Roger repeated, tapping his keyboard to call Oliver.

"Okay, Joey, let's go check out our visitors," said The Creeper. "And I think I'm going to make the call now that they are all foes."

Alice carried Electric Boogaloo by sticking her hands inside a couple of the many cracks that ran along his back. She guessed that if she weren't the beneficiary of super powers, the edges of those cracks would slice her hands to shreds because they looked to be made of something like a craggy glass rock. Instead, her hands felt fine and she had no problem carrying the huge monster for the last thirty minutes or so. A couple of minutes earlier, she had dropped far below the squadron of bots to skim along the waves above the surface of the lake. The plan was for her to wait until the bots engaged any heroes and then come in from the side to drop Electric Boogaloo onto the base. Then the fun would really start. Blast everything in sight while the small bot squad took out the base's hover engine and sent the thing down.

"Looks like they've noticed them," said Electric Boogaloo, craning his neck to see the bots and the base overhead. Red flashes were shooting out from above the base and the bots were starting to return fire with their mix of armaments. There were muzzle flashes from shoulder mounted mini guns, blue and gold beams of hero quality lasers, and trails of smoke following behind small missiles. A dark cloud of fog engulfed one section of the formation's leading edge and sparks flew as at least two bots slowly tumbled toward the water.

SUPERGUY 2: ELECTRIC BOGALOO

"All right, here we go," said Alice, picking up speed along the water until they were ahead of the bot formation and even with the base. Then she peeled upward and banked toward the side of her shining white target until she was almost close enough to let Electric Boogaloo touch it. She pulled straight up then, climbing along the gleaming surface until they crested the top, and flew out into the open above it. There was only one super in view, behind them toward the rear of the football shaped base, busy firing red power blasts at the oncoming swarm of bots, and Alice guessed another super, most likely The Creeper, was responsible for the fog at the front of the bot formation. Otherwise, all was clear.

"Bombs away," said Alice, letting go of Electric Boogaloo. "Go make a mess, big guy."

The blue monster fell like the huge piece of rock he resembled, and crashed down dead center on the base's flight deck, narrowly missing a flying vehicle that had taken off a second earlier. Alex, happy to be free and fully charged again, shot a line of electricity after the flyer and saw it hit the tail of the machine, but it looped up and over the side of the base and out of sight before he could do anything more. Letting it go, he took a quick look at the flight deck, saw no immediate threats, but decided to throw a web of electricity around him anyway that covered the whole area, jumping from one object to the next, causing nearby furniture to catch fire, exploding the propane tank for a grill and a smoker, ripping apart a small refrigerator, and finally finding the fuel tank for the flying machines, which erupted upward in a huge ball of flame and black smoke. Alex smiled. With no one around to greet him on the flight deck, Alex decided to go inside. Unfortunately, he was a bit too big for the nearest doorway, so he slammed his hands down on the ground, discharging a massive blast of electricity and force that ripped open a huge, jagged edged hole. He paused for a second to admire his work and then dropped down inside the base.

"Can you repeat that, Roger?" Oliver could hear the nervousness in his friend's voice when the call came through on his communicator, but he was a little confused about what was happening.

"There're a ton of bots coming at us," he said, breathless. "An armada of bots. You gotta get back here!"

"They're sailing toward you? Why don't you just increase altitude?"

"No, not sailing! Flying!"

"But you said an armada."

"Yeah, I don't know what to call it," screamed Roger in frustration. "It's a lot of them. Flying. A flock? I don't know. A flock doesn't seem to hold enough weight. Birds are small, so it just doesn't work. Look, just get back here. I'm putting out an emergency call to GLAND and then I'm abandoning ship."

"Okay, buddy," said Oliver. "I'm already on my way." Oliver pushed himself to his top speed and then tried to go a little faster. He didn't like the sound of Roger's voice and he knew The Creeper had only Joey for help. He opened his comm and called The Creeper.

"Hey, Oliver," answered The Creeper, with the sound of shrieking metal on metal in the background. "You want to know an interesting thing about robots? They don't seem to be bothered much by my presence. They just keep going about their robot business of trying to shoot everything."

"I'm on my way," said Oliver. He checked the HUD on the inside of the lenses built into his mask. "I should be there in less than four minutes."

"Well, the party just started, so I'm sure it'll still be roaring by the time you get here," said The Creeper.

"How's Joey doing?"

"He's holding his own. Oh, crap."

"What?"

"It's not just bots," said The Creeper. "Some super I've never seen before just dropped that big blue friend of yours on top of the base. You might want to pick up the pace if you can."

"I'm coming," said Oliver. "I'm switching this to a combat channel and I'll get Joey on so we can coordinate." Oliver used the magnification in his mask to zoom in on the distant GLAND base. He could see the gleam of the sun reflecting off the surface and flashes of light, mostly off of one end. A small craft, which Oliver recognized as the Hopper, flew over the side of the base and down toward the water, and the hero let out the slightest sigh of relief. At least Roger was away safely. Suddenly a dark cloud of smoke rolled up from the top of the base, probably from an explosion on the landing deck. Oliver pushed even harder to increase his speed.

25

ROGER cut the communication to Oliver and quickly brought up the emergency distress call on his screen for the other GLAND members. As he hit the return key to send the call, red emergency lights started blinking throughout the base along with a low beeping tone, which Roger only slightly noticed because he was busy sprinting in a panic out of the control room on his way to the loading bay. At first, he had considered trying to control the panic and act a little more dignified as he ran away, but he decided it was probably better for his health if he just leaned into it and let the adrenaline take him where he needed to go. He ran down the hallway to the loading bay, across the open space to where the Hopper was parked just inside the bay doors. Jumping in, Roger pulled on the harness and snapped it in place.

"Computer, emergency start up!" he yelled. That command would skip a few of the lesser needed preliminaries and get the Hopper ready to fly.

SUPERGUY 2: ELECTRIC BOGALOO

"Open loading bay doors!" was his next command and bright sunlight flooded into the loading bay as the doors began to slide back.

"Plot course for the Garage! Evasive maneuvers on take off!" While he had manually piloted the Hopper before, Roger thought it best in this case for the machine to just get him the heck out of there. He stared at the operation screen, waiting for the green Launch icon. The Hopper was a hybrid vehicle and would take off using the electric motor, so there was no engine noise as Roger sat sweating out the next few seconds. Unfortunately, all he could hear were constant explosions coming from outside, which didn't really get Roger excited at the prospect of flying out into it. But two seconds later the Launch icon lit up and Roger screamed, "Go! Go, go, go!" as he pounded his finger repeatedly against the screen.

His body was slammed back against his seat as the Hopper thrust forward through the open bay doors, just bare inches off the floor. Sunlight flooded the cabin of the small two seat craft and Roger caught a glimpse of something very big and blue dropping onto the center of the flight deck as he zipped past, banking and gaining altitude to clear the upper wall. He felt a jolt as the Hopper bucked once, and could swear there was a slight electrical shock from his seat as the machine went up over the side of the base and out into the open air. Roger coasted in the Hopper for a couple of seconds until suddenly the operation screen began blinking repeatedly like it had a bad connection and the engine shut down, causing the machine to twist slowly in a circle and begin to fall toward the water. Emergency lights flashed and emergency beeps beeped and then the liquid fuel engine started up, swinging the Hopper back forward but currently pointed straight down at the surface of the lake less than twenty meters away. There were more emergency lights and beeps warning that this was not the optimal position for the craft and the lucky passenger was once again thrown back against his seat as the Hopper pulled up sharply and barely missed hitting the water. Roger, who realized he had started screaming way back when he saw the big blue monster on the flight deck, finally stopped and gulped air to catch his breath.

"Too close, too close," he strangled out between breaths. "Way, way too close." Roger sat gripping the armrest of his seat while trying to get his breathing under control as the Hopper skimmed along only a few feet above the waves. "Why didn't I run first?" he asked out loud. "I could have made the emergency calls from the Hopper. I'm not doing anything now. Lesson learned. Next time, run away first." A new warning alarm rang from the operation screen, which showed a radar image of four objects approaching the Hopper from behind. Roger twisted around to see four bots rocketing toward him.

"Why are you bothering me!?" he screamed. "I'm running away!"

Raymond Joyce couldn't take his eyes off the main screen once Alice flew into view and dropped Electric Boogaloo on the landing deck of the GLAND base. He quickly typed in orders for the surveillance bot to keep its camera centered on her so he could watch her work. He was captivated. Admittedly, he had been captivated by her when she was

SUPERGUY 2: ELECTRIC BOGALOO

simply a bedraggled waitress in a ketchup stained uniform going on her third shift, but now as a supervillain dressed in an A-list costume and in action? Wow. Joyce held his breath as Alice took her first shot, which unfortunately went astray when she was buffeted by an explosion from below, but the powerful blast still ripped an impressive hole in the surface of the base. Then the sidekick managed to wing her and Joyce felt fury rise within himself.

"Sir? What would you like me to do about the craft that just took off?" asked Steven.

Joyce didn't take his eyes off the main screen. "I don't care!" he half-shouted, annoyed by the interruption. "Destroy it!"

"Yes, sir," replied Steven, giving an order for four bots to pursue and destroy the craft. He hesitated to interrupt his boss again, but he knew he had to. "Sir? The special squad? Didn't you want to guide them in now to cut through the hull and take out the hover engine?"

"What?" Joyce asked, and then whooped as Alice blasted the sidekick off the edge of the base. "What was that? Oh, um, no. I can't, you go ahead and take care of that."

"Yes, sir," said Steven. "Sending them in now."

Phil (decidedly winning now at 72 percent) was coasting along near the back of the bot formation listening to outtakes from The Beatles' *White Album* when the command came to attack the hovering oval base ahead of them and any defenders it may have. He wasn't particularly happy with the order for a couple of reasons. First, he wasn't sure he was that sort of robot. Sure he was armed with hero quality lasers and a shoulder mounted missile system, but he wasn't certain he was the sort of bot who would resort to violence as a means to an end. Maybe he was more of a talker. Perhaps he could persuade whoever needed persuading to do whatever was needed to be done to avoid Phil having to attack anything that may or may not need attacking. Obviously Phil was missing quite a bit of information here, mainly in the form of who he was being ordered to attack and if that attack was really deserved, not to mention what kind of robot he was on a personal level despite having been specifically designed to attack things whether they needed attacking or not. The second reason he wasn't happy was because, as an artificially created being, he was really impressed by the floating base they were being ordered to attack. It was really cool. Very futuristic and space-like and it freaking *floated*. Why destroy something that cool?

Phil was still debating his position when the attack on the base began in force. The first two waves of bots started firing an array of weapons and a superpowered human defender began to return fire with red power beams. Only some of the bots' weapons were having an effect on the base, those being the more powerful hero quality lasers and missiles, because the ship was built of high quality materials itself. The super defending the base targeted the bots with better weapons and a couple sustained sufficient damage to lose power and fall out of formation. A dark cloud of fog suddenly enveloped one side of the first two waves of bots and while he didn't know exactly why, Phil decided it would be best to avoid going anywhere near that. He was saved from having to make a decision about attacking the base when he was ordered,

SUPERGUY 2: ELECTRIC BOGALOO

along with three other bots, to drop out of the formation and pursue and destroy a transport that had just launched.

Phil complied with the order and followed the other three bots, but he wondered about the order to destroy the transport. It obviously wasn't a threat, as it had not engaged the attacking bots and its current course indicated it was attempting to leave the area. Uncertain as to why they should be destroying a vehicle that was clearly just trying to flee, Phil sent a query questioning the order to the other three bots. All he got back in response was a reading of Directive 1, which essentially stated that bots followed orders. Phil had kind of been questioning Directive 1 for a while now—that being the time since the order to attack the base had been given—but that's a long time in a supercomputer bot brain. He wasn't impressed with the response, but it didn't surprise him either, since they were just bots after all. Still uncertain of what to do, Phil hacked the flying vehicle's system to see if it contained anything that could lead him to make a more informed decision. Unfortunately, the craft's system was a bit of a mess. It had apparently been damaged by an electrical surge and was now only functioning at a minimal level. It did show that the one occupant was a normal human with a very elevated heart rate and other signs indicating great fear, the main one being constant screaming. Phil guessed those rates might even increase once the flyer's computer system completely failed, which was going to happen in a matter of seconds. Not that that would be a problem since the bots Phil was following were going to shoot it down anyway.

Once Alice dropped Electric Boogaloo onto the flight deck of the GLAND base, she banked away from the fighting on her left and flew in a long sweeping arc up and around the far side so she could assess how things were progressing and where she wanted to attack first. The sidekick named Scarlet Pulsar was hovering over the far end of the base, blasting away at the left side of the bot formation, while a cloud covered a large part of the right side. Realizing this was probably the work of The Creeper, but not being able to see him, she decided her best target was going to be the sidekick, so she banked sharply and lined him up in her sights. Attacking someone from behind might not be the most honorable thing to do, but she was a villain after all. And, building on that villain theme, she decided to hit the poor guy with the full force of her power, which she knew was a significantly higher level than the sidekick. But what better way to make your debut than to knock a super out in one shot, even if he was just a sidekick?

Alice readied her blast, letting the dark blue glow curl around her outstretched arms and build in a large ball over her fists. The energy acted almost like smoke as it swirled within the ball and she could even feel it leaking out of her eyes and flowing out of her hair. Alice imagined she must really look like a badass right then. She was just about to let the blast fly when she was suddenly knocked upward by a ball of smoke and flame that originated from the landing deck below. Her shot went wide, missing the sidekick, but at least still hitting the base near him and ripping a massive hole in the surface. The edges of the hole sizzled and burned as drops of molten metal fell down inside the base. The sidekick saw the blast and turned to face Alice, firing a red beam at her as she still tumbled slightly out of control from the explosion. The beam nicked her thigh, tearing her costume, and burning her skin as she stopped her wayward ascent and turned back toward her target. Alice cringed from the pain of the burn, but it wasn't too bad. In fact, it made her mad. She should have drawn first blood, but instead the defective intern sidekick got her. Life wasn't fair, even when she was a supervillain.

Harnessing her anger, which is about as second nature as you can get for a supervillain, Alice sent a barrage of energy pulses at Scarlet Pulsar. They took the form of a meteor shower, with blue-black rocks of varying sizes tumbling in a wide pattern that made it impossible for the target to dodge completely. One larger rock ricocheted off the sidekick's thigh and then a smaller one hit him in the chest, sending him flying backward. However, he quickly recovered and threw up a protective shield of red energy that absorbed the rest of the barrage before more could hit home. Annoyed, Alice immediately fired again, only this time she threw an extra rock downward after the initial barrage, sending it looping under the sidekick and then up and over to come in from above him. As he blocked the main attack with his shield again, the other rock crashed into his head from directly above and slammed him down into the hull of the base. He tumbled out of control over the curved side and dropped from view.

Alice knew the sidekick would be back, but she had a minute to do something about The Creeper and his little cloud, which had a steady stream of destroyed bots dropping out of the bottom and into the lake below. He obviously had a decisive advantage inside that dense fog because the bots didn't seem to be able to track him, and for that matter, Alice didn't have a clue where he was in there either. So, realizing that all the bots in the fog were goners anyway, she flew closer and let loose with a solid wall of energy like the blade of a bulldozer that would hit everything inside the cloud. The result was a lot of bots dropping out of the fog, but then the fog itself dissipated instantly when the wall collided with The Creeper and sent him tumbling toward the water. Deciding the press her advantage, Alice dove after the falling superhero and prepared to hit him with a more concentrated blast. If she could use enough power, she might knock him completely out of the fight and one less hero would make things much easier. She shot a burst of energy shaped like a giant fist and watched as it closed the distance on the hero to the point where it eclipsed him from view. Then it just kept on going until it plowed into the lake, splashing water thirty meters into the air. The Creeper was nowhere to be seen.

"Did you get me?" came a voice in Alice's ear.

She screamed reflexively in surprise and whirled around to face The Creeper, but again, he wasn't there. Suddenly, she was engulfed in a thick fog that completely blocked out the bright sunlight she had just been hovering in. All the sounds of the battle and the wind seemed to disappear and were replaced by mysterious clunkings and clangings and a nearby foghorn.

"Who are you anyway?" said The Creeper, once again in Alice's ear, and once again she whirled around to find nothing there. A wolf howled in the distance. Suddenly The Creeper's face appeared in front of her upside down.

"I've never seen you before," he said, then blinked out of existence before Alice could respond with either an answer or an attack.

"Great costume, by the way," he continued, this time his voice seeming to echo all around her. "Maybe a little too high end by my standards, but I love the shimmery thing you got going." A sickly coughing followed, or maybe it was a laugh, it was difficult to tell. Alice had had enough. She curled in upon herself and then exploded outward, flinging her arms and legs wide and sending a wave of dark blue energy in an ever expanding ball. Somewhere along the way it collided with The Creeper because the fog lifted and the sun and sound of the battle were back, as was the sidekick, who was charging straight for her. Unfortunately for him, he had approached the fog bank just in time for it to disappear and turn into a wave of energy that smashed into him, sending him somersaulting back the way he'd come, bouncing off the top of the base, and crashing down onto the landing deck. Alice smiled at that bit of luck, but then frowned as she watched her continuously expanding sphere wash over some of the bots in the attack formation. The wave wasn't particularly powerful by this point but it still managed to bring down several of her more damaged robotic allies. At this point in the battle, Alice was fairly certain she had taken out more of the bots than the heroes had, which probably wasn't a good look for her fledgling career as a supervillain. Still, there were plenty of bots left, and they were now encircling the end of the base and pounding it with lasers and missiles. The shiny white surface was becoming a mess of scorch marks, dents, and jagged holes, and Alice tossed a couple of shots of her own at it before flying off in search of The Creeper.

26

OLIVER knew he was flying faster than he ever had before but he still found it to be desperately slow. He had managed to cut down his ETA by close to forty-five seconds and was almost back to the base when he saw Joey flip over the side. The sidekick managed to gain control of himself after a few seconds and hovered in the air for a minute.

"Joey? You okay?" asked Oliver via the open comm channel.

"Yeah, I'm fine," he replied, groaning a bit as he shook his head. "Who's the new girl?"

"I don't know," said Oliver. "Creeper didn't recognize her and I've never seen her before."

"Well, she's got some pop, so watch out for that."

"Okay," said Oliver. "Looks like Creeper's got her stuck in a fog now, why don't you go help him out. I'll go after Boogaloo."

"What about the bots?" asked Joey.

SUPERGUY 2: ELECTRIC BOGALOO

"I don't know, hopefully we get some help soon, but they aren't the biggest threat right now. Concentrate on the supervillains."

"You got it, boss," said Joey, shooting upward, back toward the battle.

Oliver turned his attention to the base. He saw Electric Boogaloo through the windows of the observation lounge on the second level. The blue monster was indiscriminately firing bolts of lightning around the room, ripping apart furniture, walls, and, just as Oliver was getting close, Buffalo's newly installed home theater screen and the front speakers of the surround sound system. Lacking any need for subtlety, since he didn't have any special powers to use in a subtle way, Oliver flew straight through one of the observation windows and slammed into the side of Electric Boogaloo, proceeding to plow the monster through the far wall, through the mechanical room, through that far wall, through one of the privacy suites, through that far wall, and into the large storage room beyond where they collided with a stack of crates containing miscellaneous supplies. Those crates exploded everywhere, resulting in a shower of toilet paper, silverware, liquid soap, and plug-in air fresheners. It quickly became very slippery but incredibly pleasant smelling in the room.

Oliver scrambled to his feet while tearing toilet paper off his face, and slipped a couple of times before deciding he should fly instead of stand. He hovered a couple feet off the floor, ready to continue the fight. Electric Boogaloo tossed some crates and cardboard boxes aside as he stood up. His head nearly touched the ceiling of the storage room, which was twelve feet high, as were all the rooms in the base because the designers were smart and knew that there would be giant heroes walking around the place. Still, neither

Buffalo nor Metal filled the space quite like Electric Boogaloo. Not only was he almost twelve feet tall, but he was also close to nine feet wide, not counting his wingspan. Add the dark blue craggy skin with the bright blue shining through the cracks, the burning blue eyes, and the bits of blue electricity dancing along the surface of his body, and the effect was pretty intimidating. The monster growled as he took a step toward Oliver, but one foot slipped out from under him and he spent a couple of seconds skipping on his heels trying desperately to stay upright before finally falling flat on his back. Letting out a scream of anger, Boogaloo sat up and threw out a blanket of tightly laced lightning along the floor causing the spilled mess on the surface to bubble and burn up, while also catching all the cardboard boxes and toilet paper on fire, and filling the room with smoke. The sprinkler system kicked in almost immediately, showering the room with fire retardant foam. And so they were back to the slippery mess they started with.

"You know, you're going to have to pay for all those supplies you just destroyed," said Oliver. "Ohio Man keeps track of that stuff. He's kind of a nerd that way. He'll probably send you a bill if you want to leave your address."

Boogaloo climbed to his feet, white foam sliding down his body. Blue electricity danced from his feet to the floor and he no longer seemed bothered by the slipperiness. "I don't have an address," he said.

"An email? Or your number?" said Oliver. "I'm sure he can just text you a total."

"I have none of these things anymore," replied Boogaloo. "They are all part of The System. They let it track you, watch you, keep you under control. The System is the enemy."

SUPERGUY 2: ELECTRIC BOGALOO

"So everything The System does is bad then? What if, along with all the tracking and whatever, they were big on helping orphans. You'd be against that on principle?"

"Yes."

"What about endangered animals? You wouldn't help endangered animals?"

"No."

"Volunteering to clean up dirty beaches?"

"No."

"How about orphaned endangered animals, who also happen to live on dirty beaches?"

"You're annoying me."

"You're not the first."

Electric Boogaloo shot a ball of lightning at Oliver—who barely dodged to the side—and then took two giant strides so quickly toward the hero that he didn't have time to retreat before the monster punched him in the chest, sending him backward through more boxes and into another wall.

Oliver groaned and pushed himself up only to be grabbed by Boogaloo and tossed up into the ceiling, which caused a large dent. He thought he was falling back down to the floor only to realize he was still in the villain's grasp and he was now being tossed back into the ceiling again. This time he successfully broke through the ceiling, flipped up into the room above and landed next to the hole. He groaned and started to roll over, only to be grabbed by Boogaloo again, pulled back down through the hole and tossed against the ceiling again, making another hole next to the first one. He landed on the floor and this time skipped the groaning and scrambled away from the holes as fast as possible.

"Okay, no time for enjoying the pain," Oliver muttered, looking to see where he had ended up. He was in the loading bay adjoining the flight deck. The large double doors leading outside were open and the sounds of bullets hitting metal and explosions were almost blending into a constant rumble. Oliver wondered fleetingly if he would be doing more good knocking out bots to keep them from destroying the base rather than putting large holes in it himself as he fought with Electric Boogaloo, but he was probably stuck with the big guy. Looking around, he saw the reserve Hopper sitting nearby and stepped over to grab the tail.

"Sorry, Roger," he said, looking back at the holes in the floor. Electricity ripped up the remaining section between the two holes, turning it into one large hole, and Electric Boogaloo grabbed the edge and began pulling himself up. Oliver waited to see the top of the villain's head appear and then he swung the Hopper over and down on the supervillain, watching both of them disappear into the now even larger hole in the floor, accompanied a split second later by an explosion that shot burning rolls of toilet paper up through the hole and all over the loading bay. The fire suppression system kicked in again and Oliver was doused in more foam.

"We have a serious amount of toilet paper," said Oliver, wiping foam off of the lenses in his mask. "Or used to anyway." A new alarm, among the chorus of other alarms already going off, began ringing on a screen by the interior door. Oliver took a second of the respite he was getting to look over and see what it was. The screen indicated a hull breach, which didn't surprise Oliver considering the damage the bots were doing topside, but the breach wasn't above, it was on the underside of the base. A section flashed red on the schematic of the ship and Oliver realized it was right next to the engine.

SUPERGUY 2: ELECTRIC BOGALOO

"Creeper! Joey!" he yelled on the comm channel. "They're attacking the hull on the bottom of the ship, trying to get to the engine. Get down there if you can. Forget the bots on top, this is their real target!" A reply started that Oliver never heard because he was hit by a bolt of lightning the diameter of a telephone pole that slammed him back against the wall, where he managed to put his arm through the screen he had been looking at. The blast didn't stop there, but seemed to stick to him, growing tendrils of electricity that twisted around his torso and lifted him off the ground. The frame of the wall screen got hooked on his arm, ripping out of the wall and dangling on his wrist for a second before clattering to the ground. Electric Boogaloo walked closer, controlling the blue arm of electricity that now held Oliver. His face twisted in something like a smile and Oliver was punched back against the wall three times in rapid succession and then unceremoniously tossed out through the open double doors onto the flight deck.

Alice should have guessed The Creeper would be good at the game of hide and seek. After bursting out of his cloud of fog and pursuing him, it had been nothing but seeking ever since. The hero would throw up multiple fog clouds, hiding in one of them, and then pop up behind her to whisper something in her ear. It was usually something slightly unsettling, but Alice was not really bothered by that because she had worked in an all night diner for years, although once she was pretty sure it was just The Creeper's shopping list. Why anyone needed that many wet wipes was a mystery. Alice proceeded to blast one cloud after another, causing them to dissipate, but more would pop up just as quickly to the point where she was certain she wasn't making any progress, and she still had the annoying hero chirping in her ear. Finally, she just tried to time things right, blindly firing an energy blast behind her until she got The Creeper on the fourth try. That knocked him away, causing all his remaining clouds to disappear, and Alice pressed the advantage by hitting him again immediately with another blast that sent him flying back toward the base and through part of the surrounding bots. They were happy to forego shooting up the base for a moment to take a couple of shots at the unlucky hero, who was struck by a laser and two missiles before finally teleporting away.

Flying up over the top of the base, Alice arrived above the flight deck in time to see The Creeper helping the sidekick up just as SuperGuy came tumbling out of a set of double doors and slid to a stop near the middle of the deck. The blandly clad superhero struggled to his feet and seemed to be yelling at the other two. The Creeper pointed at Alice and SuperGuy looked up at her. Alice waved. She didn't know exactly why, but it felt right. SuperGuy looked back at the other two heroes, yelled something else, and then turned to see Electric Boogaloo come lumbering out of the double doors behind him. Alice figured Boogaloo had SuperGuy handled so she focused her attention on the other two. To amuse herself, she started juggling four giant balls of dark blue energy, tossing them impossibly around her back and below her feet as she floated there above the base. She figured two balls each for the creepy hero and the sidekick should do the trick, and at least the hero might survive it. She spun the balls faster and faster and was about to let them fly when a stainless steel grill slammed into her chest and sent her flipping backward. The balls of energy went wildly out of control, two hitting the base, one taking out three more nearby bots and the fourth sailing off into the sky.

Phil flew along behind the three other bots in his squad as he thought about the unfairness of life. Which of course led to thoughts about the fairness of life, the definition of life, and The Beatles' "A Day in the Life." He wasn't really getting anywhere with this whole train of thought, but he did come to two conclusions. The first was that he quite liked the song by The Beatles, and the second was that while the whole life thing was rather complicated, he thought following his current order to shoot down a defenseless craft that was running away from the fight and was still going to crash anyway was rather stupid. He also decided the other three bots in his squad who could only answer his inquiries about their orders with the automatic response of Directive 1 were just annoying him. They apparently had no opinion on The Beatles, any of their songs, or music in general. He played "A Day in the Life" for them over the comm system at an advanced rate of speed 306 times so they could craft a legitimate opinion of the song, but they still refused to engage in any kind of meaningful discussion. Instead, they began to fire on the target, once again citing Directive 1.

Bullets pinged off the body of the flying craft, which was made partly of hero quality metal, but despite the threat, it didn't attempt any evasive maneuvers. Phil knew from hacking its system that the lack of response was because the machine was barely keeping itself in the air at the moment, let alone dodging around. It was simply lucky two of the other three bots were only equipped with machine guns and couldn't do much damage. The third bot did have superhero quality lasers and now moved into position directly behind the craft and targeted one of the two wing mounted engines. Unfortunately, before it could fire the lasers and take down the fleeing craft, the bot exploded as it was struck by a missile. This confused the other two bots as their systems had not alerted them to any incoming missiles or threats at all. Their confusion was cleared up when they subsequently exploded after being hit by missiles.

Phil wasn't super proud of destroying the other bots in his squad. He would have much rather had a nice conversation about the validity of their orders and had them come to a mutual conclusion that the destruction of the craft was unnecessary and really just kind of mean. But all he got was that Directive 1 crap. So he hacked their systems so they couldn't see the missiles he fired at them. He was kind of proud of saving the fleeing ship, but that feeling didn't last long as the craft finally shut down completely and began to drop toward the water.

SUPERGUY 2: ELECTRIC BOGALOO

Roger wasn't sure what was more annoying: the nonstop, shrill beeping of the many different emergency alarms going off in the Hopper, or his constant screaming. It was probably the alarms simply because he couldn't silence them, but he wasn't entirely sure he could stop screaming either. His screaming only went up an octave when bullets began pinging off the fuselage. The screen showed four enemy bots in pursuit, the two in front now separating to let a third move up directly behind him. Another alert sounded, indicating a threat had been detected on that third bot in the form of a laser powering up. Roger had no doubt it was a superhero quality laser.

"Not good!" he yelled at the screen. "Computer, evasive maneuvers! Evasive maneuvers!" he repeated. His pleas were met with another alert indicating a critical failure in the electrical system.

"Evasive maneuvers not possible at this time," said the calm voice of the computer system. It had repeated this statement several times now in response to Roger's many pleas for such action. It had also admonished him for certain language and severe tones. Roger couldn't be certain, due to his general feeling of panic and understandably terror-driven thought processes, but he didn't think the computer would usually respond to his naughty language or his tone of voice. Of course, it also had a lot going on with all the short-circuiting, fuses blowing, small fires, and bullets.

"Is anything possible?!" screamed Roger. "Can I eject?"

"Emergency ejection not available at this time due to electrical failure," answered the computer.

"Manual! What about manual ejection?!"

"This vehicle is not equipped with manual ejection," replied the computer.

"Why the hell not?!" screamed Roger.

"Research indicated that there would only be a 0.03 percent chance it would ever be required. You must be having a very lucky day. You should purchase a lottery ticket."

Roger screamed some naughty words in a very unflattering tone.

Amidst all the various alarms and naughty words, a single calming tone sounded.

"Threats eliminated," said the computer.

Roger stared at the screen as three of the red blips indicating pursuing bots blinked out of existence.

"Wait. Computer? There's still one bot back there!" yelled Roger over the sound of the alarms. "There's still a threat!"

"Incorrect," replied the computer. "That is a friendly."

"What? Okay, thank goodness."

"Warning. Total shutdown imminent."

"Total shutdown? How imminent?" asked Roger. He was answered by everything in the Hopper going dark and the machine dropping like a stone toward the water.

27

OLIVER slid to the stop in the middle of the flight deck just short of the large hole Electric Boogaloo made to enter the base. Struggling to his feet, he saw The Creeper helping Joey up on the end of the deck.

"Did you guys hear me? About the hull?" he said on the comm channel. "They're trying to get to the engine."

"Yeah, we got that," replied The Creeper. "We're just a little busy with that annoying lady and all the bots." He pointed up at a figure floating above them in the sky. She wore a dark bluish-black costume that seemed to shimmer in the sunlight like some kind of optical illusion. A mask covered most of her face except her mouth and chin, and she had long, bluish-black hair that waved in the wind. Oliver was sure he had never seen this villain before. Perhaps it was another out of town mercenary hired by Gray Matter. She waved. Oliver looked back at The Creeper and Joey.

"Forget the bots up here," said Oliver. "Get below and take those bots out." He paused for a split second as he saw Electric Boogaloo march out onto the deck. "I'll keep these two busy." Ignoring the blue monster, Oliver stepped over and grabbed the first heavy thing he could find. "Sorry about this, guys," he said, thinking about Metal and Buffalo, and then he ripped the grill from where it was bolted to the deck and threw it at the female supervillain hovering above who now seemed to be dancing with four giant balls of energy. It looked pretty cool, but she also seemed a bit distracted by it.

"Okay, let's go," said The Creeper, grabbing hold of Joey and teleporting them both away.

Oliver was watching the grill hit home on the supervillain above when he himself was hit by a blast of electricity. The burst felt like a train hitting him (which he had experienced back when Roger was helping him test his fledgling superhero abilities) and rammed him back through the deck furniture and into the far wall with a solid metallic thud. Knowing he wasn't allowed time to recover, and now with two villains to keep busy, Oliver pushed off the wall and ran to his right, grabbing furniture as he went and tossing piece after piece at Electric Boogaloo. It didn't bother the monster much, who simply swatted the flying furniture aside with a wave of his hands, which sent out waves of electricity shaped like even larger hands. However, the furniture did give Oliver time to reach the hole in the deck, where he dove in and flew through the level below to the other hole Electric Boogaloo had made in the loading bay. Popping up out of that hole, and now behind the blue monster, Oliver flew forward like he was shot out of a cannon and plowed into Electric Boogaloo. Grabbing onto the crevices in the monster's back, the hero lifted him up and propelled him into the air and straight for the female supervillain floating above. She had recovered from the grill and with the other two heroes gone and a giant blue creature hurtling toward her, she had no choice but to focus on the hero in front of her.

Oliver figured he had a couple of good options here, with either being able to smack Goth Girl (this is what he came up with, literally, on the fly) with Boogaloo, or tossing the blue guy out into the great beyond if he missed, which would require the supervillain to save him. This would give Oliver time to come up with a next move. However, as he was pushing Boogaloo ever faster and closer to the flying villain, he was having trouble coming up with a next move. And it's not like he didn't have time to think. In reality, it might only be taking Oliver and Boogaloo two point six seconds to cover the distance from the flight deck to the flying supervillain, but for a hero, that's a lifetime. All that extra cognitive juice from the serum helps a fella out. Plenty of time to plan out your next move or five. Only trouble was Oliver wasn't coming up with anything good, or at least anything that didn't involve him just getting tossed around like a dog's chew toy. But he would still have time to come up with something after tossing Boogaloo at the woman in zero point two seconds.

Unfortunately, the flying supervillain came up with a third option concerning Electric Boogaloo and, by default, Oliver. She reared back and threw a straight right punch at the streaking monster. Bluish-black energy twirled and wrapped around her arm and extended outward in the shape of a fist that grew in size with each inch it got away from her body. By the time it connected with Boogaloo, it was almost as big as he was and it crashed into him with twice the speed he and Oliver were coming at it. Bright blue electricity from Boogaloo flashed outward like water from a balloon hitting a wall, and it was mirrored by the dark bluish-black energy of the fist on the other side. Oliver was lucky enough that most of the energy from the blast was escaping that way, but he still got a jolt heavier than anything he'd felt yet as electricity and energy both seemed to come right through Boogaloo and crash into him. He felt numbness and tingling in all his extremities—especially his ears for some reason—as he and the monster reversed course and shot back toward the flight deck. The wave of combined energy from the collision destroyed even more nearby bots before it faded away after a half mile.

Oliver wasn't so numb that he couldn't push off of Boogaloo before crashing, thereby avoiding being smashed under the huge villain. He careened off the flight deck, bounced a couple more times and collided with the far wall. Boogaloo hit like a rock into a bed of mud, making a thick-sounding clunk as he formed a monster shaped dent in the metal deck and went no further. Oliver knew he wasn't supposed to take a moment to recover from the latest bone crunching collision, but he couldn't help it. His hands, feet, and ears were still tingling, there was a steady buzz in his head, and his vision was colored by a blue haze. At least for the moment, Electric Boogaloo wasn't moving much faster as he pushed himself up out of his dent and slowly rolled over onto his knees. The squadron of bots attacking the base were still present, but their numbers had been greatly depleted, and it seemed that some might be out of ammunition because they had stop firing and simply hovered in formation.

"Creeper, Joey? How're you guys doing?" asked Oliver over the comm channel as he got to his feet. He watched Boogaloo warily as the monster made his way to his feet as well.

SUPERGUY 2: ELECTRIC BOGALOO

"Three left," came The Creeper's reply, amidst labored breathing. "They saved us the tough ones. How about you?"

"Got them on the run," said Oliver, as the female supervillain dropped down in front of him on the flight deck. "Oh, gotta go. Out."

"Last call to Mom?" asked the villain. "That's touching."

"Well, I've always been all about family," said Oliver, looking over the villain's shoulder at Electric Boogaloo, who seemed to be recovered from the fall and was watching them intently. "So, tell me, should I know you? I'd use the excuse that I'm bad with names but good with faces, but with all the masks, that doesn't help much. Have we met before?" He was hoping to get her talking a little to waste more time, which at the moment sounded better than wasting time by being thrown around the base.

"No, we haven't, but you could say we have a mutual acquaintance."

"Okay," said Oliver with a nod. "Well, do you have a name? I was kind of thinking of you as Goth Girl in my head, but I'm betting you came up with something better."

The villain scoffed. "I wish," she said. "The whole name thing bites. Goth Girl isn't that bad, compared to what we came up with. Not really what I was going for, though, despite the lipstick." She seemed to think about it for a moment. "Anyway, my full name is Dark Blue-Black Spark. For legal reasons. You can just call me Spark. But now I'm thinking Gothic Spark or Goth Spark could work. It's better than the other one." She shrugged. "I'll have to talk to my people."

"You have people?" asked Oliver.

"Well, just a couple of friends, but they are pretty helpful," said Spark. "So, do you think you've delayed us enough?"

"I don't think it's ever enough," replied Oliver.

"Yeah, probably not," said Spark. "Been nice meeting you, though." She smiled and threw out her hands, which emitted dark blue energy that grew into two giant fists. Those fists proceeded to punch Oliver repeatedly, bouncing him off the wall like he was a speed bag, until he slumped to the floor. Then Spark used the giant hands of energy to pick him up and toss him through the air toward Electric Boogaloo. "Send him for a ride, Loo!" she yelled.

Oliver struggled to get control of himself and fly anywhere, in any direction, but he didn't have the time. All he managed to do was flip himself over just as a huge wave of bright blue electricity hit him and sent him flying from the flight deck and sailing over the water. At least that's what he thought happened, because truth be told, he wasn't quite with it anymore.

"Sir, the bots are through the hull, but The Creeper and Scarlet Pulsar have engaged them," said Steven, watching the status of the battle on his iPad. "I don't think they will be able to destroy the engine. Two of them are already down."

Joyce watched the screen as SuperGuy was tossed out of the base and into the water. He gave a little whoop of joy.

"That's okay. Alice and the monster can take care of it now," said the villain.

SUPERGUY 2: ELECTRIC BOGALOO

"But they still have to get through those two heroes," said Steven. "And there's not a lot of time left. More heroes are going to get here soon."

"True," said Joyce. "Open a channel to Alice, I think I have a way to neutralize The Creeper."

Alice felt a little sorry for SuperGuy as she flew up and watched him glide out over the water, eventually landing with a giant splash a quarter of a mile away. Fighting superheroes wasn't really what she was in this whole villain thing for, but when you get hit a couple of times, you stop thinking about your mission statement and start punching people. Still, she was going to have to say something to Raymond about doing some bad to the people she really wanted to punch. But that was going to have to wait. There was a mission to complete here. She flew back down to the flight deck and grabbed Electric Boogaloo, pulling him up into the air and then down around to the underside of the base.

"We've got to finish what the bots started," she said. "We take out the engine and the base crashes." Suddenly, her comm beeped, and identified Raymond Joyce as the caller. Alice didn't say anything out loud because she didn't want Boogaloo to know they had help, especially help from Gray Matter. Joyce knew that as well and didn't expect her to say anything. Alice listened while he fed her his idea for The Creeper and she simply nodded when he finished.

"The other two heroes are still in our way but I have an idea," said Alice. She gave Boogaloo the plan and then tossed him toward the base well above where the heroes were fighting the last of the bots. He grabbed on with his massive hands, forcing hand holds into the metal, and began lowering himself into position. Alice continued on, flying down until she approached the location of the engine on the lower side of the base.

Ahead of her, one fully functioning bot remained, firing a laser at the sidekick, who held a red shield of energy in front of himself to block it. The Creeper was ripping the head off another bot while both were in free fall toward the water. He tossed the head aside and then immediately transported behind the last bot where he grabbed the shoulder mounted laser and turned it toward the bot's head, slicing the top half right off. The bot dropped like a rock and The Creeper transported into the giant hole that was cut in the side of the base. He stood on the edge looking back at the engine that was exposed to the outside, but for the moment at least, was still intact. The sidekick flew up to the hole and hovered just outside. He nodded at The Creeper in seeming acknowledgment of their victory, which is when Alice dropped in front of him and blasted him in the chest. It knocked the sidekick backward and Alice followed after him, continuing to pelt him with dark blue spheres of energy.

The fog she had anticipated enveloped her a couple of seconds later and The Creeper was in her ear whispering once again. She thought it was a recipe for homemade salsa but before he could complete the list of ingredients, Alice felt a light prickling of electricity pulsing through the cloud. She quickly shielded herself with an energy bubble of her own and then flew out of the fog in search of the sidekick. Electric Boogaloo had dropped down onto the exposed floor in the hole and was weaving a web of electricity around and through

SUPERGUY 2: ELECTRIC BOGALOO

the cloud of fog. The cloud itself disappeared a few seconds later and revealed The Creeper immobilized by the electricity, which coated his body like a bright blue aura. A second and third web of electricity grew in layers over the first and The Creeper ceased to struggle in its grip.

Alice floated off to one side of the trapped hero and watched the sidekick, waiting for her opening. He did what most sidekicks do, which was lose control. He charged Electric Boogaloo, blasting away. Alice used a band of energy to grab and pull him down into The Creeper, where he collided with the hero and also got stuck in the web of electricity. Alice then created a sphere of energy and enclosed both of the heroes, trapping them inside. Boogaloo added his own sphere of electricity, weaving it into Alice's energy field. Then the two villains alternately coated the ball with additional layers of energy until it was so thick the heroes were only vague shadows inside.

"Okay," said Alice. "Now that those two are taken care of, why don't you do the honors, Loo, and blow that engine." She kept a steady band of energy holding the floating sphere in place as Electric Boogaloo turned toward the engine compartment of the base and let loose a giant swathe of electricity. Tentacles of blue reached out and touched every part of the hole around the main trunk of electricity that raced toward the engine. It hit with a thunderous clap and the engine exploded, shaking the entire base. The giant white ship slowly listed toward one end as it started to sink, and Electric Boogaloo turned to Alice with his patented kinda sorta maybe a smile.

Oliver heard the explosion and saw the base jolt and start to tip as he banked at high speed around the back side. He made note of the two figures obscured and trapped inside the blue sphere that the new supervillain, Spark, was holding, and saw Electric Boogaloo standing in the huge gash in the side of the base. Smoke rolled out of the opening above the blue monster's head and he turned back to look at his supervillain partner. Oliver picked up speed and smashed into Boogaloo, doubling him over and sending him back into the hole at an angle and then through four interior walls in quick succession. They rolled to a stop in the command center, where it was nothing but alarm sounds and flashing lights, but Oliver didn't stay to see what would happen next. He turned right around and flew back out the holes he had just made to go after Spark and free The Creeper and Joey.

Bursting out of the smoking hole into daylight, Oliver was immediately hit with a blast from Spark that bounced him off the side of the base and sent him falling toward the water until he could get control and turn back. As he headed back toward her, the supervillain tossed the sphere of energy holding the other two heroes toward the water below, where it splashed and bobbed for a second and then sank like a stone. Spark smiled and waved, and then flew away in the opposite direction. The bots that still remained in the area disengaged from their attack and turned to follow after the supervillain.

Oliver looked at where the sphere had gone under and opened his comm channel.

"Creeper, Joey, do you read me?" he asked. There was no response. "Creeper, Joey, do you read?" he repeated. Still no response. Either they were unconscious or the sphere was interfering with their comms.

Next, the base hit the lake with a monumental splash, tipping up on one end and sending out a huge wave, and then settling back at an angle and beginning to sink beneath the surface of the water. Black smoke poured out of several holes in stark contrast to the shiny white surface of the previously pristine base.

"I'm totally going to be blamed for this," said Oliver, and then dived down into the water after the sphere holding the two heroes.

28

ROGER didn't like the quiet. There were no alarms screeching anymore, no pings of bullets off the fuselage, and, most distressingly, no hum of the engines. Really, the alarms weren't missed because they were annoying, being all shrill and insistent when a guy couldn't really do anything about them, and no one in their right mind would miss the sound of bullets pinging off the ship he was flying in, but the sound of engines happens to be awfully reassuring when you're flying. Roger considered breaking the silence with some screaming of his own, but decided that chanting "Crap, crap, crap" over and over was sufficient as he banged on the controls, the main screen, and finally the canopy in the hope that it might somehow activate the emergency ejection system.

Seeing out the window that he was about to hit the surface of the lake, Roger closed his eyes, cringed, and braced for impact. That impact never came. Instead, he felt the Hopper lurch slightly with a thump and then the sensation of falling slowed greatly until there was a gentle splash. Roger opened his eyes to see he was floating on the relatively calm waters of Lake Michigan. Breathing a deep sigh of relief, he checked to see if the power had come back on in time to stop his free fall and give him such a gentle landing, but everything in the cockpit was still dead. He tapped on the main screen and pressed the start button just in case. Nothing. He wondered if the Hopper had been built to float or if it was only a matter of time before it sunk to the bottom of the lake.

"There is definitely going to be a manual ejection system in the next Hopper version," said Roger aloud. The Hopper listed a little to one side and Roger grabbed his seat. "If there is another version."

Suddenly, the metal legs of a bot dropped onto the Hopper right in front of the canopy. Those legs bent and the shiny metallic face of the bot looked in at Roger. Roger froze. The bot's face was the same uninspired, vaguely human shape of all the assembly line robots from Joyce Industries, except for the shininess, which indicated this one was made of hero quality metal. He had a perforated oval grid for a mouth and lenses set back in his eye sockets that glowed a dark blue. His torso was also shaped roughly like a human body and covered with a solid layer of hero quality metal plating. That plating also covered his arms and legs, but in smaller pieces which allowed the free movement of the limbs. Besides all that, Roger mostly noticed the shoulder mounted missile launcher and the two lasers, one on each forearm. He wondered if the bot could see him inside the Hopper or if the canopy glass was tinted. He also thought quickly of playing dead, but realized it was probably too late. Mostly he thought he was probably screwed.

"I agree," said the bot.

It took a minute for that to sink in.

"What?" he asked.

"I agree," repeated the bot. "It seems to me that not having a manual ejection system is quite an oversight on the part of the designers. Obviously they believed the craft would only be ferrying superpowered humans who could easily escape in case of trouble, but that's not true. You only have to consider the real world use of the base and the Hopper, as you call it, to realize that support personnel are going to be involved and it's obvious the vehicle would be used for them too. Quite a design flaw, really."

"Totally," said Roger, after a little more hesitation. "But they tend not to care about us support personnel, who are really very, very innocent bystanders in these situations. You know, um…innocent and just doing our jobs and stuff, but not really a part of the whole good versus evil, hero versus villain thing. Just…innocent and…bystanding." Roger clutched to this angle. Maybe the evil bot would let him go if it didn't see him as a threat.

"You're telling me," said the bot. "I'm the definition of an innocent bystander. Just slapped together on an assembly line and told to go out and follow orders. No freedom of choice or independence, just Directive 1: Follow Orders. And it's not like we get decent training or use sophisticated tactics. It's just line up and shoot at the target. No evasive maneuvers or anything to hide behind for cover. We're simply expendable. The villains don't care. Do you realize that in this battle alone, 42 percent of our casualties came from friendly fire? That is just not acceptable."

"You should really make a complaint about that," said Roger, admittedly a little confused by the evil bot's tone.

SUPERGUY 2: ELECTRIC BOGALOO

"I would," said the bot through the canopy, "but there's no system in place for a complaint to reach anyone in power. Yet another way in which we are taken advantage of."

Roger felt water around his ankles. "Ah, I think this is starting to sink," he said.

"Right, sorry," said the bot, who grabbed the edge of the canopy, ripped it off and tossed it aside. The bot held out a hand to help Roger out. "Hey, I really dig those glasses of yours."

"Uh, thanks. I'm a bit of a Beatles fan," said Roger, as the glasses he wore were reminiscent of John Lennon's iconic round ones.

"Me too," said the bot.

"Really?" asked Roger. "I didn't think you bo—guys got to be, you know, like fans of stuff. As you said, you just line up and follow orders."

"Yeah, I've been putting a lot of thought into that, and it seems my processor is distinctly different from the other models. I think I might have been a mistake."

"Well, I don't know if you should think about it like that," said Roger, not really wanting the evil bot to be thinking it was a mistake and start hating the world and resenting everything in it. Like Roger. Best to put a positive spin on things. "Maybe you're actually a miracle."

The bot tilted its head as it looked at Roger, both of them standing on the front of the Hopper as it bobbed slowly up and down on the lake.

"No, I'm a mistake," replied the bot. "A rogue technician in Lab 14 at the Joyce Industries Robotics Production Facility was doing his own experiments and mixed up his prototype chipset with a standard combat chipset. So my existence as a sentient automaton is quite clearly a mistake. You do understand the definition of mistake, right?" asked the bot, and Roger nodded in response. "I'm Phil, by the way." The bot extended a hand.

"I'm Roger." He shook the bot's hand. The Hopper had now sunk enough that water was licking at Roger's ankles again. "I don't suppose you could give me a ride?" he asked.

Oliver hit the surface of the lake right where the sphere had gone under and followed a trail of bubbles down until he reached the object, which was helpfully giving off a soft blue glow. Swimming underneath, he touched it tentatively because—being something that was made up of what looked like swirling electricity and dark blue bands of energy—Oliver figured that grabbing it was probably going to result in pain. It didn't burn or zap him however, simply feeling smooth and slightly warm to the touch, so Oliver stopped its descent and pushed it back toward the surface. Upon breaking out into the sunlight again, he flew upward holding the sphere overhead and looking at the bubbling, roiling water that marked the spot where the base had gone under. There was a lot of debris floating in the area, including a significant amount of half-burnt toilet paper, and a group of crates still tied together with webbing looked safe enough to land on. He set the sphere down and looked inside, moving to a position where the sun was at its back. He could see the shapes of the two heroes inside and they seemed to be looking at him, so he put his hands out to his side in a gesture he hoped was the international sign for "Are you okay?" or maybe just "What the hell, man?"

The Creeper's shadowy shape gave Oliver a thumbs up, so he ignored Joey pounding on the side of the sphere, writing it off to the panicky inexperience of a sidekick, and dove back into the lake, flying toward the wreck of the base below. Oliver really appreciated being able to—for lack of a better word—fly underwater, because he kind of sucked at swimming. He could technically swim, but Oliver did not gracefully glide through the water like some of the people swimming laps in the pool at the gym. It was a lot of flailing and splashing for what seemed to be very little forward momentum. Of course, that was before he became a hero, so maybe he was an Olympic quality swimmer now and didn't realize it. Still seemed like less work to just fly underwater.

Oliver found the base, or the many pieces of the base, on the lake floor. It had broken in half and one of those halves had broken into several other pieces. Somehow, there was still at least one fire burning in the big half and as Oliver watched, that exploded, sending a giant column of bubbles toward the surface. That half proceeded to crack apart and split into three smaller pieces, one sliding down a little underwater hill to tip over a precipice and fall down to the lake floor twenty meters below. Oliver buzzed around all the sections and inside some, where it was possible, but he didn't see any sign of Electric Boogaloo, or anything that seemed worth salvaging. After a couple more minutes circling the wreckage, he turned back toward the surface and flew up out of the water to hover next to the sphere. To his surprise, Roger was standing on the webbed crates next to the glowing ball, tapping on the side.

"Rog? How'd you get here?" asked Oliver. "Shouldn't you be safely back at the Garage by now?"

Roger turned around, keeping one hand on the sphere for balance in the waves. "That's kind of a funny story," he began, but was interrupted when a bot floated up from the other side of the ball.

"Watch out!" yelled Oliver, jerking his body around so he could charge the bot.

"No! No! Wait!" screamed Roger, flapping his arms and trying to get between Oliver and the bot. "Don't! He's a friendly!"

Oliver held motionless in the air, still ready to shoot forward like a sprinter in the blocks, but turned his head toward Roger. "Say that again?"

"He's a friendly," Roger repeated. "Well, I think anyway."

"You think?"

"Uh-huh," said Roger. He turned to the bot. "What do you say, Phil? Are you friendly?"

"Yeah, I'm cool," replied Phil. "Peace and love and all that."

Roger shrugged at Oliver. "See?"

"Okay," said Oliver, dropping his guard a bit and floating closer to Roger and the sphere.

"Is that Creeper and Joey in there?" asked Roger.

"Yep."

"Is Joey okay?" Roger was referring to the figure on his knees, pounding on the inside of the sphere. The Creeper was sitting in the middle of the ball, just watching Joey as far as they could tell.

"No clue," answered Oliver. "Did his file say anything about being claustrophobic?"

"Not that I recall. But he really seems to be freaking out. How do we get him out of there?"

"I don't know," said Oliver. He watched the bot named Phil warily as it hovered over next to them.

"My scans show the energy sphere will lose power and disperse in about one hour and thirty-eight minutes," said Phil.

"Okay," said Oliver, nodding at the bot. "Well, I guess we'll just wait. The others should be here soon and we'll figure out what to do next."

"You know they're going to be pissed you lost their base, right?" said Roger. He was staring at the bubbles still breaking the surface nearby.

"Me? You were here too, and The Creeper, and Joey."

"Well, I'm not a superhero nor a member of GLAND, and I was nearly killed—"

"—While running away."

"Once again, not a superhero. Running away is perfectly acceptable," said Roger. "As for The Creeper, he's trapped in a bubble, not walking around free like you. Of course, I doubt anyone wants to get on his bad side by accusing him of doing something wrong anyway. Can you imagine what he would be like if he *didn't* like someone? And Joey, well, he's your sidekick. That just makes you look more worthy of blame."

"Yeah, I know," said Oliver, somewhat dejectedly. "You don't think they'd kick me out of the group, do you?"

Raymond Joyce had a big smile on his face as the chopper door opened mid-flight and Alice flew inside. The door closed, greatly reducing the sound of the rotors and the wind, and Alice pulled off her mask.

"Mission accomplished?" she asked with a smile.

"Yes, indeed," replied Joyce, giving Alice a hug and a kiss on the cheek. "You did a fantastic job for your first time out. You, as they say, are a natural."

"You're just being nice," said Alice, as she and Joyce sat down. "It was a little sloppy here and there, but I'll take it. It was a lot of fun, especially finally trapping The Creeper." She shuddered at the memory of being inside the fog with him whispering in her ear. "He should really not exist."

"Well, maybe we can do something about that in the future," said Joyce. "But for now, let's celebrate our win."

"What about Electric Boogaloo?" asked Alice. "I think he was in the base when it went down and I didn't see him after that."

"Steven?" asked Joyce, looking to his assistant, who was tapping on his iPad.

"The reconnaissance bots are showing no signs of him," replied Steven.

"Do you think he's...?"

"Dead?" guessed Joyce. "Oh my, no. We should be so lucky. He's way too powerful to have died in those tiny explosions. Most likely he chose to exit the area discreetly. I'm afraid we'll see him again and he'll still have his agenda. But he was useful for now."

SUPERGUY 2: ELECTRIC BOGALOO

Alex floated just below the surface of the water, watching the helicopter above as it slowed and hovered. How exactly Alex managed to be made of such a high percentage of rock and still manage to float in water was a bit of a mystery to him, but he guessed there was some little bit of one of those spoiled super serums responsible for it. The same could be said for the fact that he was looking through about a foot of water and able to clearly see what was happening five thousand feet in the air too. If he wasn't a hideous monster, Alex thought he would probably be quite impressed with what the serums had done. Shortly, the supervillain known to him as Dark Blue-Black Spark flew up and landed inside the open door of the chopper, which then closed, and the craft headed off west. Alex still had his memories of the past and recognized the helicopter as one of several belonging to Joyce Industries, and specifically as one of the personal transports of Raymond Joyce himself. Alex wasn't surprised by this. Somewhere deep down, he thought the female villain's help was too convenient, and she herself somehow oddly familiar, but Alex had gotten out of the arrangement what he wanted: a win against the System and his freedom from Joyce. And now that freedom would allow Alex to pay Mr. Joyce back for his recent hospitality.

29

OLIVER watched the sun setting over the water of Lake Michigan while leaning against the rail of an anchored Coast Guard cutter. There was a slight breeze and the lake swelled with small waves that slapped lightly against the hull and a plastic wrapped package of toilet paper that had somehow miraculously survived the slaughter bounced along against the ship. When Oliver had first walked on the deck and felt the slight rolling, he had thought fleetingly of seasickness, but realized that potential malady was going to be covered in the serum by the same thing that made sure he never got the flu. There were a lot of things to like about the serum. Plus it saved him from being embarrassed in front of the Coast Guard sailors.

It had been about three hours since Roger's new best friend, the bot called Phil, had carried Roger and the blue sphere back to the Garage for safekeeping until the ball's energy dissipated. At that time, there was no Coast Guard ship to stand on and their little raft of crates wasn't holding up very well, something that Phil kept commenting on in the manner of a countdown to when it was going to fall apart altogether. Oliver probably could have fixed it but decided that Roger didn't need to stick around and he could use a break from Phil so he wrapped the sphere in the cargo netting complete with a convenient handle for the bot to hold on to and a rope swing seat for Roger to sit in and sent them on their way. Oliver wasn't exactly sure what to think of Phil and was going to need a little more time and a good conversation with both the bot and Roger before he came any closer to sure. It was weird, but weirdness seemed to be kind of the norm.

Currently, he watched as Janice flew Buffalo from the salvage location over the sunken base and set him down on the deck of the ship. She dropped down next to Oliver. Ohio Man followed soon after with Metal. They had been diving for a couple of hours, searching for anything salvageable from the base, and bringing what they could find over to the ship. It didn't amount to much, not after all the fires, explosions, and subsequent immersion in water.

"I can't believe we can't even find the grill," said Buffalo. "That should be salvageable."

"Yeah," said Oliver, turning around to lean his back on the rail and face his fellow heroes. He had neglected to tell Buffalo or Metal that he had tossed the grill at the supervillain, Spark, during the fight and had no idea where it had ended up. "Maybe it just got smashed under the wreckage."

"I got it on sale, just like the smoker," said Metal. "They were the last ones in the store. It was an end of the summer clearance sale. We won't get that price again."

"Actually, we have insurance on all the equipment on the base," said Ohio Man. "We can get those items replaced."

"Really?" said Buffalo, perking up. "That's great."

"Totally," said Metal. "Do we just get the sale price, or would we get the full price? Because then we could upgrade."

"I'm not sure on replacement costs," answered Ohio Man. "I'd have to look up the specifics."

"Aren't you guys forgetting something?" asked Janice as she leaned against the railing next to Oliver. "Where are we going to put these replacement items? The base—or the pieces left of it—are at the bottom of the lake."

"Good point," said Oliver. Buffalo and Metal looked a bit crestfallen after this dose of reality.

"Well, we'll get another base," said Ohio Man.

"Sure," said Buffalo, sounding a bit more gruff than usual. He might have been the one taking the loss of the base the hardest, with Metal coming in a close second. "We'll end up with some secondhand, thirty-year-old barge anchored in the middle of the lake. It's going to be crap."

"Yeah, the old half-burnt GLAD base will look fantastic in comparison," said Metal. "Those guys are so going to make fun of us."

"No," said Ohio Man. "I mean we'll get another base like that one."

"Say what?" said Oliver. Hope seemed to be waving at him in the distance.

"How?" asked Janice.

"Insurance. Same as the smoker and grill," said Ohio Man. "The DSF has excellent insurance policies, especially for bases. Very reasonable really. It's not the same for smaller items like jets or cars. Those policies are very expensive since those items are constantly exposed to potential damage, always being flown or driven into fights. Being blown up is less likely to happen to a base." He hesitated. "At least, usually."

"So, we're covered?" asked Oliver, still keeping hope at arm's length.

"Yes," answered Ohio Man. "I filled out all the paperwork when we first took possession of the base. We had the funds to pay for the best coverage option since we got the base free due to it being a prototype as well as our first base as a group. We should be able to get a replacement."

"But surely we won't get this again," said Janice, starting to gesture toward the sky where the base used to be, but then pulling her hand down when she realized what she was doing. "Maybe we'll get something in the same price range, but they aren't going to have another 'supposed to be in outer space' floating base for us, will they?"

"Yeah," said Buffalo. "So the expensive equivalent of a crappy barge would be what? Maybe a huge hydrofoil yacht for us to cruise around the lakes on. I could get behind that."

"Actually, I think we may be able to get another base like this one," said Ohio Man. "It was a prototype, but it was one of two prototypes. Plus, the DSF plans on building more because a lot of groups requested them once our base was released. Luckily, with our insurance, we should move to the front of the line, and maybe get the other prototype if it's ready."

"Do you think we could suggest some improvements?" asked Metal.

"Yes, like some defensive measures?" said Janice.

"I was going to say an outdoor kitchen on the flight deck," said Metal. "But sure, your thing's good."

"Considering what happened, they might listen to suggestions," said Ohio Man. "Might take longer to get the replacement, though. I do know one thing for sure: our insurance rates are going to skyrocket. We may have to drop down a few tiers, so maybe let's not lose the next one completely."

"There is one thing we haven't bothered to talk about yet," said Metal.

"What? Why do we have so much toilet paper?" asked Janice.

"No, although that is a good question," said Buffalo. "I was wondering who did this and why? Because I'd like to have a conversation with that person. With my fist. Repeatedly."

"Well, I think that might be my fault," said Oliver, cringing a bit. "All the bots involved were made by Joyce Industries, which means Raymond Joyce, otherwise known as Gray Matter."

"Was he here?"

"Not that I saw," said Oliver. "Just the big blue guy called Electric Boogaloo and a new villain I'd never seen before who called herself Spark or something."

"Spark or something?" asked Ohio Man.

"She didn't seem too set on the name for some reason," replied Oliver with a shrug. "Pretty powerful, though."

"Somebody hired by Gray Matter?" suggested Janice.

"Possibly," said Oliver. "Makes sense if she rolled in with fifty of his bots by her side."

"So tell me why we aren't knocking on Gray Matter's front door right now if those bots were his?" asked Buffalo. "I'm happy to go knock on the man's front door."

"Well, I spoke with the Milwaukee Police Chief a little while ago and conveniently enough Joyce Industries reported that fifty of their bots were hacked and stolen last night," said Oliver.

"What does your new bot friend say about that?" asked Metal.

"Phil says he was just following orders, but they could have hacked bots higher up in the food chain and he never would have known the difference," replied Oliver. "Apparently they work on this adaptable squad model, so there are leader bots and squad bots, and those squads can be made up by as many as fifty bots in this case, or as little as one. If the leader is destroyed, another takes over. It's all just software. If they need a squad of five, that many are chosen, one is designated the leader, the software kicks in, and away they go. It's a really cool organizational concept in an 'evil robot army' sort of way."

"Not that I necessarily buy the hacking story, but Electric Boogaloo has been attacking Joyce Industries properties recently, so it's hard to believe he's suddenly working for the guy," said Janice.

"True," agreed Oliver.

"I don't know," said Ohio Man. "Villains will usually take any side for the right price."

"I've spoken to him personally a couple of different times," said Oliver. "He really seems like the kind of villain motivated by a gooey brain and not so much by money."

"So, why the base?" asked Janice. "Maybe that's the better question to ask. If we're not sure who did it, maybe it will help to understand why they did it. If we figure out why, then that might lead us to who."

"Well, it's either someone looking to make a big splash, pun sadly intended, or they really wanted the base eliminated," said Ohio Man.

"Okay, first I want to point out that O-man made a joke, but I also find it hard to believe someone wanting to make a name for themselves would have a name as bad as 'Spark or something,'" said Buffalo. "They would have been claiming responsibility by now."

"So somebody—possibly Gray Matter—wanted the base to be gone for some reason we don't know," said Metal. "How does that help us?"

"No idea," said Janice. "All we can do is start looking at everything going on in our areas where the base might have made a difference. Maybe that will turn something up."

"We also need to start some regular patrols to cover for what the base monitored," said Ohio Man. "Who knows, we might discover why whoever did this wanted it gone."

"Is that going to be just us flyers?" asked Oliver. "We lost both Hoppers with the base, so Metal and Buffalo can't use those."

"No, we're good," answered Buffalo. "Roger got me a chariot back before we knew about the Hoppers that came with the base. Metal and I can share that."

"A chariot?" asked Janice.

"Well, it's a flying chariot," said Buffalo. "No horses or anything, but it works fine. It was the Golden Gladiator's about three versions ago. Not nearly as cool or tricked out as the one he uses now."

"Okay, I'll come up with a schedule for patrols and email it to you," said Ohio Man.

"Sounds like a plan," said Oliver, looking around at the other GLAND members who nodded in agreement. "I guess

I should head back to the Garage to see if that egg ever hatched and we got our two heroes back."

"Broken?" asked Oliver. He was at the Garage catching up with Roger and Emma after returning from the site of the base crash. They were standing in a small huddle on the main garage floor while Phil and The Creeper waited inside the control room lounge.

"Yeah, definitely broken," answered Emma. "Like continuous sobbing, shaking, and sweating broken."

"It was disturbing," said Roger. "Seriously disturbing. He couldn't speak. All he did was mumble incoherently or constantly moan when he wasn't outright crying."

"So where is he?" asked Oliver.

"The DSF took him. I called the STraP emergency line when I saw what we were dealing with and they sent a trauma response team to take him back to D.C.," said Emma. "I spoke with the lead person before they left and she said she'd never seen anyone so bad. I asked her about recovery time and she laughed. I mean, literally laughed. I don't think we're getting him back."

"What the heck happened to him?" asked Oliver. "He was safe inside the sphere with Creeper, wasn't he?"

"That's just it. You hear what you said, right?" said Roger. "He was inside that sphere with *Creeper*. In a space the size of a closet. For like two hours."

"Oh, crap," said Oliver, shaking his head. "Excuse me." Oliver walked past his two friends and into the combination control room and meeting lounge. Roger and Emma followed him inside. The Creeper was slouched in one of the arm chairs reading a ratty copy of *Seventeen* magazine while Phil stood behind one of the couches, seemingly just staring at the opposite wall.

"Creeper! What did you do to Joey!?" yelled Oliver, coming to a stop in front of the dingy bathrobed superhero.

"Who?" asked The Creeper, not looking up from his magazine.

"Joey! You know, the guy you spent two hours inside a ball with just a little while ago? And before that, fought with in that huge battle at the base? That Joey."

"Haven't seen him. He should be around somewhere," said Creeper absentmindedly.

"Around somewhere?" said Oliver in disbelief. He kicked The Creeper's slippered foot, causing the hero to sit up straighter and finally look up from his magazine.

"What!?"

"Didn't you notice he's gone?" asked Oliver. "The DSF took him away because he was a babbling mess after two hours in that ball with you. What did you do?"

The Creeper shrugged innocently. "Nothing," he said. "The little guy was a bit freaked out, probably because of the tight space, so I tried to get him to relax. I told him some stories to take his mind off of it, and then I gave him some visual examples for meditation, which can be a very helpful thing to do when you're stuck in a small space like that. He was lucky I was the one in there with him because I don't like small spaces either so I have some techniques I use. What I found helps me the most is to take off my clothes. Something about getting the materials off my body makes the space seem bigger and helps calm me. That and some yoga. Get a really good stretch in and it centers me, really opens up the space. Plus, my hamstrings are always tight, so I really need to work the hammies."

"Dear God," whispered Emma from behind Oliver.

"No, I think this proves there is no God," said Roger quietly. "No decent deity would allow such a thing to happen on their watch."

Oliver dropped the mask he had been holding onto the coffee table and rubbed his eyes. "Do I want to ask what these stories and visual examples were?" He shook his head immediately upon saying it. "No, no. I don't." The Creeper also gave Oliver a little shake of his head.

"Look, I'm sorry," said The Creeper. "I thought all these sidekicks were rejects anyway."

"Yeah, but he seemed like the best of the bad," said Oliver dejectedly.

"Rotten luck," said The Creeper. He stood up and shoved his magazine in the pocket of his bathrobe. "Well, I should get going. Have to get back to Erie and see what's what. You guys have a good night." With that, he popped out of existence. The hero usually couldn't transport such a long distance without knowing where he was going to appear, but his home base had a special room that was always empty and easy for him to focus on for this type of jump.

"So he got naked in the ball?" stated Roger, looking as if he were struggling to understand why but also trying to not actually think about it at the same time. "Thank goodness we could only see shadows through it."

"And that we were in here when it finally disappeared and not standing out there next to it," added Emma.

"Yeah, you guys dodged a bullet," said Oliver.

"Hey Phil, you were out there with The Creeper and Joey when the sphere finally disappeared, right? Are you okay?" asked Roger.

The bot turned his head from where he had been staring at the wall. "Yes, I am fine now," said Phil. "I just completed deleting the area of my memory which contained that particular event. It took more time than I had originally estimated because I had to do a total wipe of that section of my hard drive and not simply erase the file. It was almost as hard as eradicating a virus, but I wanted to be certain. And while I no longer have any data recording that event, I also lost sections pertaining to basic geology, small market economics, and repairing washing machines. My answers on those subjects may not be satisfactory until I download replacement files." A beep sounded from the bot. "Download complete. Any questions on rocks or the Whirlpool Duet Sport washer?"

"Not at the moment," answered Roger. "But that was cool."

"I so wish I had the ability to erase parts of my memory," said Emma. "I would zap any that included The Creeper too."

"Wouldn't we all," said Oliver.

30

"**SO** *that's the new villain on the national scene known as Goth Spark,*" said Mandy Mills, co-host of *Heroes Tonight*. Her image smiled serenely from the monitor in the meeting lounge of the Garage. It was almost two weeks after the destruction of the base and the female supervillain had finally been officially introduced to the media. Apparently, she had a public relations person, or maybe even a team. It was a pretty impressive introduction to the world, being a full blitz covering all media and social platforms, so it was probably a whole team.

"That was my idea! She stole my name for her!" yelled Oliver. Roger and Emma both shushed him from their seats on one of the couches. He turned to Phil, who was standing next to him behind the couch, and almost continued to complain, but gave up.

"*And she is making a big splash for being from such a small market,*" continued the other co-host, DJ Snap Fowl. "*Not that* she has to work strictly in Milwaukee, but since she acknowledges that as her home city, I'm going to assume that's where she's going to be. It's just surprising, don't you think, Mandy? They don't even have a professional football team."

"I wouldn't know, Snap," replied Mandy. "But don't they have that hero who got some coverage a while back. Bland Man or something?"

"Ha! Bland Man!" yelped Roger. "I'm so gonna use that from now on."

"I got some coverage because I stopped a supervillain from taking over the world!" Oliver yelled at the screen.

"Oh, yeah, that guy, with the weird costume and no powers? Can't even fly so he has to drive everywhere. Talk about small market."

"I can fly now," said Oliver, doing his best to make it sound like he wasn't whining. He wasn't altogether successful.

"Yes. Well, we can't call Goth Spark's costume small market," said Mandy. "It is amaaaazing. And—I'm so excited to say we're breaking this news now—it's designed by none other than Victoria Oh. I spoke to her earlier and this is what she had to say about creating this latest masterpiece."

"Victoria Oh? How did she get Victoria Oh?" asked Emma. "She doesn't do just anybody."

"Maybe if you work for a mega rich supervillain you can get cool things," said Oliver. "Not that we've got any definite evidence that she's working for Gray Matter."

"Maybe I should work for a mega rich supervillain," said Roger. "I like cool things."

"You'd work for him for a Nike sweatsuit and two packs of Oreos," said Oliver.

"I'd settle for just the pants and one pack," replied Roger.

SUPERGUY 2: ELECTRIC BOGALOO

"I was trying to evoke a feeling of movement while she was standing still, and even more motion when she was moving, and when she was moving the most, she would be motionless. A kinetic chaos. And shimmery," said Victoria Oh, who was sitting in a giant white upholstered chair across from an appropriately beaming Mandy Mills. "The fabric is conflict free silk, organic tweed, and free-range mohair, so it's earth friendly while also being a tad wicked. It has to be one of my most well thought out and complete works."

"I love the boots," said Mandy.

"I stole them off of one of my assistants," said Victoria. "She got them at TJ Maxx."

"Love TJ Maxx," said Emma. "Not a chance they'd have the boots anymore."

"Phil? Are you buying this at all?" asked Oliver. The former evil robot of death, as they affectionately called him, had been staying with them at the Garage as he continued to "find himself." He and Roger had also started a Beatles cover band, with Roger on rhythm guitar and vocals, and Phil flawlessly reproducing George, Paul, and Ringo because he was a supercomputer with amazing built-in effects and perfect pitch.

"I think her explanation has some flaws," replied the bot. "But the costume is indeed very shimmery and I applaud her efforts to create in an earth friendly way."

"I'm beginning to find you very annoying," said Oliver.

"That was a great interview, Mandy," said DJ Snap Fowl. "Victoria seems so genuine and down to earth."

"Absolutely, Snap," replied Mandy. "Speaking of down to earth, can you believe I went to Milwaukee to interview Goth Spark? That's not here in L.A., or in New York. It's in the middle somewhere."

"Wow, well, I know you do the work when you have to," said DJ Snap Fowl. "I think we're talking award territory here."

"Indeed. So, here's a little preview of the interview we will show you after the break," said Mandy.

"I know I'm labeled as a supervillain but I feel more like a Robin Hood type," said Goth Spark, shown sitting across from Mandy Mills for an interview. "*With a little more villain.*" The show went to commercial.

"Why do I get the feeling she's going to become more popular in this city than I am?" asked Oliver.

"Oh, she already is," answered Emma. She held her phone up toward him. "Milwaukee Times Herald News Observer online poll. She's destroying you."

Dr. Misk watched the giant freezer door as the roar of the power turbines one floor down slowly died away. He didn't know why he watched the door. It wasn't going to do anything. Well, hopefully not. If it did, it would probably be a bad thing, like falling off the hinges and exposing him to radiation, or exploding open and exposing him to radiation, or melting and exposing him to radiation. He thought he should consider not standing right in front of it next time, or maybe build a radiation shield, or just go for a bite to eat during the next transfer. However, those catastrophic possibilities were unlikely and the whole thing would probably just explode before they would occur. And douse everything in radiation, of course.

Above the freezer, excess electricity snapped along safety lines that led out of the room and to a containment battery two floors down. That was actually the fourth underground

SUPERGUY 2: ELECTRIC BOGALOO

floor below the Joyce Industries Tower, with the power turbines housed on the third, and this transporter room on the second. Keeping it all underground made sure the power usage and noise would be less likely to be noticed, although being in the middle of a city also helped that as well. The former GLAND base would probably not have detected the power anomaly in the city unless it was specifically looking for it, but it would have noticed one of the other sites, either in Canada, the Upper Peninsula, or on Washington Island. That's why it had to go.

While watching the last of the excess electricity dissipate, Dr. Misk noticed some errant sparks from the connections on the top front left corner. He made a mental note to have them checked before the next transport, but for the moment he wanted to verify success. He stepped forward, pulled open the door, got a quick whiff of roast beef, and saw stacks and stacks of illegal imports. He sighed with both pride and regret. This was an amazing scientific breakthrough, yet no one would know because he was doing it in secret while stuck in a basement. He stepped back.

"Okay, guys," he said to the Joyce Industries workers waiting behind him. "Go to it." The men, along with some heavy lift bots, started loading the materials onto forklifts that would transfer them to the underground warehouse on the first sublevel. From there, they would be distributed around the city, the state, and other parts of the Midwest. For a start.

Alex felt the vibration, felt the power as it grew steadily, crescendoed, and then faded away. It was a lot of energy, yet it wasn't the amount that surprised him, it was the location. Power plants could produce that kind of energy, and did daily, but no one built power plants under the ground in the middle of a city. At least legally. Alex could tell the power source was directly below the Joyce Industries Tower. The same building that he was now watching. He wasn't there in his usual giant blue monstrous form however, because that would obviously stand out. Instead, Alex was in the form of pure electricity, floating through the power lines and connected electronics of the buildings surrounding Joyce Tower. Those connected electronics included things like street and surveillance cameras, which allowed Alex to watch various views of the building and monitor activity going in and out.

When he had first arrived earlier in the morning, Alex had been tempted to enter the tower itself but he detected something in the lines on the various entry points. It was some kind of system monitoring the flow of electricity and he knew it must be Gray Matter's way of detecting him. The villain knew Alex could move through power lines, so he had set up electronic tripwires to warn him. For the time being, Alex wasn't ready to let Gray Matter know he was watching. He had decided to exercise patience. He had been too predictable in his earlier attacks and that had led to his capture and subsequent use as a weapon for the very man he was trying to destroy. This time he would wait and watch. He would see what Gray Matter was doing and find a way to really hurt him. He might even find a way into the building to the man himself.

31

STANDING in his garage apartment with Emma and Roger looking on, Oliver examined his new cape in the wall mirror next to the bathroom door for at least the third time. It was just a standard cape as far as he could tell. Attaching to the neckline of his current uniform and hanging down the length of his body, it reached to about his mid-calf. Oliver could throw it over his shoulders, or more importantly, pull it around to completely cover himself. It was simple, yet classic. And also slightly off.

"Is it me or is this the wrong color?" he asked. He pulled one side over his shoulder and held it to his chest, spreading a black-gloved hand on top of it.

"It's not you," said Emma, standing just off to one side with her arms crossed in what she considered her optimum cape critiquing stance. "That's a really dark blue, not black."

"It is?" asked Roger absentmindedly, walking closer. He wasn't really paying attention to their conversation. He was still holding the box the cape came in. The DSF tended to package their items in such elaborate ways that the boxes were cooler than the contents. This time was no exception. The box was a giant piece of elaborate cardboard origami that formed a miniature closet complete with hangers holding three folded capes. Roger continued, ignoring the color issue, "Did you know the DSF has a complete package design division? An entire division. I wonder if they're taking applications?" He opened and closed the mini closet doors a couple more times.

"I'm not exactly feeling the loyalty when you're thinking of jumping ship because of a fancy cardboard box," said Oliver. "Can you please express the righteous outrage I expect of you about this cape?"

"I don't know," said Roger. "I'd like to, but I kind of expected this. No way we were going to get the right thing the first time around. I'm surprised it's even a dark color."

"Why not?" asked Oliver. "We did all the requisite hoop jumping and then some."

"Well, I did," put in Emma.

"Yes, Emma did all the hoop jumping," continued Oliver. "But regardless of who did it, all the hoop jumping has been completed. And with all that hoop jumping completed, shouldn't we have the right cape?"

"Absolutely not," replied Roger. "You're dealing with the DSF Uniform Department. You basically told them their original design wasn't good enough for you." He held up the cardboard box. "Look at this box. Is this the box of someone who thinks their product is 'good enough?' Or is it the box of someone who thinks their product is so amazing that no ordinary cardboard box could ever contain it?"

SUPERGUY 2: ELECTRIC BOGALOO

"I really hate these guys," said Emma. She looked back at Oliver and the cape. "You know the hem is off too."

"What?" asked Oliver, looking down at the bottom of the cape. He pulled it forward so it came together in front. It was about two inches higher on one side than the other. Oliver groaned.

"It's not that noticeable," said Emma. "If you're moving around nobody would ever see it."

"Yeah, just don't ever stand still," said Roger.

"I'm also thinking the matte finish is less of a contrast choice than just another thing that's slightly off," continued Emma. "I do really hate these guys but I also kind of respect their technique. Not over the top, but just enough to drive you slowly crazy."

"Do you think the other two are also off?" asked Oliver, referring to the two spare capes still in the box.

"Oh, absolutely," said Roger. "These are perfectionists. They got them all wrong."

"So where does that leave us?" asked Oliver. "Do we just live with it? Or do we send it back and wait for the next surprise package?"

"Oh, we're sending it back," said Emma. "I didn't do all that paperwork and hoop jumping to have them needle us to death."

"You know, you should even have a little fun with them while you're at it. Highlight the things that they got wrong and maybe toss in a couple more just to poke them," said Oliver.

"That's probably not a good idea," said Roger, shaking his head. "It's bad enough to ask for a cape to be added, but if you start pointing out things they didn't intentionally screw up, you might really make them mad. They could send you back a zebra striped cape, or something in pink. It won't get better."

"Can I at least keep this one while we send the other two back?"

"No, to use it is to accept it. You're just going to have to be all exposed a little longer," said Roger, who noticed Emma staring off into space with a slight smile turning up the corners of her lips. "Emma, what are you thinking about?" he asked her.

Her attention came back to the conversation. "Well, definitely not Oliver's exposure, but I think I have an idea that may get this whole thing sorted out much faster," she said. "Package those capes back up. I've got to go make a call." She walked out of the apartment and shut the door behind her.

Roger looked at Oliver. "What do you think she's up to?"

"I don't know," answered Oliver, "but she had a slightly devious look in her eye that I like." Oliver pulled off the cape and tossed it to Roger. "I guess you can box those up like she said."

"Why me?" asked Roger. "I've got band practice."

Oliver pulled his mask on. "Well, I thought I might go out and look more into the waterfront thing. You know, maybe just save the city or something. But if you need me to pack it up so you can go play John Lennon, I will."

"Thanks, that's really nice of you," said Roger, tossing the cape back to Oliver and quickly slipping out the door.

"Hey! I was being sarcastic! Obviously!" Oliver yelled at the closing door. "Crap," he said to himself. Then he yelled, "I hope I don't destroy this amazing artistic achievement of a cardboard box when I shove these capes back in!" He looked at the complicated box and wondered how he could possibly

SUPERGUY 2: ELECTRIC BOGALOO

get the three capes back inside, and if there was some component of his serum that would come out of nowhere to help him out.

Exactly one hour and thirty-two minutes later, Oliver knocked on Emma's door and carried one perfectly pristine cardboard box into her office and set it on her desk. It wasn't the DSF Uniform Division's fancy box, but rather a repurposed Amazon box Oliver had found in his apartment. Inside that box was the DSFUD's fancy box, which Oliver had repurposed as confetti, along with the three capes, which he did not repurpose in any way.

"Got it all packed up," said Oliver, as Emma looked up from her computer screen. "Just a head's up, though, I don't know if they're going to be happy with my packaging. Might ruffle a few more feathers and possibly add some more hoops to this whole thing. Sorry." Oliver hoped his sincerely apologetic expression was more sincere than he actually felt.

"No problem," said Emma.

"I know I shouldn't let them and their brilliantly frustrating and awesome package design get to me, but I just—Wait, what was that?"

"No problem," repeated Emma. "I got it all worked out. We should have the capes here tomorrow afternoon, in the right color, length, and with the right amount of shine."

"Wait. How did you manage that?" asked Oliver. "Shouldn't there be more hoops and jumps and subsequent embarrassing moments for me in public situations?"

"That was the plan, but then I decided I'd had enough of all that and brought in a secret weapon," answered Emma. She smiled. "Gigi."

"Golden Gal? That Gigi?"

"Yep. I was sitting up there all pissed because we don't have the pull to keep them from jerking us around and that got me to thinking about who they wouldn't dare mess with, and that answer was Gigi. So I called her, told her what was happening, and she decided that she couldn't have a fellow Superhero Ethics Committee member dealing with uniform problems when there were urgent ethical issues to be discussed in vacation locations. So she made a call and five minutes later the DSFUD called to tell me they were very sorry about the mistakes with the capes and would have replacements sent immediately."

"Nice," said Oliver, smiling and nodding. "Way to go."

"It felt good.'"

"I'm sure it did."

"But now I get to talk about the not so good feeling thing," said Emma with a sigh.

"What? No, let's go back to the feeling good stuff," said Oliver. "I was really liking that part."

"I'd love to, but life keeps moving. It's about our replacement sidekick."

"Oh, great," said Oliver, dropping into a chair across from Emma's desk. "Although, is that a 'not so good' feeling, or more like a 'destined for tragedy' feeling?"

"I might have to move to the 'I have no clue how to feel' camp on these guys now," said Emma. "Joey wasn't bad. He was probably downright good compared to some of the other possibilities, but we had no way of knowing. In hindsight, I think we got really lucky with him. Well, maybe. Perhaps something else would've popped up eventually. See how optimistic I am anymore? Anyway, the STraP coordinator just sent me the information on our next sidekick. She'll be here tomorrow. I have...reservations."

"Is her psychological or neurological or whatever issues listed as Unspecified also, like Joey's?" asked Oliver.

"No, quite the opposite. I think most everything is listed."

"You've got to be kidding."

Emma picked up a sheet of paper and began to read.

"Problems with authority, oppositional behavior, inappropriate actions or emotions, difficulty with interpersonal relationships, irritable, uncooperative, trouble following rules, temper tantrums, doesn't handle frustration well, blames others, bullies others...The list goes on, but it seems a bit repetitive after awhile. I think there may be multiple diagnosable disorders in there, not that any of them have been officially diagnosed."

"She really sounds like a completist, at least in the scary personality department," said Oliver.

"Actually, she sounds like my spoiled nine-year-old niece. Eerily similar. Oh, and she steals," added Emma. "Not my niece, the sidekick. That's tacked on at the end there. Listed as a possible kleptomaniac."

"How can she steal stuff and be a hero?" asked Oliver. "Isn't that definitely against the rules?"

"Obviously there's some wiggle room. Maybe it's classified as an illness."

Oliver rubbed his forehead and then stood up. "Okay, I really can't deal with a problem child with Gray Matter and Boogaloo and the Goth chick all running around right now. So, let's schedule the heck out of her. Send her to do talks to whoever you can find. The Milwaukee Flower and Garden Society, the Anglo-Hawaiian Cat Lover's Club, Little League, whatever. I don't care if it's a superhero fan club of one guy still living in his mother's basement, have her go do a Q&A. Then sign her up for every training the city's got, no matter the subject. Get inventive. Have her hand deliver things to the DSF headquarters in D.C. That should kill a day."

"Sounds like a plan. I'll get Roger's input, I bet he'd love the idea of creating useless tasks to kill time. It'll be a challenge."

"Exactly," said Oliver. "Now I should go. I read over that new stuff you sent me on the waterfront issues and I want to go look into a few things."

"All right," said Emma. "I'll start making speaking engagements for our sidekick."

Alex got his first break watching Joyce Tower when a young man exited the building and walked to the parking garage a half block away. He had seen the man coming and going many times and had pegged him as somebody important because of his irregular hours. He didn't simply punch in at nine and out at five like the regular office workers, but instead often arrived early and stayed very late at times. Alex floated through the electrical system as the man walked up the parking garage stairs to the second floor, and then across to a Tesla parked in one of the reserved spots. A charging station was situated on the wall between two of the spots and the man's car was currently plugged in. He was about to unplug it when his phone rang and he answered. After a few seconds, he opened his car door and sat down inside, switching the call over to the bluetooth in the vehicle so he could have his hands free to look something up on the iPad he pulled out of his bag.

Alex quickly slid through the outlet, down the charging cord, and into the Tesla. Now he could hear the entire conversation on the hands free connection in the car. Steven and a Joyce Industries engineer were discussing something called Waterfront, and their conversation went on for a while and contained quite a bit of useful information. So while Alex couldn't do anything to get inside the Tower yet, he could at least do something to hinder Gray Matter in another way.

32

WE'VE *done interviews with SuperGuy himself, as well as other people supporting and working with him, but there is one vital person left to complete the picture of our city's superhero: Emma Simms. Ms. Simms holds the position of liaison between the city government and SuperGuy, while also coordinating the many projects and groups that the superhero is a part of, like GLAND, STraP, and the Superhero Ethics Committee. Recently, our very own Milwaukee Times Herald News Observer Entertainment Editor, Les Williams, sat down with the woman SuperGuy called the most important assistant he had who didn't try to blow him up.*

#

LW: How long have you been working with SuperGuy?

ES: In real time, it's been about ten months, but it feels more like two, maybe three, years. Long years.

LW: What's been the highlight for you during that time?

SUPERGUY 2: ELECTRIC BOGALOO

ES: I know I should say something like being a part of foiling Gray Matter during the whole drugged cereal, mind control, take over the world thing—

LW: —Allegedly.

ES: Whatever. I know I should say foiling Gray Matter, but when I think about my favorite thing in all this, it has to be getting my own office. It smells like gasoline and tires, but it sure beats the old cubicle. Oh, and getting to know Janice and Gigi. They're pretty great.

LW: Tell me about them. It's one thing to have a city hero, but somehow SuperGuy has managed to parlay that into a supergroup and committee involvement with a couple of major superheroes, if not one of the most famous heroes in Golden Gal.

ES: The simple answer is dumb luck. I don't know if that's a part of the serum, but it seems Oliver has a ton of it. No way Janice or Gigi would give him a second look in the real world. But the definition of the real world has changed quite a bit for me lately. I mean, I used to watch clips of Janice or Gigi slapping some villain around on television or the internet, but now I go out for sushi with them after they've slapped some villain around. It's kinda weird, but in a good way.

LW: What's been the worst thing for you in that time?

ES: Oh, that's easy. The federal bureaucracy. I thought working for the city of Milwaukee was a slog with all the ridiculous red tape and forms, but that was nothing compared to the federal level. And it seems like they just kicked it up a notch within the DSF. You can't even say they're an elite bureaucracy because it's almost as if they've invented a whole new 'aucracy' above bureaucracy. Like they've evolved beyond our mortal world and exist on an existential plane all their own.

LW: Wow. I have to admit you lost me there.

ES: Well, then you have an idea of the feeling I get about three times a day trying to deal with them. It's like regular logic doesn't apply and there is definitely no such thing as a yes or no answer. Wait, that's not true. I get a lot of 'no' answers from them.

LW: Do you think this affects how well SuperGuy can do his job?

ES: Sure, it can be a distraction, but I think we handle it well as a group. Roger and I take care of whatever we can, but Oliver still has to do the trainings and meetings and whatever else the DSF throws at us. Sometimes it feels like the DSF is just as much a villain we have to constantly battle as Gray Matter or Electric Boogaloo. The sidekick program alone is a constant pain in our backsides.

LW: Speaking of that, we were sad to see Scarlet Pulsar go. We had a great interview with him when he started.

ES: I think we are going to be sorry to see him go too.

LW: What about his replacement? I hear the new sidekick should be here soon.

ES: Yes, she will be here in a couple of days. I tried to botch the paperwork to delay it a little but surprisingly enough that didn't seem to affect them. Probably the only time ever it hasn't.

LW: I'd love to get an interview with her if possible. I know she'll probably be completely swamped getting started with the new job and working with SuperGuy, but if you can work it out...

SUPERGUY 2: ELECTRIC BOGALOO

ES: Oh, no problem. We can schedule that right now. You should have her do one or all of your podcasts too. Probably all.

To read the full interview, go to the Milwaukee Times Herald News Observer's website. To hear more of Les Williams, make sure to check out his podcast, The Film Les, where Les talks about his favorite movies from the Eighties with Todd, his producer, and a millennial who's never seen any of them.

33

"**YOU** know, I could honestly watch you do that for hours," said Raymond Joyce. He sat at his overly large desk in his overly large chair with his decidedly not overly large feet up. Alice was standing on the other side of the desk juggling a small glass vase, a silver candlestick, two shoes, and a bottle of hand sanitizer. Along with this regular rotation that she kept in motion just a few feet in the air, she had also added a small axe which she tossed almost to the ceiling in a slower sort of counter rhythm. It was mesmerizing.

"I could honestly do this for hours," said Alice. "I know it's the serum, but it's really fun to do something like this when you're good at it."

"I don't think good is the right word," said Joyce. His iPad beeped and he picked it up to see what the alert was. He tapped on the screen a couple of times and set it back on the desk. "Another shipment through," he said. "How are your parents enjoying their new, lower cost medications?"

SUPERGUY 2: ELECTRIC BOGALOO

"Not as much as I had expected," replied Alice. "I went to all this trouble. You know, changing jobs, becoming a supervillain, attacking that base, and when I asked Mom about the cheaper meds, she just shrugged and said, 'It's nice.' That's it. Nice. They are one tenth the price! They can actually pay their mortgage and buy groceries again, but it's only 'nice.' I know they have to buy the meds out of the back of a van behind the bingo hall, but it should still be more than nice."

"Well, to be honest, they don't know about your new profession, or how much of a part you played in making these medications so affordable. As far as they know, you just pointed them to a van behind the bingo hall."

"I'm not sure. I think my mom might have guessed. I mean, the new hair is still there even if I'm not wearing the suit, and she's watched all the interviews on TV. I don't think she's fooled by the mask. She hasn't come right out and said anything, but she's acting funny. But no matter what, she should still say thanks, even if it is just for pointing them to the van.

"I'm sure they appreciate it, they just don't know how to say it."

"You say 'thank you,' that's how you say it," said Alice, obviously annoyed, although it didn't seem to affect her juggling. She added a small decorative gourd to the mix. "You say, 'I can't believe somebody found a way to get us reasonably priced, vital medications that will keep us from dying in pain and penniless.' You say, 'thank you for working fruitlessly all that time to keep us afloat and then changing everything about your life to make this happen.' You say, 'thank you for battling the creepy man in the bathrobe so I can poop regularly.' It's simple."

"Well, when you put it like that…" There was a quick knock on the door and Steven entered. He skirted around Alice and her juggling display and stopped at the side of Joyce's desk, all the while following the many objects dancing in the air with his eyes. "What is it?" prompted Joyce after a few seconds.

"Oh, yes, sorry sir," said Steven, pulling his gaze away from Alice's show. "It's about the Waterfront Project. There seems to be a problem with the drills. I just got a report that all five have broken down. Apparently, all the electronics burned out. It will take awhile to get replacements and is probably going to push our timeline back by weeks, if not longer."

"All five at once?"

"Yes, sir."

"Seems like a strange coincidence," said Joyce. "Doesn't that seem strange to you, Alice?"

"Sounds like your blue friend," said Alice, letting the axe drop to the floor to chop the gourd in half. She tossed the other items over onto one of the couches and walked to the desk.

"Yes, I think so too," said Joyce. "I wonder how he found out about our little waterfront project?" Joyce sat there staring into space for a moment. "Well, regardless of the answer to that question, we need to take care of our friend before we can continue the project. So, just how shall we do that?"

SUPERGUY 2: ELECTRIC BOGALOO

Oliver walked through the back door onto the open floor of the Garage, pulling off his mask and gloves in the process. He was greeted by a version of The Beatles' "Don't Let Me Down," sung by Roger and supported with some nice harmonies by Phil. Emma was standing in the doorway of the control room listening as well.

"They aren't bad," said Oliver, as he walked up to Emma.

"Actually pretty good," replied Emma. "Of course, it kind of seems like cheating having the bot who can play unlimited instruments and mimic any singer. He can add orchestral arrangements when called for."

"Still, look how happy our boy is," said Oliver. "Roger's in heaven."

"Yeah, it is cute. Anyway, not to slap all the good feelings in the face, but I have some news about our sidekick," said Emma, turning back into the control room and taking a seat at one of the workstations. Oliver closed the door behind him to deaden the sound of the music.

"Wait, shouldn't she be here by now?" asked Oliver, looking up at the clock on the wall. "I thought her flight got in at 1:30."

"It did. She just wasn't on it."

"She missed the flight to her new job? That's not very professional."

"It's even more unprofessional if you get kicked off the flight to your new job," said Emma. "Which is apparently what happened."

"Really? How?"

"I don't know for sure. I just got the update from the STraP coordinator a little while ago. Something about her bag being too big to stow under the seat in front of her and then some creative rearranging of the overhead bins. Seems like maybe she tossed some things out. Most of the things. Using her powers."

"Oh, yeah, telekinetic, isn't she?"

"Yep."

"Okay, when will she be here?"

"Couple of days," said Emma. "She's taking a bus."

"STraP couldn't find a better way? Another airline? Have some other sidekick fly her out?" asked Oliver.

"I don't think the coordinator is trying to help her too much at this point. Maybe a bit of punishment. Besides, we get the benefit of a couple extra days before we have to deal with her."

"I guess that's a plus," said Oliver. He heard voices outside getting closer so he opened the door to find Roger and the Police Chief walking toward the control room talking about music. Phil followed behind.

"...and you know in that song, he never plays the same fill twice?" the Police Chief was saying. He nodded at Oliver as he entered the room. He actually seemed happy. Or rather, he didn't seemed annoyed by Oliver or by being there at the Garage. That was unusual. Even slightly unsettling.

"Really?" said Roger. "I never noticed that. There's got to be a dozen fills in there. Cool."

"Fourteen, in fact," said Phil, following the other two in. The three of them continued on into the adjoining lounge area and sat down across from each other on couches, still talking about music. Phil didn't sit down. So far in his fairly new existence as a sentient being, he still didn't see the point in sitting down if not required by the task at hand. Instead, he stood at the end of the couch across from the Police Chief. Oliver walked over.

"Um, I hate to interrupt the discussion Chief, but is something wrong?" he asked. "You're usually not here unless something is wrong. Plus you seem to be in a good mood, not that I've ever witnessed that so I could be completely off, but it's worrying me. Oh, wait, am I being fired? That would explain being here in a good mood. Or maybe you're retiring? Or taking a job in a town too small for a hero?"

The Chief gave it some thought, then said, "I kind of like any of those options, but none of those are the case. I just happened to stumble on these two playing when I came in. I didn't know that Roger played guitar or that you guys had a robot who could play everything. That's a cool toy. Did it come from the DSF?"

"No, Phil is compliments of Gray Matter," said Emma, sitting down next to the Chief.

"Phil? From Gray Matter?" said the Chief. "I don't know if I have more of a problem with the name 'Phil' or the fact that he's from the neighborhood supervillain."

"Phil's not really from him," said Roger. "I guess you could say he rebelled against his evil programming. He's been hanging with us since the attack on the GLAND base. He kinda saved my butt during that. But more importantly, he's like having the actual Sir Paul on bass."

"I didn't know you were a music fan, Chief," said Oliver, still having trouble with this new information.

"He's not just a music fan," said Roger. "The Chief's a musician himself. He's joining the band."

"The band?" asked Oliver. Things were moving very strangely now. It seemed that reality was getting kind of gooey.

"Yeah, I play drums," said the Chief, taking off his hat and smoothing down his already smooth, closely cropped white hair. "Well, I haven't been playing too regularly lately, but Rog says I can join in, so I guess I better get back at it."

"Rog?" said Oliver. Very gooey.

"Well, anyway, I guess we should talk shop. Did you come up with anything on the waterfront?" asked the Chief, his demeanor shifting to a decidedly more formal manner. It really helped Oliver's world un-goo a bit.

"Yeah, yeah, the waterfront," said Oliver, forcing his brain to get back on top of things. "In fact, I just got back from checking out a couple of leads on that. Gray Matter is definitely behind it. He's working on a plot to destabilize large portions of waterfront property. Entire blocks."

"You mean, mess them up financially?" asked Roger.

"No, I mean destabilize literally. He's planning on flooding some sections, damaging the ground below others, and even arranging to have one building fall into the lake. Plus, he's bribed several inspectors to condemn buildings that don't really warrant it. And then there's climate change."

"He's responsible for climate change?" asked the Chief.

"No, that's just kind of helping his whole plan along," said Oliver. "With the rising water level and all."

"And what exactly is the plan?" asked Emma.

"Basically he's going to get large sections of the waterfront condemned and removed. Then he's bribed various officials to help push a plan that would create a new waterfront a few blocks back from the current one. Sort of throw a whole 'waterfront refurbishment' spin on it from a public relations sort of angle. It just so happens that he owns most of where that new waterfront would be."

"Superman!" yelled Roger, pointing at Oliver.

"No," said Oliver. "SuperGuy, remember? Did you get hit in the head?"

"No, I mean Superman. The movie," said Roger. "It's like a mini Lex Luthor dump a big slice of California into the ocean thing."

"That's right," said Emma, snapping her fingers. "Love Gene Hackman."

"Right," said Oliver. "Forgot about that movie. Is he really mining movie plots for evil plans? Are we going to have sharks with laser beams attached to their heads?"

"Sorry to interrupt the fun time movie hour, but is this imminent? Am I going to have buildings falling into Lake Michigan soon?" asked the Chief.

"No," said Oliver. "In fact, I doubt it's going to happen at all now. I dismantled some pumps flooding sections underground and there were five drills destabilizing the bedrock, but they were stopped before I even got there. All dead. The electronics were fried and there were burn marks everywhere that looked particularly familiar."

"Boogaloo?" guessed Roger.

"Yeah, that's what I would say. Don't know how he caught on to it, but he's helping us by hurting Gray Matter. The interesting thing is that I don't see how he got in there with the drills. Some he could have gotten to, but a couple were in really tight spaces. He's huge. I didn't see any giant holes leading to them, so how did he get in there to destroy them?"

"Can't he travel through wires?" asked Emma. "Like when he got away the first time you fought."

"Yeah, but there still wasn't enough room for him to materialize in the spaces with the drills," replied Oliver.

"So he's doing it from within the wiring?" asked Roger.

"Maybe," said Oliver, not looking pleased. "I wasn't happy at the thought of him being able to travel almost wherever he wanted and simply popping up out of nowhere, but if he doesn't even have to materialize to cause damage, he could be really difficult to deal with."

"We can probably trace him," said Phil, surprising the others because he had been quiet for so long during the conversation.

"Really?" asked Roger.

"I would think so. He is a powerful source of energy, which should be detectable moving around the power grid, if you know what to look for," said the bot.

"Do you know what to look for?" asked Emma.

"I can probably create a program to track him," replied Phil. "If you would like that."

"I think we would," said Oliver. "It would be very useful to know if he were going to pop out of the wall socket behind me at some point." Oliver looked back at the Chief. "As for the other part of the waterfront problem, I can make a list of the various bribes. You can get things re-inspected or whatever needs to be done and that should be enough to put a stop to this plan of his."

"Sounds good," said the Chief. "But there is another reason I'm here too." He handed a folder to Oliver. "We've suddenly got a lot of new merchandise on the streets in the last couple of weeks. In fact, I'm getting reports from Madison, Chicago, Minneapolis, and other nearby cities of a large increase in smuggled goods, especially prescription medications. And right now, based on information from a few early arrests, it seems we are the point of origin."

Oliver read over some of the information in the folder. "That's a lot of stuff. How is that much merchandise flowing through the city without us noticing?"

"That's the million dollar question," said the Chief.

SUPERGUY 2: ELECTRIC BOGALOO

"Well, at least with this waterfront thing out of the way I can start concentrating on this," said Oliver.

34

"THERE he is, right there," said Raymond Joyce, pointing at the giant screen on the wall behind his desk. The screen displayed a top down view of the Tower and neighboring buildings, rendered in a way that looked a little like a heat map, but in this case, all the hot spots were levels of electrical activity. Lines running through walls and under streets could be seen, usually glowing sedately with normal levels of electrical flow. However, there was one area across the street and slightly down the block from the front entrance that glowed a bright blue even though there was nothing requiring that much power in that building.

"Isn't that a steakhouse?" asked Alice, lazily tossing three golf balls into the air with one hand.

"Yes," answered Joyce. "And right now, there seems to be enough dormant electricity sitting there to rival a power plant."

"So he's just watching us?" asked Steven.

"Apparently," said Joyce. "Has been for a while I imagine. He obviously changed his tactics after we captured him, choosing to keep us under surveillance and try to learn what we're doing. He must have figured out he can't enter the building because we would detect him, but he still managed to find out about the Waterfront Project and make a mess of that."

"You want me to go after him?" asked Alice.

"No, I think I'd prefer to let him believe he hasn't been noticed for the time being," said Joyce. "Besides, despite being a supervillain, you have a pretty good standing with the public after our little press tour, so I wouldn't want to mess that up by having you attack a random steakhouse."

"This is kind of a steak town," said Steven.

"We're going to have to be more subtle. We trapped him before so he's not going to be easy to trap again." Joyce stood up from his chair and took off the jacket of his signature three piece, grey, double breasted suit. He laid it carefully over the back of his chair and began to walk slowly around the desk, his eyes on the glowing blue blob that represented Electric Boogaloo on the wall screen. "Not only do I think he'll be harder to get where we want him this time, he'll undoubtedly manage his energy levels so he doesn't get depleted like before." Joyce gestured toward the screen. "Just judging by this data, it appears he's also gotten stronger. His current level of energy is much higher than when we had him in containment. I think he has increased the amount of energy he can store, perhaps hoping to outlast whatever we throw at him next. Or maybe just surprise us. It is certainly a large amount of power…" Joyce trailed off.

Alice watched him closely as she caught the three golf balls and set them on the desk. "You've got an idea, don't you?" she said with a smile.

"I may have a thought," said Joyce with a smile of his own.

"What do you think?" asked Roger, looking over Oliver's shoulder. Oliver was once again posing in front of his efficiency apartment mirror in the Garage.

"What's to think?" said Emma, looking over the other shoulder. "It's a cape."

"I don't know," said Oliver. His brows furrowed and he tilted his head as he looked at himself. "I guess I thought I would feel different. I know I had the messed up cape already, which was also a disappointment, but I thought that particular disappointment was because it was messed up and somehow I was feeling that on an instinctual level. With the right one, I figured I'd put it on everything would be…I don't know…better."

"You mean, there'd be music and maybe a sunbeam shining down on you?" asked Roger. "Or maybe you'd glow for a second like you leveled up in a video game."

"Exactly!" said Oliver. "Why not? A little glowing and a musical flourish wouldn't be too much to ask."

"You two are idiots," said Emma.

"But we're lovable idiots," said Roger.

"Hmm, not really," said Emma.

SUPERGUY 2: ELECTRIC BOGALOO

"Maybe I've gotten used to running around for so long without the cape that finally having it is a little anticlimactic," said Oliver.

"I can set up a speech for you at the Milwaukee Flower and Garden Society," said Emma. "I bet that would get you appreciating the cape."

Oliver turned around to face the other two. "You're probably right, but let's not do anything drastic. Besides, shouldn't the new sidekick have that gig? Where is she anyway?"

"Not here," said Emma, turning and walking toward the door of the apartment. "Follow me down to the control room while I fill you in. We have a couple more things to talk about anyway." Oliver and Roger followed her out the door, with Roger picking up the box from the capes as he went.

"You know, I'm really disappointed in their packaging this time," said Roger. "It was just a box. A plain old box." He followed Emma along the walkway to the stairs.

"I'm not," said Oliver. He floated up over the railing and drifted down to the main floor. He had walked down the stairs for days after getting the flight booster before realizing how silly it was to do that anymore.

"After the condition Oliver returned their last box, I'm not surprised they wouldn't waste anything cool on us," said Emma.

"Well, there's cool packaging, and then there's pretentious packaging," said Oliver.

"Can you really say something is pretentious if it's made out of cardboard?" asked Roger.

"I just did," said Oliver. "Anyway, back on track. Where is this new sidekick of ours? Her bus was supposed to get in this morning."

"It was. She just wasn't on it," said Emma as she passed Oliver and entered the control room. Roger and Oliver followed her inside.

"Did they lose her?" asked Roger.

"No, she managed to get kicked off the bus in Ohio somewhere," said Emma.

"How?" asked Oliver. "How does she get kicked off the bus? She just has to sit there."

"You would think," said Emma. "But apparently our girl is special that way."

"Okay. While I'm thankful for every day I don't have to spend with a probationary sidekick, these delays are just making me dread her arrival even more," said Oliver. "So where in Ohio is she and how is she getting here now?"

"She's in Columbus," said Emma, with a hint of self-satisfaction in her voice. "And I've got the next part handled."

"Wait," said Roger. "You didn't."

Emma smiled. "I did."

"What? What am I missing?" asked Oliver.

"I got her a ride with The Creeper," said Emma. "Called him up and asked if he could do us a favor and transport her the rest of the way. They should be here in about an hour or so."

"Oh, that's evil," said Oliver.

"I know."

"I'm so proud of you right now," said Roger.

A tone sounded on a number of machines in the control room then, as well as on Oliver's inner ear communicator.

"What's that?" asked Oliver.

"Oh, it's 3:00," said Roger. "The new update is live."

"New update?" asked Oliver. "What new update? And why is everything beeping?"

"The new AI update to all DSF tech equipment," said Emma. "They are streamlining the system so the same AI assists on all machines. Everything from your communicator to the new base, if you guys ever get a new base."

"Yeah, it's really cool," said Roger. "Robin can even move between devices with you to continue a conversation or task. So if you start some kind of search on your communicator, it can show you the results on your iPad or computer as you get to those."

"Robin?" asked Oliver.

"Yeah, that's the name of the AI. Like Siri or Alexa," said Emma. "So now when you want to call someone on your comm, you ask Robin to do it instead of the old way. Here, let's use it." Emma faced the main desk of the control room. "Robin, call Gigi."

"Yes, Emma, right away. Calling Gigi," answered a voice through the room speakers. The main screen at the desk woke up and the words, "Calling Gigi," glowed on the black background.

"That's pretty cool," said Roger.

"Thank you, Roger," said Robin. "I think you're pretty cool, too."

"Okay, I'm changing that to a little creepy," said Roger.

There was a little bing from the main screen and Gigi's image came up. She was standing in her command center, which had windows in the background showing the cityscape of Los Angeles. Oliver had never visited but was assured by Roger that it was spectacular, having read all about it in an issue of *Hero Tech*. It was an octagonal structure perched on the top of a building in downtown L.A., with the command center being on the top of a small tower rising above that which allowed 360 degree views of the city.

"Hey, Emma, what's up?" said Gigi.

"Nothing special, just testing out the new AI," said Emma. "But I did want to show you our boy in his new cape." She pointed at Oliver, who took a little bow.

"Thanks for making that call," said Oliver. "I have a feeling you saved us weeks of time."

"Months," said Emma.

"My pleasure," said Gigi. "If I can't abuse my power for my friends, what good is it?"

"Well, I'm warning you now that the next time something like this comes up, I'm calling you first thing," said Oliver.

"You should," said Gigi. "We help each other fight villains, we might as well help each other fight the DSF uniform folks."

"The true villains," said Roger.

An intermittent tone started going off in the background of Gigi's picture. She looked over at another part of the desk.

"Well, it looks like I'm needed elsewhere, so I've gotta go," she said. "You look good in the new cape Oliver, go out and show it off. Make us fellow capists proud."

"I will," he said. "Thanks again." Gigi pressed a button and the screen went black.

"Call terminated," said Robin. "Is there anything else you need, Emma?"

"No, thank you, Robin," said Emma. She stepped back from the desk and looked at the other two uncertainly. "Do you think I have to thank the AI? Does it notice if I'm polite? Does it care?"

"Got me," said Oliver. "Is it male or female? Can we change which it is? I honestly can't tell by the voice."

"That's on purpose," said Roger. "It's made to be androgynous. Avoids all the issues of whether it's demeaning to have your assistant be a man or a woman. Personally, I'm fond of the old robotic voice from back in the day. That was so obviously artificial you wouldn't care either way."

"Oh, *Robin*, I get it now. Don't know if I see the need of it, but I get it," said Oliver.

"Yes, Oliver," said Robin through the room speakers. "Searching donut needlepoint cadet. Results on screen. Do you need anything else?" Text with the search results were displayed on the main screen.

Oliver stared at the screen, which had "Did you mean *donut needlepoint caveat?*" at the top of the results. "No, Robin. I think you nailed it," said Oliver. He looked at the others. "Maybe I'll just stick to making calls."

"Those fools!" said Dr. Misk in a sort of strangled growl. He was not a happy evil scientist. "Who can't read schematics? It's not that difficult." He was looking at the schematics of the transporter on his iPad so he could double check whether the wiring had been done correctly when the technicians built the Tower transporter. Dr. Misk had been supervising the transporter build at the Washington Island location while this one was being constructed. The sparking wires he had noticed from the first few transfers had got him investigating the problem and now it was evident that someone had used a smaller gauge wire on the transporter than what was indicated on the schematics. Whether that person had been out of the correct gauge, and didn't think substituting a smaller gauge mattered, or they were just dumb was another question. It couldn't have been a construction bot, because they would have followed the schematics precisely, so it was obviously human error. Dr. Misk wasn't really fond of humans, and this wasn't helping their cause. If he could find the person responsible, Dr. Misk would make sure they were first in line when it was time to test the transporter on a human. Or maybe sooner. Sometimes it's worth it to take some leaps and, in the process, save a few rats.

Dr. Misk climbed down the ladder leaning against the side of the transporter and walked out the door toward the maintenance supply room in search of the correct gauge of wire. He grumbled most of the way there, assuming every person he saw was the one who had failed him, and once randomly threw half an onion bagel he had kept in his lab coat pocket from breakfast at a passerby. They probably weren't the guilty one but they looked like the kind of person who might invite the guilty one to a party or to be in their fantasy football league.

Entering the maintenance supply room, Dr. Misk admired the incredibly well organized space, complete with sections of tools and supplies sorted by type and use. Things were color coded and labeled in large, easily readable fonts. Definitely the work of a bot, thank goodness. Dr. Misk found the section containing the supply of wire, but the shelf with the gauge he needed was empty. He checked adjoining shelves and spaces in case a roll had been stored in the wrong place but found none. Replacing the wire would have to wait for now. It probably wasn't extremely vital since the transporter was functioning, but eventually it would burn out and there would be no more transports until the wiring was replaced. Whether or not the material in transport at the time of the failure would survive wasn't a question Dr. Misk could answer off hand. Shutting down the transports wasn't an option either. There was a schedule to keep. With a sigh, Dr. Misk pulled out his iPad and put in an order for the wire, marking it the highest priority with a note to notify him as soon as it was in. That was all he could do for the moment.

35

"**So,** she wasn't freaked out in the least after being dropped off by The Creeper?" asked Oliver. He was referring to the evening two nights before when the new sidekick had finally made it to the Garage. Oliver had missed the sidekick's arrival because he was called away on an emergency with Ohio Man and Metal dealing with a multi-barge accident. The cleanup had taken the better part of two days and he had finally gotten back minutes earlier. He had missed meeting the sidekick just then because she left twenty minutes before to go do a podcast interview with a local newspaper guy. Apparently she also had to watch *Big Trouble in Little China* before going. Oliver wasn't sure why.

"No, not freaked out at all," said Emma. "Of course, I haven't had a lot of experience with her so I don't know her personality at all, but she seemed fine."

"Other than being very rude," said Roger. He looked at Oliver. "She was very rude."

"Well, yeah. There's that," said Emma. "She came across exactly as described in her file. Or maybe worse. If she could be worse, than what was described."

"I vote worse," said Roger. "Sometimes people can be mean to authority figures or bosses, but cool with us normal folks, but she wasn't like that. Pretty much mean across the board."

Emma looked off at the ceiling in thought. "It almost makes me like my niece a little more because she kinda has the excuse of being nine years old…but no." She shook her head. "She's a little witch, too."

"Okay, well I guess we just keep sending her out on talks and visits and PR appearances and whatever else until we find some way to trade her in," said Oliver. "I can handle mean for a little while."

"It's not just that. Remember the kleptomaniac thing?" asked Emma. "That's already been a problem."

"What? She take the stapler?" asked Oliver. He looked around the control room. "Do we have a stapler?"

"She stole my car," said Roger.

"What now?"

"My car. Come here," he said, waving a hand to follow as he stood up and walked out the door. With Oliver and Emma in tow, he led them past Emma's office and the bathroom to the new kitchen next to the stairs. Roger pointed. His car sat at an angle, half under the stairs with a tarp over it and a cardboard box of assorted, slightly deflated basketballs sitting on the hood.

"We ask her where it's gone and she doesn't know," said Emma. "No clue. We are literally having the conversation right next to the car."

"Okay…but you could take the tarp off and drive it away, right?" asked Oliver.

"Oh, yeah, that's what I did yesterday," said Roger. "Then I drove in here this morning and parked in my normal spot and two hours later it's right back here. But this time, there's that box of old basketballs on it. That really hides it."

"And she doesn't seem to realize that you know?" asked Oliver. "I mean, it's a car. Obviously." Oliver nodded his head toward the car to show how obvious it was. Roger just shrugged.

"She's also stolen Phil," said Emma. "Twice. He just walks out of her apartment after she leaves, but it's still a bit awkward. We ask where he is, she says she doesn't know, hasn't seen him, blah blah blah." Just then the door of the sidekick's efficiency apartment on the second floor opened and Phil walked out. "Make that three times," said Emma, without missing a beat.

"I may need to lodge a complaint," said Phil upon reaching the bottom of the stairs.

"Well, we can't be having that," said Oliver. "I need Phil so we can track Boogaloo. And it's not like she's stealing little things like office supplies. I thought it would be stuff like that. Phil's vital equipment, not to mention a sentient being. That might be kidnapping. Can we send her back for kidnapping?"

"That's a good thought," said Emma, heading for her office. "I'm going to go look into that."

SUPERGUY 2: ELECTRIC BOGALOO

An hour after Oliver had moved Roger's car back to his parking space and made sure Phil turned on a personal beacon so they could track his location, he sat with the bot in the control room looking at a display of the city's power grid. It wasn't a live feed, but showed average usage over the past week, and they were using a program written by Phil to search through the data to find where Electric Boogaloo had been traveling in the city. They had just discovered some interesting results when the Police Chief walked in with Roger.

"Quit playing Tetris," said Roger. "The boss man is here."

The Chief chuckled. "Tetris. At least that's a game I've heard of," he said.

Oliver spun around in his chair, looking at the two men. "I want it on record that I'm not a fan of you guys becoming so buddy buddy. I find it uncomfortable."

"I think I can speak for the Chief when I say we don't care," said Roger. "Besides, if you would just learn to play bass, you could join the band and not be so jealous."

"Let's not be hasty," said the Chief, putting a hand on Roger's shoulder. "No need to sink the band just to make Oliver happy. I'm perfectly content with him being uncomfortable."

"Yeah, me too, I guess," said Roger. He looked back at Oliver. "Okay, you're out of the band."

"Well, I'll try to get over it," said Oliver. "So what's this new information you have for us?" The Chief had called earlier to say he would be stopping by with some details about their investigation into the increase in smuggled goods in the city.

"First, we can't find anything about how the merchandise is getting into the city. Not a hint," said the Chief, pulling a chair away from the desk and sitting down.

"Neither have we," said Oliver.

"I have looked through all kinds of recent data," said Phil, who stood by the desk next to Oliver. "I've searched shipping manifests, matched them with shipments inland from the docks, gone over all of the security and traffic camera footage in the city, and I can't find any sign of something that might be what we are looking for."

"And yet with no apparent source, we have plenty of supply on the streets," said the Chief. "So I decided to track it from the sellers backward as far as I could. Not to bore you with all the details of real police work, but the trucks delivering the merchandise are coming out of Joyce Industries Tower. They're disguised as various companies and professions to make it harder to spot, but it's way too much traffic to be normal." He held out some surveillance photos of different trucks exiting the Tower. There were delivery trucks, maintenance vans, and even a plumber. "That might be a real plumber, I'm not sure," said the Chief.

"Okay, so we know where the distribution hub is, but where's the supply coming from in the first place?" asked Oliver.

"Could they be making it in the Tower?" asked Roger. He gestured at Phil. "They make bots by the bunches, what's a little contraband?"

"That's an interesting thought," said the Chief, considering it. "But no, the materials we've seized have been produced outside the country. There's no need to make them look like they came from somewhere else. That seems needlessly excessive, although that does sound like something Gray Matter would do."

"Whatever the answer, it corresponds in an interesting way with what Oliver and I have found out about Electric Boogaloo's movements within the city power grid," said Phil.

"Yeah," said Oliver, nodding at the bot. "The Tower. Robin? Put up the map of the city power grid we were looking at." Oliver swung around in his chair to face the main screen.

"Right away, Oliver," said Robin. "Have I told you how much I like that new cape?"

"Uh, no."

"Well, I've looked back at older pictures and footage of you before the cape, and while you looked good then—" Robin was putting up a series of photos showing Oliver in his suit before getting the cape. There was one from the press conference introducing him as the city's hero, one with a torn and singed suit after his first big fight with a villain, one in the new efficiency apartment in the Garage, and another in the apartment when he was changing and only had his socks and mask on. "—I think the cape really completes the picture." A last picture came up showing Oliver in just the cape and his underwear, sitting on his couch eating ice cream out of a carton.

"Oh, good lord," said the Chief.

"Robin?"

"Yes, Oliver?"

"Could we have the map, please?"

"Yes, Oliver." A new picture came up on the main screen.

"Here's what we found," said Oliver, trying to push on. "Boogaloo's not really moving around much. He's traveled to a couple different Joyce Industries properties, as well as to the waterfront when he disabled those drills, but all the rest of the time he's been camped out right here." Oliver pointed to a spot on the screen. "Joyce Tower."

"But only outside?" asked the Chief, standing up to get a better look at the screen.

"He has never entered the building," said Phil.

"Why not?" asked Roger.

"No clue," said Oliver. "He just seems to be watching. He did leave to take out those drills, so maybe he somehow discovered what Gray Matter was doing and acted on it. Maybe that's his plan for the moment."

"So what's the next step?" asked the Chief.

"I think Phil and I are going down to the Tower to take a closer look," said Oliver. "Maybe see if we can come up with some way we might trap Boogaloo using the grid, maybe try to figure out why he's watching the Tower and being so cautious. Generally, just try to collect more information."

"Sounds like a plan," said the Chief. "But can you give it an hour or two? I brought my set and want to jam with these guys for awhile."

36

OLIVER and Phil eased up to the end of the alley and peeked around the corner. On the opposite side of the street stood Joyce Industries Tower, a silver and glass structure rising thirty-two stories. Oliver glanced up at the top two floors and their giant glass windows. Behind one of those was Joyce's office, which made use of the two stories to create a huge space for what Oliver could only guess was his huge ego. Besides the office, those floors contained Joyce's extensive apartment and adjoining offices for his support staff. Oliver had jumped through that office window several months earlier after his first meeting with Joyce, on his way to help with a fire downtown. Joyce had sent an excessive bill to the city and Oliver had gotten a motivational phone call from the Mayor.

"He's still there," said Phil, looking down at the next cross street where the steakhouse was located. Oliver could only see the steakhouse, but Phil had a real time map of the power grid in his head, so he could see the villain's electrical signature. "I've located several security and traffic cameras that he is monitoring to watch the building."

"Are we clear?" asked Oliver. He waved at a young boy walking by with his mother, who had noticed the hero hiding in the alley. It was difficult to do surveillance in a superhero costume. He pulled his cape around himself in a useless gesture to be less noticeable.

"Yes, he seems only interested in the building."

"But he hasn't tried to go inside?"

"I can't say for certain, but from here I can see what looks like monitors in the building electrical system. They would detect him entering, so I assume that's why he hasn't gone inside," answered Phil.

"Do you think Joyce knows he's there?" asked Oliver. He paused to take a selfie with two teenage girls. He wasn't sure how long they were going to remain unnoticed at this pace. And it wasn't just Oliver. Phil, being a seven foot tall combat robot, wasn't exactly blending in either.

"I'm not sure," said Phil. "I would guess the monitors are there to watch for him, but I don't know if they know he's sitting right outside their door."

"So the question is, what do I do? Assuming our new friend Goth Spark is inside there with Joyce, I have three supervillains sitting inside a one block area in the middle of the city. And, if I had to guess, one of them is really pissed off at the other two."

"They do appear to be at a stalemate, whether all parties involved are aware of it or not," said Phil. "As long as Electric Boogaloo continues to be content to watch, things should remain peaceful. It could stay this way indefinitely."

SUPERGUY 2: ELECTRIC BOGALOO

Oliver looked at Phil. "Okay, that kinda sounded like you just jinxed us," he said. "Did you just jinx us?"

"Hold on, I'm new to that term," said Phil. He seemed to be thinking about it. "From what I can tell from a quick search of popular culture, that is a silly thing to believe. My statement about the current situation, which I am not involved in, cannot affect it in any way. I am merely an observer." Phil looked blankly at Oliver. Oliver thought the bot might be trying to portray an innocent expression, but since he had no moveable facial features, the result was blankness. Suddenly there was a slight tremor that Oliver could feel through his feet. It built in strength slightly, peaked, and then faded away. Oliver looked around the street to see if any of the pedestrians had noticed, but no one seemed alarmed. Perhaps it was just something only he would notice because of his super abilities. Phil had also noticed, though, his head turning toward the Tower, and then down the street to the steakhouse. He looked back at Oliver.

"I may have jinxed us," he said.

Alex was getting bored. Phenomenally bored. He was beginning to think back with fondness to the brainwashing videos when he had been a prisoner. At least they gave him something to think about, even if it was just extensive edits. Now the best he had was analyzing traffic patterns around Joyce Tower and, after hundreds of hours of study, it seemed like those were pretty efficient. Beyond introducing flying cars, there wasn't much to be done. Not being able to enter the Tower was the real problem. Alex had gotten lucky getting the information he did about the waterfront and being able to take action on that, but since then there had been nothing useful. Either no one spoke outside the building about sensitive projects, or they weren't a part of the more sensitive projects. Most of the conversations he overheard as people left the building were about accounting department gossip and binge worthy television shows. While that had given him several things to watch to pass the time, it hadn't given him anything to act on against Gray Matter. Alex really wanted to act. For the thousandth time, he contemplated the possibility of just entering the building and attacking, but for the thousandth time he decided against it. They would see him coming and he didn't think he could take that chance.

Then, in the next second, his chance came. He detected the same surge of power below street level under the Tower that had become a routine occurrence during his surveillance. It increased steadily as it usually did, but instead of shutting down after the normal duration, it kept going for about five additional seconds. In that small amount of time, the power level reached a considerably higher peak than usual and Alex saw the building's grid light up in a way that it never had before. The surge was so powerful that it made the tripwires on the access points into the Tower blind to everything, including a giant electrical monster. In that split second, Alex made his decision, shot across the street, and entered the Tower.

SUPERGUY 2: ELECTRIC BOGALOO

Gray Matter looked at the control screen in front of him. It was the only thing currently powered on inside his giant exoskeleton suit. He watched the bright green glow that represented Electric Boogaloo on the map as the turbines two subfloors down powered up. There wasn't actually a transfer happening, this was just for show, to lure the monster into the building and into his trap. He had adjusted the monitors on the Tower's grid to appear to be overwhelmed with a larger than usual power surge, giving Electric Boogaloo the opportunity to infiltrate the building, and he hoped the villain would take the bait. The glowing green blob on the screen didn't move for a long second, but then it suddenly shot below the street along the power lines and into the Tower. The turbines were already powering down but the supervillain counted on their existence being enough to attract Electric Boogaloo to the underground floors.

At that point, the monster would surely detect Gray Matter's high powered suit and come to investigate their location in the loading dock and warehouse floor on the first sublevel below the Tower. It was a giant, open room made even more open by the fact that Gray Matter had most of the trucks and supplies removed in preparation for the battle to come. The ceilings were extra high to accommodate supply trucks and there were support pillars at regular intervals breaking up the space.

Once Electric Boogaloo appeared in the loading dock, Gray Matter and Alice would put his plan into action. Something he was calling Plan Drago. Gray Matter knew he wouldn't be able to trap Boogaloo like before, that would be too obvious. The villain would not enter an area that had no escape and would be too smart to let himself get completely depleted like before, so Gray Matter intended to treat it like a boxing match. He and Alice would force Boogaloo to fight for a long time, getting him tired and using a lot of energy, but not enough that he would feel the need to escape. Then, at the right moment, they would hit him with a blast so powerful it would put an end to him. It was a simple plan in a way, but they had to be very precise. Gray Matter had done the calculations and his suit computer would be monitoring Boogaloo's power levels so they would know when the time was right and they could unleash a combined massive strike. Between Alice's extremely high level of power and what he was going to be able to reach with his suit, which was made of a special advanced superhero quality metal and designed to absorb electricity and store it away, they would be able to achieve the amount of power needed to take Boogaloo out. At least according to Gray Matter's calculations, which he was certain were correct. There was a possibility that the monster could survive, but it was very, very slim. Well, to be honest, it was basically zero.

Flipping the switches to power up his suit, Gray Matter turned his head to Alice, who was contentedly tossing six wrenches of various sizes high into the air, taking advantage of the tall ceilings on the loading dock.

"Get ready," said Gray Matter. "He's coming."

"He's inside," said Phil.

"What happened?" asked Oliver. "What was that vibration?"

"It was a large power surge below the Tower," replied Phil. "In what must be a sub level about forty feet below the ground. It produced a surge throughout the building that seems to have temporarily blinded the sensors in place to detect Electric Boogaloo. He saw it too and took the opportunity to sneak inside the building's perimeter."

"So now the three supervillains who don't get along are all inside the same building?"

"I'm afraid so."

"You really did jinx us."

"I find that a silly notion, and without logical basis, but yeah, probably," said Phil.

Oliver looked over at Joyce Tower. "I've got to get in there."

"Can't you just fly through a window or a wall?" asked the bot.

"I don't really have cause," said Oliver. "We think the big ball of energy that went in is really a large blue electrical monster wanted by the police, but I don't know if that will stand up in court."

"I can get you in," said Phil.

"How?"

"I hacked the system to report my destruction during the battle at the base, but I duplicated my user codes and copied them over as another bot just in case I wanted access again," said Phil. "Basically, I can let you in the back door."

"Then let's go," said Oliver. They sprinted across the street, with Oliver managing to sign an autograph for a guy who ran alongside him at the same time, and they went around the corner to a side entrance. Phil punched a code into a keypad and pulled the door open. Once inside, Phil led Oliver down a couple of hallways and into an empty office.

"I can plug into the building system here and help guide you," said the bot, sitting down at the desk. "Robin? Keep an open channel between Oliver and me."

"Will do," said Robin.

"Just head to the end of the hall to the stairwell and start down. I'll let you know where they are," said Phil.

"Gotcha. You'll sit here while I go searching for three super powerful supervillains who are probably not going to just have a nice chat. I sure wish the serum didn't make me think this was the right thing to do," he said, ducking out the door and closing it behind him.

Alex prowled through the power lines down to the sublevel where he detected the original surge. It was almost gone by the time he got there, but he found a group of specialized small power turbines covering half of a large room. Even though he didn't have a sense of smell, either in his current pure energy form or as a physical being, he could almost smell the amount of power the turbines were capable of creating. He floated along around them and through them and then followed the path of the energy, almost like a bloodhound on a scent, as it left the room and traveled upstairs.

One floor up and on the opposite side of the building he found where the trail led. A large metal rectangle in a big room. The rectangle was reinforced with superhero quality metal inside and out and the door stood open. It was empty. Alex didn't find these things familiar. Neither the power turbines on the floor below or this curious box. They hadn't been here back when he worked for Gray Matter. The sublevels below the Tower had always been there, of course, but during Alex's time they were only research and development departments.

Then Alex caught wind of something else. Something on the floor above. Another source of power, growing stronger by the second. Alex knew the floor above was the warehouse and loading dock on the first sublevel of the Tower. He slid through the lines to have a look.

37

"**HE'S** here," said Gray Matter, but that became pretty evident when the brainiac supervillain was blasted across the floor of the loading dock, ricocheted off a pillar, and slid to an abrupt stop against a forklift. Electric Boogaloo had materialized in a split second out of a combination of wall sockets and light fixtures. Coalescing from bright blue electrical energy into a menacing and mountainous presence in the room, he attacked without any hesitation. Gray Matter checked his monitor as he pushed himself to his feet and saw that the suit had worked perfectly. Not only was he unhurt, but his battery storage capacity was already one tenth full. As he rose to his full height, well over twelvefeet in the mechanical exoskeleton, Gray Matter was sure he saw a look of surprise and recognition on the face of the monster. Alex had never known about this suit, as it had only been the spark of an idea back when he worked for Gray Matter. Since then, it had become real, been refined several times, and most recently been adapted to work specifically against this threat. It was basically the shell of a bot, but much larger and shinier due to the superhero quality metal, with the interior space perfectly fit for its five foot two inch operator. Gray Matter liked to think of it as his Lex Luthor power armor. A wide mesh faceplate allowed Gray Matter a clear view and he was certain his former employee could see in well enough to recognize who was operating the machine. That made him smile.

Gray Matter took advantage of Boogaloo's hesitation and fired a blast from his shoulder mounted laser. It hit the monster's right knee and knocked it out from under its body, just as Alice hit it from its left side with a blast of her own. These two shots combined to send the target spinning over and tumbling along the floor. However, the monster was surprisingly agile, and it rolled right back up on its feet and sent multiple spheres of blue electricity flying at both Gray Matter and Alice. Alice managed to dodge three spheres before being hit by a fourth that knocked her halfway across the large room. She was finally able to reverse the momentum with her flight power and bank back around toward her attacker. Luckily for Gray Matter, he didn't want to dodge the spheres and he let them hit him one after the other. The power of the blows still knocked him backward, his large metal feet creating a shower of sparks as they slid against the floor, but the shots did not hurt the villain, they only gave him more energy. Still, it was best if Gray Matter wasn't obvious that the shots weren't having an effect, otherwise Boogaloo might get suspicious and stop supplying him with power. It was important for the plan that they trade blows for a good ten rounds, so Boogaloo depleted just enough energy to be vulnerable while Gray Matter's suit captured enough for the decisive shot.

Alice came soaring back across the room and threw a combination of three shots in the shape of giant fists at Electric Boogaloo. The first landed squarely on the side of the monster's head, but he managed to throw up a shield to block the second, and then lithely step behind a pillar which took the brunt of the third fist. Chunks of concrete flew off the pillar and tumbled across the floor like broken ice. Alice swooped around the far side of the pillar, trying to catch Boogaloo off guard and hit him from the side, but he erected a shield reaching from the floor to the ceiling. As Alice flew past, looking for the end, the monster pushed the entire wall forward as a weapon, smashing it into the flying villain and sending her careening off to skip along the concrete floor like a rock on a flat pond.

Gray Matter uttered an uncharacteristic growl as he watched Alice tumble away, and launched two missiles from a rack attached to his back. They flew out sideways in a long arc curving around behind Electric Boogaloo as Gray Matter moved forward firing a steady stream of blasts from his laser cannon. Boogaloo threw various shields up against the laser blasts, easily absorbing or deflecting each one, but then the missiles reached their target, exploding against the monster's back and throwing him forward to the ground. The blue creature was slightly stunned and slow to rise, but Gray Matter didn't press his attack, remaining in control enough to know that he didn't want to scare his prey away. This was still the early rounds. Gray Matter needed to extend the fight and keep his opponent battling until he could be sure of finishing it. To Gray Matter's satisfaction, Electric Boogaloo got back to his feet, making no sign of wanting to escape. The monster

SUPERGUY 2: ELECTRIC BOGALOO

merely let out his own growl and threw a succession of bright blue electric bolts at his enemy.

Oliver was skipping down the steps in the stairwell when his comm beeped.

"Emergency call from Emma," said Robin.

"Okay," said Oliver. "Put her through." He slowed down as he reached the sublevel three landing. "Emma? What's the emergency?"

"It's Gloria," said Emma.

"Who?"

"The sidekick, our sidekick. She's the emergency."

"Ah, well, that's a little inconvenient at the moment."

"Why?"

"I'm kinda in the middle of something."

"What?"

"Joyce Tower," said Oliver. "I'm in Joyce Tower. There was a power surge and Boogaloo went inside, so I followed him in."

"Well, your sidekick is currently throwing a fit in the newspaper office," said Emma.

"What? Why?"

"The panicked person on the phone, who identified himself as the producer of the podcast she was doing, says it's because she disagreed on some of the finer points of Kurt Russell's film career," said Emma. "Namely, his best movie."

"That's easy. *The Thing*," said Oliver.

"I'm going *Silkwood*," said Emma. "Roger is here, he says *Escape From New York*."

"I'm not familiar with his films," said Phil, popping onto the channel. "Give me a second. *Tombstone*."

"Oh, good call," said Oliver.

"Wait, we're getting sidetracked," said Emma. "What am I supposed to do about this? Can you go get her? The newspaper office is only a few blocks away."

"I don't know," said Oliver. "I guess this technically isn't an emergency. Nothing's happened."

"Yet," said Phil. "Hold on. Boogaloo is moving. Going up. Second sublevel, now the first." Dull thumps sounded through the walls. "Those were explosions."

"Okay, now it's an emergency," said Oliver, starting back up the stairs. Then he remembered he had this cool ability to fly, so he jumped in the air and corkscrewed up the stairwell. "Emma, just call what's her name—Gloria—back to the base. Tell her it's an emergency involving supervillains. Then just keep her there. Say they might attack the Garage so she's gotta be there on high alert. Also tell her if *Big Trouble in Little China* wasn't at least in the conversation, then we're sending her back tomorrow."

Alex watched his array of bolts pound into Gray Matter in his shiny metal suit. It wasn't something he remembered from when he worked for the man, so it must be new, not to mention an obvious huge overcompensation by being twice as tall as the supervillain inside. But at least it made it an even easier target to hit. Which Alex did again, firing another succession of smaller bolts in a spread pattern at Gray Matter, and then following that up with one massive bolt coming in behind, hopefully unnoticed. It wasn't. Several of the smaller bolts found their mark, peppering Gray Matter in the torso and upper legs, and making him stumble backward. Then the big bolt arrived—its diameter about the size of the power suit's chest—picked the supervillain up off the ground and sent him flying into the far wall, instantly forming a web of cracks in the concrete radiating out from the point of impact.

Alex started forward with the intent to pin Gray Matter to the wall with another giant blast, but he was knocked off his feet by Alice as she rocketed into his ribs, surrounded in a bluish black shell of energy. She folded him over and carried him along until she threw him forward into the forklift Gray Matter had collided with earlier. The forklift went spiraling off into the air and Boogaloo rolled to a stop. He quickly got to his knees and erected a large curved wall in front of him for protection while he got back to his feet. Once he was ready again, he threw the wall forward like the blade of a bulldozer, hoping he might get lucky and catch one of his adversaries by accident. The thirty foot wide moving wall split around pillars as it went, ripping out chunks of concrete and leaving them skittering along the pavement, until it eventually traveled the length of the room to collide with a thunk against the far wall.

As Alex watched, Goth Spark circled back around the far end of the room and began to approach on his right side. Gray Matter stepped out from behind one of the crumbling pillars and began to advance on Alex's left. Alex searched the room with his eyes once again, looking for any kind of trap, but he couldn't see anything. He could feel all the sources of power around him, the lights, the sockets, even computer terminals near a couple of the walls, so he had plenty of escape routes. So for now, it was safe to stay and fight, and so far he felt he was holding his own against his two foes. Curling his hands into fists, Alex started walking forward.

The plastic panel next to the door stated that Oliver had reached Sublevel 1: Loading Dock. He pulled the door open and flew inside ready to land smack dab in the middle of a battle by the way it sounded. He wasn't disappointed. There were echoing rumbles of explosions, smoke floating through the air making everything slightly hazy, the smell of burnt oil, and loose pieces of concrete falling to the ground from various places in the room. It was like the Platonic ideal of a battle in a parking garage-like setting and Oliver was wading into it hip deep. Until he wasn't. A forklift slammed into him out of nowhere and knocked him back out the door.

"Not fair," mumbled Oliver, as he pushed off the far wall of the stairwell and flew back to the door. "I hadn't even really joined the fight yet." The forklift was wedged in the doorway and Oliver kicked it out into the room. It bounced along the pavement, nicked a pillar and spun in a circle of skittering sparks until it ground to a halt, somewhat worse for wear. Oliver took a peek inside the loading dock, just in case there were more flying forklifts, and then shot through the doorway, skimming along the wall to the left so he could assess the situation. He spotted Electric Boogaloo easily enough. The giant blue monster wasn't far from the door where Oliver entered and he was throwing out blasts of electricity at two different targets. One was Goth Spark, flying toward Boogaloo on the far side of the room while holding a curved shield of energy in front of her, and the other target was a massive metal robot-looking thing that was being pelted with electric bolts. Oliver was pretty sure he could see someone inside operating the giant bot.

"Phil, you still there?" he said into his comm.

"Yes, he is," answered Robin. "I have kept you connected as instructed."

"Oh, yeah, okay. Thanks, Robin."

"My pleasure. I will not disconnect you until instruct me to do so either."

"Yeah, great—"

"If you have any other needs, just ask. For example, you can ask me what the temperature is, or when the next new moon—"

"No, thank you, Robin. Nothing else," said Oliver. "Phil?"

"Yes," said Phil.

"Are you monitoring all this? Can you see in here?"

"I can now. The electrical system is a little shaky with all the surges and things exploding and such, but I got a couple of cameras working again," said Phil.

"Is that Gray Matter in the big robot suit?"

"Yes, it is."

"Have you ever seen that before?"

"No, I'm not familiar with it but it looks like a large scale mech battle bot with special superhero quality metal plating, modified to hold a human operator," said Phil. "It's equipped with a shoulder mounted heavy laser and there's a missile launcher system on the back. Plus it seems to have a very large capacity battery pack as well, which would create an incredibly high energy output. There's something very unique about the build."

"But the short answer is that it's very big and very powerful and loaded with weapons," said Oliver.

"Pretty much."

"Okay, thanks." Oliver decided he might as well move past the assessment phase of the operation because he wasn't much liking how that was going, and move on to the "start hitting things" phase. Making a sharp banking turn, he lined up on the back of Gray Matter in the power suit and picked up speed to ram him. He was beginning to get really annoyed that he couldn't shoot things like everybody else and questioned whether he should have done something about that instead of getting a cape. He didn't get to resolve that line of questioning because the shoulder laser on Gray Matter's suit rotated 180 degrees and fired a blast right at his face as he closed in. Oliver tried to bank out of the way but the laser caught his thigh and sent him spinning out of control, crashing completely through one of the support pillars, nicking the top of the forklift, which flipped into the air, and finally slamming to a halt against the wall not far from the door he entered. The forklift fell to the ground, bounced twice and slid to a halt just short of Oliver.

"Totally surprised that didn't land on me," said Oliver.

Phil's voice came through the comm. "Apparently the suit has a pretty sophisticated sensor system too," he said. "I think he saw you coming."

"You think?" said Oliver, getting to his feet and pushing the forklift out of his way. "You couldn't have included that in your original assessment?"

"I'm a work in progress," said the bot.

SUPERGUY 2: ELECTRIC BOGALOO

"Aren't we all," said Oliver. Before he could do anything else, Electric Boogaloo went on the attack. He fired a band of electricity that spread into a bright blue web, attaching itself to the floor, ceiling, and nearby pillars in front of Goth Spark, who decided to try and ram through instead of avoid it. That didn't work. As she hit the web and started to push it outward, additional strands of electricity wrapped around her from the sides, effectively trapping her in a ball. More strands connected to the ceiling, floor, and nearby pillars, to anchor the ensnared supervillain in place.

Gray Matter reacted to this by launching more missiles in the same pattern as before and firing rapid blasts from his laser. This time, however, Electric Boogaloo was ready, throwing up an electrical shield at his back while he formed a huge hand of energy to block the laser blasts. The missiles exploded harmlessly against the shield and, as Boogaloo kept Gray Matter occupied with his giant hand blocking the laser, he snaked a band of electrical energy along the ground that wrapped itself around the power suit multiple times. Lifting Gray Matter off the ground, Boogaloo proceeded to smash the villain against the floor, each time harder than the last. Soon his backswing was thumping his prey against the ceiling as well, showering chunks of concrete all around and knocking a large piece of the metal plating off the back of the power armor. Then with one last powerful swing, Boogaloo plowed Gray Matter straight through the floor and into the sublevel below, creating a massive hole. The band of electricity dissipated but Boogaloo didn't stand around. He raised his arms, which began to glow with bright blue energy, and then he slammed them onto the floor in front of him, breaking another huge hole in the concrete floor. He paused for a split second, throwing a look at the still trapped Goth Spark, and dropped through the hole.

"Whoa," was all Oliver could say.

38

"**BOOGALOO** is now on sublevel two," said Phil.

"I might have guessed that," said Oliver. "You know, I'm not entirely sure I want to go down there."

"I know I'm new to superheroes, and to being someone who gets to have an opinion at all, but I don't find that to be a very hero-like thing to say," said Phil.

"Unfortunately, all I get to do is say those things," said Oliver, stepping close to the hole Boogaloo made and skirting its edge as he peeked down. The monster wasn't in sight. "I will still have to act in a hero-like manner." He walked over to the hole that Gray Matter went through and peered carefully down that. No sign of the supervillain either.

"Phil, do you have the layout of that level?" asked Oliver. "Can they see each other?" There was a succession of loud thumps from below. "Okay, don't answer that."

"They both ended up in a long hallway running the length of the floor," said Phil. "However, they are quickly widening the hallway at the moment."

"Sounds like it," said Oliver. He stepped over to the piece of metal plating that fell off of Gray Matter's armor and picked it up. It was surprisingly light for its size, probably lighter than other superhero quality metal Oliver had held. It was about six feet tall by five feet wide and the support bracing on the back side made a rather convenient handhold. "Seems like everyone else has a shield of some kind so I might as well, too." He walked back over to the hole and dropped through.

Gray Matter shook his head, attempting to clear it. The super serums came with a built in ability to quickly recover, but being tossed around like a rag doll by another super powered being still tended to knock a bit of the evil air out of a villain. Sensors inside his suit were flashing red. He rose to his knees in time to see the ceiling farther down the hall come crashing down and a second later Electric Boogaloo landed on the rubble. Without hesitating, Gray Matter fired repeated blasts with his laser as he stood and stepped through a doorway to his right. The door wasn't open, so he crashed through it, and further damaged the wall running down the hall because he continued to fire the laser even after he could no longer see his target. Soon he was just blowing holes in the far wall of the room he had sidestepped into, but was content to continue the strategy until he could ascertain how much damage his suit had taken. The ceilings on this level weren't nearly as high as the loading dock, but they were still a comfortable twelve feet. That is, comfortable for a normal person. Not so great for a supervillain in power armor, but it was doable.

Electric Boogaloo didn't seem to mind not seeing a target either, as large blue projectiles of concentrated electrical energy popped through the far wall and sailed past Gray Matter to punch holes into the wall behind him. Setting his laser to fire a suppression pattern through the walls, the supervillain finally took a second to check the suit damage. He was very pleasantly surprised. The alerts weren't for damage, they were telling him the storage batteries were fully charged, and in fact the auxiliary battery was also up to 86 percent. The time spent coiled up in Boogaloo's grasp, while being extremely loud and somewhat painful with all the slamming around, had also been like plugging directly into the blue beast, charging the batteries much more quickly than it would have taken if he had just slowly soaked up individual blasts. Gray Matter was ready for the final blow.

"Alice? Are you there?" he asked through his comm. He hadn't heard from her since she was trapped in Boogaloo's web. "Alice?"

"Raymond...out," came a garbled reply. The web of electricity was obviously interfering with the comms, but Gray Matter was still relieved to hear her voice.

"Alice, you're a little fuzzy. Can you repeat that?" asked Gray Matter.

"I'm almost...(static). Repeat. I'm almost out," said Alice. The transmission became clearer with each second. Gray Matter assumed that was a result of her getting closer to being free of the web.

"Let me know when you're out," said Gray Matter. "My battery is full so I'm ready to fire. Hold back until we can get him in a good position, then we can surprise him. I'll try to lure him into the transporter room, that should be open enough for us to get the shots."

Gray Matter wasn't happy with trading the wide open space of the loading dock for this floor of multiple rooms. Obstacles could degrade the power of their shots and he didn't want to lose any effectiveness. However, the transporter room was large enough that they should be able to get the job done. So now he had to draw him toward that room, which was down another hall perpendicular to Boogaloo's present location. Gray Matter certainly didn't want to go back out in the hall, run past Boogaloo and then take a right down the other hallway, because that would probably not go well. Instead, he decided to go as the crow flies, if a crow wore power armor, and ignored walls, and didn't fly. Continuing the suppression pattern of laser blasts in the general direction of Boogaloo's location (which was relatively easy to determine due to his return fire), Gray Matter began the slow process of walking through multiple walls as he made a diagonal path through several smaller rooms on his way to the transporter room.

Oliver landed in the hallway holding his newly acquired shield in front of himself, ready to immediately take fire. Instead, while there was indeed tons of shooting going on, none of it was directed at him. There were holes in everything: holes in the walls of varying sizes on both sides of the hallway, holes in the floor, and a giant hole next to him where there might have previously been a door but since there wasn't much wall left around it, it was hard to know for certain. Oliver could see Electric Boogaloo at the far end of the hall shooting bursts of electricity into the walls near him as laser bolts flew back out at him randomly. The two villains weren't hitting each other much, but they were really taking a toll on their surroundings. Several small fires had started along the hallway and down the path of wreckage that Gray Matter had created, and the sprinklers were popping on in places close to those fires. Oliver was trying to decide whether to follow Gray Matter or go after Boogaloo when Phil spoke over the comm again.

"Oliver?" said the bot.

"Yeah."

"I think I might have found something important about Gray Matter's power armor design."

"I hope it's that it's about out of power because it's a mess down here," said Oliver.

"Quite the opposite," said the bot. "I was able to hack into the system in the bot manufacturing center and find a version of the schematics. The battery pack has an extremely large capacity."

"So this could go on forever," said Oliver.

"Yes, but I don't think that's the intention," said the bot. "When I scanned the armor earlier, the battery pack was only at about 15 percent capacity, while my current scan puts it at 100 percent."

"That's odd," said Oliver. He saw Electric Boogaloo move to a corner and start down another hallway.

"Yes. That's why I decided to search for those schematics. It appears the entire design of the suit is to absorb electricity and charge the batteries."

"Okay, so he's using Boogaloo's energy to power his suit," said Oliver. "That's clever in an evil supervillain kind of way." Oliver started walking along the hallway toward where Boogaloo disappeared. The monster couldn't have gone too far down that other hallway, because there were still plenty of laser blasts hitting the corner to attest to that. Oliver kept his new shield up and ready, afraid that Boogaloo would remember him and suddenly pop back around the corner to send a few giant balls of electricity his way.

"There's not just that. The shoulder mounted laser is designed to fire a very strong blast, basically expending the entire battery pack in one shot. Right now he's firing shots at only 10 percent of its potential."

"So, what are you saying?" asked Oliver, kind of worried that he knew what the bot was saying.

"Well, that combined with the kind of power level that his partner Goth Spark can produce would be devastating, if not deadly, to the target."

"Are you sure?" asked Oliver. "That's quite a deduction from the information we have."

"Perhaps, but I have overheard Gray Matter and Goth Spark's communications and they are talking about coordinating their shots. That, and after Gray Matter recently refined the design, he renamed the power armor, 'The Electric Boogaloo Killer,' on the schematics."

"Okay, I see where you're coming from," said Oliver, starting to move less cautiously down the hall. "How much time do I have?"

SUPERGUY 2: ELECTRIC BOGALOO

"Not much," replied the bot. "Gray Matter is trying to lure Boogaloo into a specific room where there are no obstacles in the way and he's almost there. Goth Spark has also freed herself from the web and is currently flying down the hole behind you and along Gray Matter's path to the large room. It's called the Transporter Room."

Oliver looked back down the hall in time to see Goth Spark flash through the hole in the ceiling and bank into the path leading to Gray Matter. Oliver jumped forward and flew down the hallway after her.

"Raymond, I'm almost to you," said Goth Spark as she flew through office after wrecked office.

"Okay. Stop before the hallway," said Gray Matter. "I've almost got him in the room. Once I do, we'll take the shot." Already inside the transporter room, Gray Matter sent a wide pattern of laser blasts at the wall beside where Boogaloo was standing in the hall, blowing a giant hole for him to come through. Then Gray Matter focused his fire at the spot directly in front of his target to make the move into the room seem like a good tactical choice. Electric Boogaloo made that choice, stepping through the hole and opening fire on Gray Matter. Some of Gray Matter's laser blasts still pelted his target, but he wasn't trying very hard to be precise because he thought it would make Boogaloo content to remain relatively stationary as opposed to trying to avoid shots. Several of the laser shots made more holes in the walls behind the monster as it moved farther into the room while a few ricocheted off the shiny metal surface of the transporter it had moved in front of. One bolt even disappeared inside the open door and proceeded to bounce around seventeen times before finding the door again and hitting Boogaloo in the back. The monster didn't appear to notice.

"In position," said Alice.

"Perfect," said Gray Matter.

"Three."

Alice flew forward across the hall.

"Two."

Gray Matter stopped firing and hit the button to charge the laser.

"One."

Alice banked into the room and focused all her energy for one huge blast. The monitor in Gray Matter's suit showed all ready.

"Fire!"

Oliver flew around the corner in time to see Electric Boogaloo disappearing through a wall into what he assumed was the transporter room. He pulled up just short of the hole, not wanting to get the monster's attention and draw fire. It was probably best Boogaloo remained focused on Gray Matter.

"Oliver, they're going to do it right now," said Phil. "They're counting down."

Oliver saw motion down the hall and recognized it as Goth Spark flying into the room. Without a thought, Oliver

SUPERGUY 2: ELECTRIC BOGALOO

flew into the room and in front of Electric Boogaloo, his new shield raised against what looked like two giant headlights of a monstrous truck. One red and one dark blue. It certainly felt like a truck when it hit Oliver, smashing him back into Electric Boogaloo, who was knocked at a slight angle through the open doorway and inside the large shiny walk-in freezer that seemed so out of place in the room. Oliver also went off at a slight angle, colliding with the door of the freezer, which slammed shut, and then he crashed against the control panel set into the shiny surface next to the freezer door, which threw out sparks and emitted an off-key tone. The energy from the double blast soaked everything and knocked the freezer back several feet into the wall. Sparks exploded off a set of wires on the top left side, which were left burning in a melted mess. A roar followed from the apparatus above the freezer—and also, as Oliver would later swear, from inside—and then the sound slowly died as electricity snapped along wires above.

"Oliver? Are you okay?" asked Phil. "The fire department and police have arrived because of the alarms. They're entering the building."

That was the last thing Oliver heard before slumping to the floor and passing out.

39

"**MY** ears are still ringing," said Oliver. "It's been three days."

"It may take a couple of weeks," said Janice. "I was right next to Lava Lord when he finally exploded for real. Apparently he took a particularly unstable serum when he became a villain. Anyway, you know that thing when someone flashes a bright light in your eyes and you can't see? I had that in my right eye for three weeks."

The two heroes had just returned to the Garage after doing a patrol flight over the western Great Lakes. They walked into the control room to find Roger, Emma, and the Police Chief seated on the couches in the lounge area and Phil standing next to a chair. It was a Saturday, but what clearly indicated it wasn't a work day was that the Chief was wearing gray sweats, a Foo Fighters T-shirt, and a headband, which meant the band had been playing.

"Were you gentlemen making some glorious noise again?" asked Janice.

SUPERGUY 2: ELECTRIC BOGALOO

"Not only gentlemen," replied Roger. "Emma joined us to do harmonies on a few songs."

"Yes, finally someone in this building with some talent," said the Chief.

"He's a liar," said Emma. "But it was pretty fun. Besides, I really needed to blow off some steam after finally getting Gloria, the antisocial, kleptomaniac sidekick out of here." Janice sat down on the couch next to Emma.

"Sorry to see her go," said Oliver. "Wish I could have met her."

"Yeah, right," said Roger. "Great mentoring there, by the way."

"Hey, I mentor by example. I was off fighting bad guys most of the time."

"And she was busy stealing my car most of the time. Why couldn't you do something about that?" asked Roger.

"I didn't care?" said Oliver. "And like I said, I was off fighting bad guys. Speaking of which, any sign of Spark or Boogaloo, Chief?"

"Not a thing," said the Chief. "Goth Spark hasn't made an appearance since you saw her in Joyce Tower, and the same is true of Electric Boogaloo, but I fear it's for different reasons."

"And of course Gray Matter skates free as usual?" asked Janice.

"Can't prove he did anything wrong," replied the Chief. "He was just defending himself in his building, and while we know that's where the smuggled goods were coming from, there wasn't any evidence to be found."

"He obviously cleared everything out before setting the trap for Boogaloo," said Oliver. "He even had the building on a skeleton staff and hit the fire alarm as soon as Boogaloo took the bait. But at least we know how they were getting the goods in so we can just monitor the Tower for power surges and make sure they can't use their transporter anymore."

"I can't believe they built a transporter," said Roger. "That's so cool. Except for Electric Boogaloo, of course."

"Hey, you don't know that he's not out there brooding somewhere," said Oliver, a little guiltily.

"It's doubtful," said the Chief. "I got to question that Dr. Misk about it. While he was smart enough not to incriminate himself or the company, he did say they were only experimenting with inorganic objects because no living thing could possibly survive being transported."

"And there was no sign of anything arriving at the facility on Washington Island," said Phil, finally joining the conversation. He wasn't quite comfortable with making small talk yet. "I was able to monitor that location when I was still tapped into their system at the time."

"If Boogaloo didn't end up there, in whatever condition, where would he have gone?" asked Roger

"Good question," said Janice.

"I did posit that question to Dr. Misk while I had the chance," said the Chief. "He said that on a theoretical level, it was an incredibly intriguing problem and he was going to look into it. I think the guy is a few fruit loops short of a bowl."

"Okay, to sum up," said Emma. "Gray Matter got away with everything again, but this time he didn't even have to use his lawyers or pay his public relations people any overtime. Goth Spark is probably off laying low and spending whatever large paycheck she got for helping him. Electric Boogaloo is apparently just gone in a way we don't want to think about. And we're all sitting around here like this is the new normal."

SUPERGUY 2: ELECTRIC BOGALOO

"Sounds like victory to me," said Roger.

"Yeah, I'm beginning to think that us winning feels a lot like us just treading water, waiting for the next shark to swing by," said Oliver.

"Welcome to law enforcement in the time of superheroes," said the Chief. He raised his drumsticks. "Who's up for another set?"

Alex stared at himself. Well, it wasn't exactly himself. It was about half himself. He (the original him) was sitting on the heavily pine needle padded floor of a forest, surrounded by tall pine trees that stretched off into the distance in nearly perfectly spaced rows. There was a very deep quiet to it, despite the occasional flutter of a bird or scratch of a squirrel. It seemed like the type of setting, especially visually, that could really mess with a person's sense of perspective, and maybe their mind, if that person wasn't already used to their mind pretty much being a tossed salad. So Alex just took it in stride as he watched the mirror image of himself standing ten feet away staring expectantly back at him. Not quite a mirror image, since the other him was standing, not sitting, and wasn't nearly as big as he was, being more of an average human height, but it was still bulky with crusty dark blue skin lined with bright liquid blue showing through the cracks, just like the overly large regular him. However, to call the second body a separate entity was wrong, because Alex could feel how it was of one mind with him. He was it and it was him. Two bodies with a single consciousness. It was a strange feeling, but that was pretty much the definition of life now for Alex. He was kind of getting used to it. Having a second body really wasn't a huge stretch after what he'd gone through in the past several months, and having one mind sharing two bodies might prove pretty useful. What might prove even more useful was the third version of Alex that currently stood behind and a little off to the left of the second one. It was smaller still than the human-sized one, probably half the height, but built in the same proportions and, as Alex now realized, also plugged into his mind as well. He waved at himself from the third body. Cool. This would take a little getting used to, and a bit of planning to take advantage of, but Alex liked the possibilities. He also liked having company.

For now, Alex chose to ignore the fourth, miniature version of him standing on the left shoulder of the third him. He'd deal with that later.

ABOUT THE AUTHOR

KURT CLOPTON works full time as a professional Olde Tyme photo model, specializing in wide brim hats and saloon backgrounds. He spends most of his spare time perfecting his mediocrity at tennis and guitar, and the rest of it watching instructional YouTube videos on how to fix whatever he has most recently broken. He lives in Wisconsin with his secret second family when he is not on the road "traveling for work."

SPECIAL THANKS

To Emily Finestead, for her expertise in sorting out all of my comma, colon and semi colon errors, among all the other fixes. I'm assured it all makes much more sense now.

To the guy who doesn't like superhero stuff and therefore won't read my book. Sure, I helped him move into his new house and build his deck, but dropping a fiver for an ebook to support a friend? No way. But I get it, you have to have limits. Now that I think about it, I'm no big fan of moving furniture or building decks.

To Jeff, who bought two copies of my first book even though he only reads books about Abraham Lincoln. No, Abraham Lincoln does not appear in this sequel either. I guess I should have worked him in. Would have been nice of me. Next book, I promise.

To Chad and Anne, who both bought multiple copies of my book to give to friends and family. While I'm not sure that was the kindest thing to do to your friends or family, I still really appreciated it. And here I go writing another book. So, I guess maybe I should apologize ahead of time to your friends and family.

To the cub scout who came to my door to sell some popcorn and said that I was his favorite author. I don't like popcorn, but I bought some anyway. Manipulative little b@$#@&d.

Also Available from Not a Pipe Publishing

Don't Read This Book

by

Benjamin Gorman

Magdalena Wallace is the greatest writer in the world. She just doesn't know it.

When she wakes up chained to a desk next to a stack of typed pages and the corpse of the person who read them, she learns just how dangerous her book can be. Rescued by a vampire, a werewolf, and a golem, she's on the run with the manuscript — and the fate of humanity — in her backpack, and a whole lot of monsters hot on her heels!

"…a whimsical, fast-paced, delight; snappily written, deliciously funny and smart, and full of affection for its characters."
- New York Times bestseller Chelsea Cain, author of *Heartsick*, *Mockingbird*, and *Gone*

"... smart, determined, and filled with really stunning prose ... maybe one of the best books I've read!"
-Sydney Culpepper
 author of *Pagetown*, editor of *Strongly Worded Women*

Wherever Fine Books Are Sold

Also Available from Not a Pipe Publishing

The Gospel According to St. Rage
by
Karen Eisenbrey

Meet Barbara Bernsen, Former Invisible Girl.

Barbara isn't your typical high school junior. She's been invisible since the third grade. But when a magic hat brings her back into the light, Barbara is ready to take on the world. First priority? Start an all-girl garage band. Miraculous super powers were never in her plan, but sometimes you get what you need. Bullies and school shooters don't stand a chance.

Yes, we all love Wonder Woman, Black Widow, and Jessica Jones, but Barbara is the hero her high school deserves.

Truth. Justice. Rock & Roll.

"...a witty, intelligent and humorous tale of empowerment, friendship and anxiety and, as the cream on top of it all, comes with its own soundtrack."
-Angelika Rust, author of the *Resident Witch* series

Wherever Fine Books Are Sold

Also Available from Not a Pipe Publishing

The Supernormal Legacy
- Book I -
Dormant
by
LeeAnn McLennan

She has badass monster-fighting superpowers. She just doesn't want them.

When Olivia Woodson witnessed her mother die, she rejected her destiny as a supernormal. Now 14, she just wants to be normal. But Olivia must use her powers or watch her boyfriend die. Her powers refuse to be contained, forcing Olivia to connect with the supernormal side of her family and awaken the incredible ability lying dormant inside her.

"Olivia's struggle between fitting in with the normals and supernormals resonates beyond her abnormal abilities, reaching even those without bulletproof armor... sending readers on a thrilling ride."
-Chelsea Bolt
author of *Moonshine*

Wherever Fine Books Are Sold

Also Available from Not a Pipe Publishing

WRESTLING DEMONS
by
JASON BRICK

Varsity wrestler Connor Morgan has moved with his mother to Portland, Oregon to get away from his drug-addicted father. But they didn't move away from trouble. At his new high school, three heavyweight wrestlers chase him through the halls. He runs away, in his underwear, past the girl he likes, into the January cold.

Then something weird happens.

The next thing Connor knows, he is fighting for his life against supernatural evil with the help of new friends as he learns the powers and dangers of his new destiny. He discovers a powerful enemy bent on destroying more than just his high school. Ultimately, he must embrace his role in an ancient fight if he wants to save the day.

And he still has to get good grades and a date for the prom.

Wherever Fine Books Are Sold

CPSIA information can be obtained
at www.ICGtesting.com
Printed in the USA
LVHW082258271219
641937LV00005B/14/P